The sky was lit by a blinding flash and a glare of orange, then crimson, shading to a fierce yellow. The shockwave reached the two fighters fractionally before the huge blast of sound boomed in their ears. The two little planes bucked and leapt through the wispy clouds and screamed away to right and left, each performing tight circles to come round again and dive towards the wreckage of the Boeing as it dropped from the night sky.

The fiery cigar shape of the Boeing's fuselage was now starkly illuminated as the fighters chased it down to the sea.

"Shot down." Naples queried.

"No!" Eagle roared, "not shot down. It just . . . exploded!"

Chapter One

Mister Smith's watch had long since been taken from him, so he logged the passing seconds in his head. Not all of them, but enough to keep him in touch with reality.

No natural light penetrated the cell, for he was a Category "A" convict, rating a top-security tomb. No everyday sounds of the world outside reached his ears through the solid old walls of Fresnes Prison.

In three years, even during his twice-daily canters around the exercise yard, not a single airplane engine had Smith heard, nor the dying snarl of a truck, nor the aimless twittering of a sparrow.

His hearing had become abnormally and selectively acute, sifting the mélange of manmade, purposeful noises for the odd accidental one to disturb the relentless pattern of normality. But these were few, scattered like grace notes through an otherwise pedestrian score. Yet still, and obsessively, Smith listened—for the catch in the footfalls of his guards that meant a broken step, for the clang of a dropped key and the curse that always followed it, for the scraping of a match as a warder unknowingly bestowed on Smith the priceless gift of lighting a cigarette outside *his* cell.

These sounds, after a while, slotted subliminally into his mind, and were used by Smith to fuel his determination to avoid mental stagnation in his solitary confinement. He owned one of the truly original criminal minds of the century, and had no intention of letting it rust into disuse.

He exercised his body ruthlessly to keep his muscles finely toned, and drilled his brain no less fanatically with complex chess and bridge problems committed to memory. And when he had dispatched these, he would reconstruct in perfect detail the greatest achievements of his long career, and go on to plan those yet to happen.

That they *would* happen, Smith never doubted. He had known with a cold certainty on the day that the forces of the United Nations Anti-Crime Organization defeated his commando army on the Eiffel Tower, that no prison could hold him beyond his calculated tolerance.

Now he had tolerated Fresnes Prison for long enough. Smith had rarely spoken, still more rarely smiled, during his incarceration. But as he sat on his bunk and squinted at the naked lightbulb which he had come to think of as a trusted friend, the ghost of a grin touched his lips.

While his brain schemed at a feverish pitch, he dropped his eyes and absentmindedly sketched with a fingernail on the palm of his hand the ragged outline of an airplane. And he whispered a name.

"Dunkels."

Dunkels was Smith's creature, dragged from the gutters of Berlin. Smith had made Dunkels rich, and fear of Smith kept the German loyal. The time had come for Dunkels to repay his master, to be the catalyst of Smith's freedom, and of the crime he would perpetrate and which would rock the Western world.

"Dunkels," Smith breathed again, drawing comfort from the sound, for sounds were precious to him. Dunkels would not let Mister Smith down. No one ever did that.

The Swissair DC-9 started its lazy descent into Zurich airport. The "No Smoking" sign came on in the first-class compartment, and Siegfried Dunkels obediently mashed his cigarette into pulp with elegantly powerful fingers.

He teased a flake of ash from the crease of his blue mohair trousers and glanced out of the cabin window. White puffs of cumulus danced on the snow-topped Alpine peaks, basking in their Christmas card complacency under an otherwise china blue sky. His thin lips twisted. Dunkels detested the smug Swiss, but envied and feared them, too, for their effortless success and smooth financial brigandry. He had been bested, cheated, by Swiss money-men in the past; it would not, he vowed, happen again.

No Zurich gnome had ever beaten Mister Smith, Dunkels mused, and he was in Switzerland on Mister

Smith's business. Nothing must go wrong. On Dunkels's life, nothing must go wrong.

A pert stewardess, confidently pretty, stopped by his seat and glanced meaningfully at his lap through lowered lids. She was merely checking that his seat belt was fastened, yet she made it seem like an invitation.

"I trust," Dunkels said in German, "that your Swiss doctors are more amenable than your bankers."

"I beg your pardon?" said the girl.

"You have it," Dunkels rejoined, stretching his mouth into a smile.

Fawn-colored sunlight flooded into the aircraft as the pilot turned in to his final approach. A priest in the window seat struggled with the shade, and Dunkels reached across him to flick it expertly down and mask the sudden glare. The priest bowed his thanks. Men of God, Dunkels thought, should not travel first class. It did not demonstrate a proper humility, though he doubted whether one such as his companion, clearly a bishop, would even bother to affect an attitude of humility.

The tension of the landing mounted in the cabin, and was reflected by seasoned travelers like Dunkels who steeled themselves for the touchdown. A sigh of relief escaped from the bishop when the DC-9's wheels rode safely on to the tarmac. The prelate crossed himself, and started to say something to Dunkels, who pretended, with an exaggerated pantomime, to be deaf.

Later, Dunkels hefted his alligator-skin case from the baggage carrousel and strolled past the deferential Swiss *douaniers* to the automatic exit doors. A uniformed chauffeur standing by a black Mercedes signaled to him with a gloved hand. The driver indicated the front passenger seat, but Dunkels pointedly waited for the rear door to be opened. Just as pointedly, he insulated himself from the possibility of small talk on the journey by leaving the limousine's plate-glass partition closed.

Dunkels did not look through the tinted window at the breathtaking scenery, but into it at his own reflection. He saw, and admired, a square-jawed, firmly fleshed face with a slightly kinked nose jutting aggressively under his deceptively mild brown eyes. The chin was adequately cleft and the forehead broad and bland. His eyebrows, like his

3

hair, were ash blond. The hair was kept short and sculpted by an Italian barber who was an artist with a razor. Dunkels drew a comb from his pocket and ran it across his scalp. In its wake, the individual hair follicles snapped smartly back into place like Prussian guardsmen.

A fleeting shadow intruded on his self-absorption. Dunkels frowned, and peered more closely. Then he grinned. It was an airplane. A Boeing 707. The undulating silhouette was not unlike the shape Smith had traced on his hand in the Fresnes Prison.

The dignified italic script on the sign said "Edelweiss Clinic" in English, and Dunkels mentally switched to English for the period he was to stay there; a short time, he hoped. Like Smith, Dunkels was an accomplished linguist—though without Smith's encyclopedic command of esoteric tongues. Dunkels had known Smith to range languidly through the alphabet from Albanian to Xhosa purely for mental stimulus.

Gravel crackled beneath the wheels of the Mercedes when it left the main road and turned into the clinic's long drive. Edelweiss, Dunkels assumed, would be an unwelcome intruder into the probably regimented sterility of the clinic, which at last came into view through the front window. It was a newish, chalet-style complex nestling in a fold of the mountain, and built out from it to overlook the vertiginous drop to a rock-strewn valley. Patients of Doctor Richard Stein who were unable to afford his treatment, or failed to benefit from it, could solve their problems simply by walking off his expensive terracing, Dunkels thought. He spread his long, spare body over the rear seat of the Mercedes and waited for the chauffeur to release him. A white-coated figure came out through the swinging doors and descended the steps towards him.

Doctor Richard Stein looked old for his years. He was an acknowledged frontrunner in the treatment of rheumatoid-arthritic complaints among the elderly and rich, as well as a gifted psychiatrist. He was also (but less acknowledged) probably the most skillful plastic surgeon in Switzerland. It was a fortunate aptitude to possess in a land where a secret access of fortune often demanded a consequential change in appearance.

Richard Stein oiled rusting joints, cleared cobwebbed minds, and restructured dangerous faces with the same impartial expertise. He was small, dark, and frail-seeming, with a prominent aquiline nose. His shoulders were bent, and Dunkels, who towered over him, saw the permanently crooked upper half of his body swivel from the waist as Stein extended a bony hand in greeting. "Physician, heal thyself," Dunkels murmured indelicately.

"Mr. Dunkels, I presume," Stein said in German.

Dunkels ran his tongue along his strong, square teeth and grinned. "There's an answer to that, I believe," he replied in English, "though I never learned what it was. Doctor Stein, it's good to meet you at last." He gripped Stein's hand with careless strength, but released it when the Swiss grimaced in pain. "Sorry," Dunkels said, "I wouldn't hurt your hands for all the money in Zurich."

"Even *with* all the money in Zurich, I doubt that you'd be able to buy their equal," Stein remarked, in excellent, though accented, English. He rubbed his abused fingers ruefully and added, "I'll lead the way, then," turning as fluidly as a man afflicted with an apparent arthritic curvature of the spine can rotate.

The Mercedes slid away, and Dunkels followed the little Swiss doctor along two uniformly pristine corridors until they came to an oak-paneled door bearing the single word "Director." Stein's office was functional G-plan, with a picture window framing the valley and mountains like an adjustable holiday photograph. Stein settled himself behind the desk and seemed to grow in stature now that he was exercising his own territorial imperative. He waved Dunkels into a comfortable low hide chair.

"You have the photographs and the anatomically detailed descriptions?" Stein asked, breaking the silence.

Dunkels nodded. "You have the candidate?"

Stein nodded. Dunkels waited for the exposition, but none came. Finally he sniffed loudly and said, "Name?"

Stein linked his fingers and laid them on the desk, leaning forward and gazing intently at Dunkels as if he were on the point of revealing a state secret. "Jagger. Cody Jagger."

Dunkels pursed his lips. "It has a somewhat theatrical ring," he mused.

"It's his real name," Stein supplied confidentially.

Dunkels sat up and leaned in towards Stein. "He's here now?"

Stein inclined his impressive head. "Would you like to see his picture?" Dunkels indicated that he would.

It was an ordinary enough face gazing out at him from the first page of the manilla folder which Stein shot across the polished mahogany desk. The ordinariness, Dunkels knew, was a bonus. It was also a strangely pliable-looking face . . . no highlights or promontories, no points of interest or focus; it could have been molded from plasticine for all the definition it carried. Another bonus. Dunkels stared hard at the face, then closed his eyes and tried to visualize its contours—and failed. He grinned, and smacked his lips approvingly.

Stein smiled, too. "I knew you'd like him. Good basic building material. There are, additionally, certain similarities already between Jagger and the subject, and for total conversion . . . well, at the very least Jagger's physiognomy creates no obstacles, as you can see. The coloring, incidentally, is identical, and his height and weight match the subject's almost exactly."

"Almost?"

"Each man is six feet two inches tall, but Jagger is eight pounds heavier than the subject. This is not a problem, since my clinic specializes in reducing diets."

"Among other things."

"As you say," Stein acknowledged, "among other things."

Dunkels flipped through the remaining pages of the Jagger file, and grunted in amusement. Stein regarded him questioningly. Dunkels snapped the file shut and remarked, "Not exactly a model citizen, our Cody, is he?"

Stein replied, "You didn't tell me you wanted a circuit preacher." Dunkels grinned. "It makes no difference what he is," he conceded, "as long as he is the man he claims to be. If he checks out, he'll do."

"He will."

"He'll have to," Dunkels said, leaving the implicit warning unstated.

Stein unlaced his fingers and spread them wide in apparent consternation. "I've never let Smith down before, have I?" he demanded.

"*Mister* Smith," Dunkels corrected icily.

"*Mister* Smith, I'm sorry," Stein apologized. "But all the same, I've always delivered. Even when it was Mister Smith's own face. I made him Javanese, if you recall. And Swedish—and Peruvian. No complaints? No." Stein's fingertips agitated like the hands of a blue-dyed matron drying a full house of painted nails.

"I gave him his present face," he protested, "the aristocratic look, that's what he wanted—top-drawer English. And that's what he got. He could pass for a duke at Buckingham Palace."

"He did," Dunkels interposed dryly.

"There you are, then," Stein exclaimed, "though of course Mister Smith's face is marvelously—eh—malleable. And unmemorable, too. He tells me he's quite forgotten what he originally looked like."

That, Dunkels admitted, rising from the hide chair, was true. "OK, Stein," he said brusquely, "I'll put Jagger through the mincer, and if he comes out kosher, he's it." Dunkels prided himself on his idiomatic English.

They lunched expansively in Stein's penthouse, which afforded an even more staggering panorama of Switzerland's greatest natural asset. When they had finished eating, Stein inquired tentatively whether Dunkels really thought they could get away with the impersonation.

"What do you think?" Dunkels replied. "You're doing the important part."

Stein explained that the assumption of the subject's physical identity was not difficult. He had made people into other people before. "Naturally," he went on, "I'll be able to offer a more qualified opinion on Jagger's chances when you tell me a little more about our subject. At present, all you've given me is his face in six different poses, for which I'm grateful, plus the information that he's connected with the American forces, though which branch I don't know."

Dunkels cracked his knuckles and drew a baleful glance from Stein. "His name is Joe McCafferty," Dunkels said slowly, as if grudging every word. "He's on loan from the United Nations Anti-Crime Organization—UNACO—to the elite Secret Service Corps forming the American president's bodyguard. Currently, McCafferty has been assigned to head the security force aboard Air Force One, which is, as you know—"

"Yes," Stein interrupted, "I know what Air Force One is. The Boeing—707, isn't it?—used by the president as a sort of aerial White House. So . . ."—he dragged the conjunction out admiringly, and whistled—"so McCafferty's an important man."

"He is."

"Then you'd better come along and see him," Stein twinkled. "I mean, of course, his potential *doppelgänger,* his look-alike, his—other self." Stein paused and added, half to himself, "How unpleasant it will be for McCafferty to discover that he has suddenly become two people."

Smith's computer "mincer," located thirty miles north of the Brazilian city of São Paolo, was extraordinarily swift and adept. It placed its imprimatur on Jagger's credentials while Dunkels was still waiting for his coffee to arrive. A courteous waiter handed him the telex, and Dunkels himself took the good news to Jagger, who was billeted in a room at the end of a wing that was private even by the reclusive character of the Edelweiss Clinic.

He introduced himself and told Jagger, "You'll be seeing a lot of me from now on." The ringer stood up and clasped Dunkels's hand. He grinned crookedly and said, "Cody Jagger—and this is probably the last you'll ever see of me as I look now."

Four hours later, Dunkels left the clinic in the same Mercedes that had brought him there. His close interrogation of Jagger had endorsed the computer's verdict: that Cody Jagger was indeed Cody Jagger. Dunkels was also satisifed, by his own and Smith's high standards, that Jagger was psychologically as well as physiologically adjusted to becoming one Joseph Eamonn Pearse McCafferty, colonel USAF, presently head of security operations, Air Force One, and assigned to the 89th Military Airlift Wing at Andrews Air Force Base, Maryland, USA.

The Alpine peaks were almost purple in the waning light when Stein knocked at Jagger's door and entered without an invitation. The ringer, who was standing before a back-lit shaving mirror saying goodbye to his face, remarked tersely, "He's hooked."

8

"Excellent." Stein beamed. "So Smith will be hooked, too. Moscow should be very, very pleased."

"So they ought to be," Jagger retorted. "This thing could be bigger than either we or they thought." He lapsed into silence, then added, "Are you sure Smith will buy it?"

"Tut, tut, tut," Stein said, waving an admonitory finger at him. "*Mister* Smith if you don't mind. That, Jagger, is your first lesson."

Smith listened to the days going by. Dunkels's last message had been affirmative. The ringer was perfect. The caper was on. His freedom lay barely a week away; then the world of sound, sight, and scent would assume its normal proportions.

But strangely, that mattered less and less to Smith as the elongated hours passed. What was important was the crime he had planned to celebrate his return to life—the big one, which would destroy the credibility of UNACO and its commander, Malcolm Philpott. Smith deeply hated the man who had condemned him to the scarcely endurable catalepsy of imprisonment—but this time *he* would triumph and UNACO would fall.

Dunkels would not let him down. Nor would Jagger, nor would Stein. Failure, as always with Mister Smith, was unthinkable. He had felt President Warren G. Wheeler squirming in his hands once before, and he would do so again.

Smith's mind conjured up anew the vision of the converted Boeing 707 that was, to Warren G. Wheeler, Air Force One. "Oh dear," he murmured, "has the nasty man taken your toy away?"

And for the first time in three years, four months, and eighteen days, genuine, unforced laughter filled the lonely prison cell, so near to his beloved Paris that Smith could almost smell the drains.

Chapter Two

Over the next four days, Cody Jagger survived the mental and physical agony of losing his persona.

He could not, though, have been in more skillful or patient hands. Stein's operating theater, in which he was joined by only two members of his staff, entirely dependent on him for money and drugs, was set up like a society photographer's salon.

Every inch of wall space was given over to huge blow-up pictures of McCafferty's face taken from six different angles, including a shot of the back of his neck, showing the precise set of flat, trim ears.

The operating table was surrounded by a forest of tripods bearing multibracketed floodlights, adjustable vertically and in their angles of concentration. Stein, bent over the table which glowed under its own bank of arc lamps, constantly barked instructions to his minions to sharpen or illuminate particular features of the subject.

Then, squinting fiercely at the pictures that charted McCafferty's face with the fine detail of an ordnance survey map, Stein wielded his scalpel on the unconscious Jagger to trade cheek for cheek, jowl for jowl, nose for nose.

With total detachment, and a square centimeter at a time, Stein sliced away slivers of Cody Jagger and molded them into jigsaw pieces of Joe McCafferty like Lego bricks of flesh, the common denominators of a man which the surgeon simply rearranged in the shape of a different man.

Finally it was done, the stitches out, the scars pink and fresh. It was 3:30 A.M. on the morning of the fifth day, and Stein, slumped cross-legged on the floor studying his handiwork in an enlarging mirror set into the ceiling, reflected sourly that in only a day and a half more, the God of Abraham and Isaac had created an entire world. "Probably had better hired help than me," Stein chuckled malevolently. He had never felt so enervated, so completely exhausted.

He looked at the taped and bandaged head. If there was no tissue infection, the bulk of the hard work was over. But Stein had sensed from the mounting urgency in Dunkels's voice on the phone that Smith's plans were coming to a head.

Stein knew he could delay no further in contacting Karilian.

The Mercedes drew up once more at the Edelweiss Clinic, midway through the evening of the same day. Stein, who had spent the intervening hours sleeping, crabbed down the steps to greet the large, square-faced man who had elbowed the respectful chauffeur impatiently aside. The driver, by inclination a gregarious type, was rapidly tiring of ferrying rude and uncommunicative foreigners to his employer.

Axel Karilian, KGB controller, Switzerland, ignored Stein's outstretched hand, grasping him instead roughly by the elbow and pivoting him around to face back up the steps. "Show me," he commanded, propelling the little Swiss doctor through the entry doors.

As a high-ranking and, by definition, high-risk criminal, Smith was customarily fed in his cell, keeping him away from contact with other prisoners. So when his evening meal tray was removed, and the others in his block (Smith subconsciously counted them, identifying the cells solely by the sounds of their doors closing and the number of steps it took to reach them), he knew that it would be half an hour to the guard's final round of the day, a further twenty minutes to complete the tour, and an additional fifteen minutes to "lights out." The regimen never varied. Smith would have been distressed if it had.

That evening, while Doctor Richard Stein was entertaining Axel Karilian in the Edelweiss Clinic's penthouse, Mister Smith ate his dinner in the prison's isolation wing with more than usual relish.

He was aware that it would be the last meal he would ever take there. He lay back on his bunk and considered the immediate and more distant future, while his mind automatically catalogued the jail's grinding routine, cell by cell, tray by tray, door by door, step by squeaky-booted step. A squeaking boot! Not two, but one! A pleasing paradox to take out with him.

Smith chuckled his delight, and in his brain the nagging metronome that kept time for him ticked remorselessly on. He fell asleep, but even as he awoke hours later his first conscious impression was of the metronome taking over again, so that he knew for an undisputable fact that the hour was drawing near.

The prison "trusty" bribed to be the prime mover in springing Smith from jail licked his lips and tried to stop his eyes from darting repeatedly to the wall clock in the maintenance block. The second hand clicked over from 3:59 to 4:00, and the convict jammed the flat of his hand down on the plunger key of the detonator device that had been smuggled in to him.

In the isolation wing, two hundred yards away, an electric spark leapt out from a junction box to join a trail of black powder. The powder spluttered into flame, and eleven seconds later a can of gasoline exploded in a linen storage closet at the end of Smith's corridor. Soon the storage area and its adjoining rooms were well on fire, and the prison staff, squeaky-boot among them, rushed to the scene. That was when Smith's cell light came on.

The alarm from the prison to the local fire station was automatic on the location of any uncontrolled outbreak, but still the firemen tended to wait for a confirming phone call. When it came, six fire trucks—two turntable tower ladder trucks, a control vehicle, and three water/foam pumpers—roared out at a reckless speed into the night.

The fire spread quickly, yet the prison warden and his deputies all had to be roused and mobilized before the order to evacuate the threatened areas could be given. The guards drew rifles and riot guns from the armory, and a nervous police commissioner turned out a cadre of the local CRS detachment, the riot police.

Arc lamps and klieg lights illuminated every cranny of the gaunt building, and Smith sat up and then leaned back on his elbows when his cell door burst open.

"Out!" the armed guard ordered. "There's a fire. We're clearing the block. Out!"

"Where to?" Smith asked, putting on a show of sudden panic.

"The main yard. Join the line. Hurry!"

Mister Smith left the place which had been his home for more than three years without so much as a backward glance.

The fire engine convoy wailed and clanged its way through the dark streets, to be joined at an intersection by police cars and outriders, adding still more manic noise to the already insane cacophony.

At the prison, shouting guards urged streams of convicts from five different directions into the large central yard, herding them into resentful chains to feed water and sand to the flames. The keening of sirens and screeching of tires announced the arrival of the police, who did little apart from get in each other's way until the firemen came.

The fire had now spread to the stretch of buildings nearest the high perimeter wall, and the two big turntable trucks quickly hoisted up their ladders above the wall. Firemen scrambled along them like mountain goats, and trained their hoses on the flames.

Unnoticed by the firemen, but ushered smartly to the wall by the police, a third turntable truck, coming from the opposite direction from the main force, also shot its ladder up over the wall. The chief fire officer in overall charge of operations in the control vehicle screamed directions at the crew for concentrating their water and foam.

The message was passed up the ladder to the man at the top, Leading Fireman Siegfried Dunkels, who acknowledged with a capable wave. Then he waved again, using both arms and trapping his hose between his knees. This time Smith saw him.

The yard was filled with smoke, clamor, and confusion, and it was easy for Smith to clutch at his throat, retch noisily, and stumble out of the line, which automatically closed ranks to fill his place.

Smith fell to his knees, apparently choking, then got up and lutched towards a patch of clearer air. It was covered by the harsh white glare of a searchlight, so the prison officer he bumped into *en route* did not trouble to turn him away from an area that would normally be strictly out-of-bounds to convicts: the foot of the wall.

Dunkels's ladder and the hoses of his men were pointed at the heart of the fire, but gradually the ladder began swinging away from the blaze and towards the yard until it centered over the crumpled figure of Mister Smith. Dunkels dropped a weighted nylon rope-ladder smack into his lap. Smith grasped it and started to scale the wall.

A guard—primed, like his colleagues, to watch for signs of a breakout—caught the unnatural movement of the human fly in the corner of his vision, and shouted a warning. As he charged over to the gyrating figure he saw the rope-ladder, and leapt for its trailing end. But Dunkels had already jerked his hose away from the flame and was swiveling it downwards. Carefully avoiding Smith, he aimed the hose, and the high-pressure jet of water took the guard full in the chest, slamming him to the ground and pinning him there like a butterfly in a specimen case.

Smith reached the top of the wall and clutched the turntable ladder, which retracted, dropped its angle, and deposited him on the ground by the fire engine. The hard-pressed fire chief also had the bad luck to notice Smith's escape. He ran in the direction of the third fire truck, the presence of which had been bothering him for quite a while.

Dunkels, in the still-retracting ladder, gave him the full treatment, bowling him over like a ninepin and then worrying him until he crawled back to his control truck, where sympathetic hands hauled him inside.

Smith jumped into the cab, and the driver gunned the motor and moved the truck away at top speed, sirens blaring. Dunkels, perched on the end of the now horizontal ladder, used his hose like a tail-gunner to deadly effect, scattering startled firemen and CRS toughs who tried vainly to stop them.

The madly racing fire engine left the city limits at an impossible speed five minutes later. In a quiet country road, it stopped. The crew got out, peeled off their uniforms, and six of them piled into a neutral-colored van which matched the name on their early-shift construction workers' overalls.

Smith, Dunkels, and the remaining three boarded a pair

of Citroën cars, where changes of clothing were waiting for them. The limousines moved off together, and Smith heaved a sigh of profound relief.

"Excellent, Dunkels," he said, "truly excellent. Now—get me a safe house and a woman, in that order."

Dunkels grinned. "Should you wish to reverse the order, sir," he said, "there's a woman in the back of the other car."

Karilian had reluctantly allowed Stein to take the lead when the surgeon ordered him to be gloved, masked, and gowned, then demonstrated beyond doubt that Jagger was no longer in the operating theater.

They reached Jagger's off-limits suite, and Stein kept the bad news from him until they had tiptoed across to Jagger's bedside. "What the hell's this?" Karilian burst out, jabbing a stubby finger at the bandaged head. "I want to see his face. That's why I'm here, remember?"

"Shhh," Stein soothed him. "Keep the noise down, I beg you. I don't want him suddenly awoken. He's still under sedation and mustn't move quickly."

Without dropping his voice, Karilian demanded when he could see Jagger properly. Stein had assured him that Jagger would wake naturally in the early hours, when the sedatives and antibiotics had worked through his system. But while there was still the risk of tissue infection, or even rejection, the ringer must remain unconscious. "Please do as I ask," he entreated Karilian. "Come and dine with me upstairs. I have some excellent vodka and Beluga caviar."

Karilian looked thunderously at him from beneath his shaggy brows, the hard, flinty grey eyes contemptuous and unblinking. Then he gave a half-grunting, half-snorting bark and growled, "Make it Glenfiddich, Dom Perignon, and a T-bone steak, and I might consider it."

Stein also relaxed, his body subsiding from warped tension into its normal question-mark shape. "But I do want to see him—tonight," Karilian warned him.

"So you shall," Stein promised, "so you shall."

The little doctor invariably won their minor skirmishes. Richard Stein, who had started life in Switzerland with the less acceptable name, in those days, of Schlomo Asher Silberstein, had known Axel Karilian for thirty-five years.

15

Stein, then a gifted young medical student, had been trapped in Poland at the outbreak of war, and was sent to the nearest concentration camp with his fellow Jews. Luckily, it was a small and indifferently run camp under a weak but perverted commandant. Stein had wheedled his way into the camp's medical unit and the commandant's confidence, and used the stepping stones to Himmler's Final Solution to advance himself into a position of power.

Stein pandered grossly to the commandant's twisted mind (and improved his own knowledge of surgical techniques) by performing ghastly and obscene experimental operations on the inmates. His greatest medical triumph had been grafting organs from a large, fully grown man on to the body of a seven-year-old girl. The child had lived for six weeks until the poisons trapped inside her literally erupted.

The Red Army surged swiftly through Poland on its way to Germany, and the commandant and his staff were unprepared for the sudden onslaught on the camp. The major in charge of the Soviet force lined up the Germans and shot them out of hand. He did the same with the weakest and most ailing of the Jews.

But Stein, neither sickly nor weak, was handed over to a young Ukrainian Intelligence captain who had just been posted to the advance armies, and so began the long friendship between Axel Karilian and the soon-to-be Richard Stein.

Stein was spirited away when the Ukrainian learned of his special abilities, and to protect him from Jewish revenge, Karilian took him to Odessa, where the Swiss Jew passed on enough of his hideously acquired skill in plastic surgery and skin grafting to enable local doctors to change his face.

Stein did not stop at that, though; he wanted his shape changed as well. And he told the orthopedic surgeons how to do it. It was an operation he had performed many times on unanesthetized Jewish children, with more pliable bones than his, transforming them from human beings into grotesque monsters. Stein laid out every step of the operation for the Russians, endured the agony, and, like Jagger, survived.

16

Richard Stein was no hapless victim of rheumatoid arthritis. He was a self-made question mark.

After the war the KGB set him up in the Edelweiss Clinic, and Karilian joined him in Switzerland as the Geneva-based controller. It frequently amused Stein, as he amassed considerable wealth with the success of the clinic, that many of his best customers now were even wealthier Jews. On them, of course, he operated with the utmost care and skill. And never forgot the anesthetic.

Cody Jagger's path to the embrace of the KGB was equally painful, and was also to involve Axel Karilian.

After a boyhood of petty offenses and a brace of unhelpful prison terms when he graduated from a more serious school of crime, Jagger made PFC in the Army and was captured early on in the Vietnam war, waging a bloody and highly personal counteroffensive north of Hué.

He was tough, truculent, a born bully, and no trouble at all to the Viet Cong torture squads, who broke him inside a month.

Jagger was selected for training by a traveling KGB recruiting officer, but far from easing his lot the new status turned Cody's life into a living hell. Physical torment and mental assault alternated in a pattern of treatment which took him to the very borders of his sanity. Only afterwards did he dimly appreciate that turncoat material was of no use to the Soviet intelligence machine. He had given in too easily to the Viet Cong; therefore, the KGB reasoned, he could just as easily revert back to the Americans. They could not afford that kind of risk, so they handed Jagger over to Axel Karilian, who had picked up any number of useful tips in his fruitful association with Richard Stein.

Karilian's program for Jagger was typical in its uncomplicated logic: the American must be cowed and brutalized into abject, unquestioning submission until he became a safe prospect.

It took Jagger three years to realize what was happening. When he did, he submitted—and meant it. Moscow sent him back to Hanoi, where the torture was increased daily for two months, to the point where Jagger lived every waking moment in constant, gibbering terror.

17

Only then had Karilian been satisfied. Thereafter, the KGB ruled Jagger by fear and fear alone.

He performed well enough for them as an agent in the States, but at a purely basic level, so that when Smith instructed Stein to find ringer material for him, and Stein had passed on the news to Karilian, even the Ukrainian had been reluctant to use Jagger. But when he reconsidered the proposition, Karilian knew that Jagger must be the perfect candidate, though Stein still had misgivings.

Stein and Karilian entered once more the bedroom of the now restlessly stirring man. Jagger's eyes opened and regarded them through the slits in his bandages. "How is he?" Stein inquired of the nurse sitting by the bed.

"Much better," she replied. "Doctor Grühner had a look at him just now. He says all the tissue has taken well, and there's no sign of infection. The scars are healing nicely."

"Have you seen his face?" Karilian asked her brusquely. The nurse shook her head. Karilian motioned towards the door with his hand. "Out," he ordered.

Stein lifted the bandages carefully away, and was arranging them on a metal trolley when the telephone rang. The call was for Karilian.

The Ukrainian spoke only his name, listened, grunted twice, and slammed the receiver back in its cradle. "That was Paris," he said, "there's been a fire at Fresnes Prison. One inmate made a daring escape. Guess who."

Stein's eyes lit up. "Then it's about to start?"

Karilian nodded. "Your waxwork doll there will be needed sooner than we thought. Well—let's take a look at him."

Jagger murmured in distress as Karilian loomed menacingly over the bed. Cody was conditioned to tremble at Russians, and at Karilian in particular. The Ukrainian took photographs from Stein's folder on the trolley and leaned in closer, holding a 10 x 1 enlargement next to Jagger's new pink ear. He rose and turned to Stein. "Good enough," he conceded.

"Good enough?" Stein bridled. "He would fool Joe McCafferty's own mother."

The telephone rang again. Stein picked it up, announced himself, and listened, also in silence. Then he said, "Have

18

no fear, he'll be ready. Yes. Until next week then. *Au revoir.*"

"Dunkels," Stein said when Karilian raised an inquiring eyebrow. Smith would be at the clinic in a week, he explained, and he wanted the ringer to be fit, unscarred, and word-perfect within five more weeks.

Karilian smiled, with no trace of mirth. "Then so do I, my dear Richard. You'd better see to it, hadn't you?"

Stein promised it would be accomplished. They had tapes of McCafferty's voice and an elocution expert as backup, plus mute and sound film of his walk, gestures, and mannerisms. Stein had a copy of Smith's dossier on the UNACO man, which was formidably comprehensive. His background, education, love affairs, close friendships, likes and dislikes . . . all were documented in detail. Psychiatric assessments and physical reports were attached, together with medical histories and dental records. Mc-Cafferty's relations with his brother officers were charted, and the file also included thumbnail pictures and mini-dossiers of the people closest to him at work, who would clearly expect instant recognition from McCafferty.

One factor was in Jagger's favor: McCafferty commanded his own unit, so he didn't have to be too unctuously friendly with anyone, superior or subordinate. Aloofness could be used to cover a temporary lapse. Nonetheless, the ringer would have to memorize not merely the faces, but the backgrounds as well, of all those men and women in McCafferty's immediate family and circle, especially the officers he had served with on his way up through the ranks. Each of them would have similar combat stories to which the ringer must unhesitatingly respond—and get the details right.

The women in McCafferty's life, Stein reasoned, could present the major problem. Affairs they knew about were fully outlined, with portraits, curricula vitae, favorite food, music, authors, and the like of the leading contenders. Sexual accomplishments and/or deviations were listed where possible, but it would be in bed that Jagger could betray himself. Several authorities rated McCafferty as a considerate and expert lover—whereas Jagger was, at best, an unfeeling rapist, with a conviction to prove it.

Fortunately, Stein had partially solved the problem by

circumcising Jagger to match McCafferty, so it would be some time before the ringer could use himself without pain. But as a general rule he would be ordered to avoid sexual contacts, pleading recurrent hepatitis, or a mild case of a social disease, or any other plausible excuse.

Again Stein asked Karilian, as they stood looking down on the scarred ringer, how good their chances were of getting away with it for any length of time.

"Can Jagger really manage it?" he insisted. "Is he that bright, that adaptable? It needs a considerable actor, you know, Axel, to carry off this part."

Karilian told him to stop worrying. "He'll do it all right," he said grimly, "and he'll do it well. I don't know why Smith wants him on Air Force One, but it's got to be something very, very big for an operator like him to go to all this expense and preparation. And for his man to be our man as well, unknown either to Smith or people like UNACO, who'll be involved now that Smith is free, is a master stroke. Moscow's in raptures at the prospect."

Stein grinned at Karilian's obvious relish, but suggested that the more Jagger was exposed as McCafferty the greater his vulnerability might become. Karilian shook his huge head. "You're wrong," he replied, "the more he plays the role the better he'll get at playing it—that surely follows."

"I don't know," Stein muttered, "I just don't know. How can you be so certain?"

"How? Simple. I know Jagger. He's terrified of what will happen to him if he doesn't do it. Something a hundred—a thousand—times worse than death. Can you imagine the depth of his fear, Doctor, a fate as monstrous as that which Jagger believes could be his? But how silly of me; of course you can. You, after all, are an acknowledged expert in pain and terror. For example, you would only have to threaten to "rearrange" him again, but without the anesthetic. It would not be the first time, would it?"

Stein flushed angrily, but could not look Karilian in the eyes. "What about the real McCafferty?" he muttered. "What happens to him?"

Karilian laughed. "If Smith doesn't kill him," he said, "then of course I will."

Chapter Three

Basil Swann, a young man with acne, horn-rimmed glasses, and a string of honors from three universities, bustled into the office of Malcolm G. Philpott, director of the United Nations Anti-Crime Organization. The bureau was located in the UN Building in New York City, and Basil was childishly proud to work there, although he would not have dreamed of showing it. He had a predictably sound future with UNACO—provided that UNACO itself had one.

The bureau had never been—and, Philpott feared, never would be—a totally secure operation, free from political pressure and financial stress. Philpott himself had proposed the formation of the top-secret group when he was a research professor at a New England university.

His specialist subjects had been behavioral sciences, but Philpott's deepest interest lay in the motivation and machination of the criminal mind. He had lobbied furiously to gain UN approval, and won it only because the US government of the day had funded the initial outlay. Philpott resisted the American patronage, and ever since then had fought successive administrations to keep UNACO independent of the American, or any other, state. The bureau must, he insisted, be at the disposal of all UN member countries, from whichever power bloc. An enlightened UN secretariat finally saw the point.

Philpott's other problem—easily foreseen but difficult to resolve—was infiltration by the UN states who were picking up the bills. Philpott fought off patently obvious attempts at penetration by both the CIA and the KGB, but the French, Israeli, British, and South African plants were sometimes trickier to uncover. Gradually, the director established his right to a *cordon sanitaire* as the only

21

effective means of guaranteeing UNACO's neutrality and disinterestedness. He managed to cope with the naturally divided feelings of his American-born operatives, who had to constantly fend off appeals to their native patriotism, and relied heavily on his assistant director, Sonya Kolchinsky, a Czech national, for ammunition against Warsaw Pact interests.

Lastly, Philpott had to persuade all his clients that UNACO was not in business to play politics . . . that the American destabilization of Chile and Jamaica, or the Soviet Union's ruthless repression of Czechoslovakia and Poland, were not international crimes in the accepted sense; deplorable, but not actionable. UNACO's enemies were criminals who challenged the security of nations and the stability of social order, and of those known to Philpott, Mister Smith came near the top of the list.

An unwanted complication for the UNACO director was the depth of his personal relationship with the US president, Warren G. Wheeler, a close friend since college days. Wheeler had to be treated as impartially as any other UN head of state, but it created a difficult tightrope for Philpott to walk. If he leaned too far in either direction, he would fall, and UNACO with him. But then, Malcolm Gregory Philpott had been trained for the risk business. And anyway, it made life interesting.

Now approaching his mid-fifties, Philpott was still a lean, trim, and handsome man, though his abundant hair was iron grey and his sharp, intelligent face was seamed, more from responsibility than age. The principal emotions showing on it as Swann walked into his office were tension and concern, rather belying Philpott's reputation as a cunning poker player.

The large room through which Swann had passed on his way to see the director housed the UNACO master computer, plus an electronically operated wall map of the world and a staff of multilingual monitors, whose continuous task was to tap listening posts in a hundred and thirty countries.

Each time a new contact was made, a red light flickered on the wall map, indicating its point of origin. An exact see-through miniature of the map rested on Philpott's uncluttered desk. Basil Swann approached the desk, stood in silence, coughed discreetly, and handed the director a computer printout. It was a brief list, no more than five lines.

USSR: Gold bullion shipment—Klvost to Moscow.

EEC: Brussels. Quarterly NATO conference.

MIDDLE EAST: Bahrain. OPEC ministers to Washington.

Cairo. Israeli-Egyptian defense talks.

SOUTHERN HEMISPHERE: Cape Town. Diamonds in transit to Amsterdam.

Philpott quickly scanned the entries and accompanying estimate of dates, and then read it over, more slowly. "Is this everything?" he inquired.

"It is a complete catalogue of the likeliest events within the next three months in which the computer considers our friend might conceivably display a criminal interest," Swann replied ponderously.

"Which friend?" called a voice from the doorway, "and furthermore, what do you mean by bleeping me at the hairdresser's? You know how sensitive Pepito is. It'd better be important."

"It is, Sonya," Philpott answered as his assistant director, newly and radiantly coiffured, sailed into the room and sank into a chair proffered by Swann. Sonya Kolchinsky was sumptuously fashioned and of above-average height, with a round face, soft grey eyes, and short brown hair, elegantly molded to her shapely head. She was a good ten years younger than Philpott, but saw no reason to permit minor considerations like age difference or their positions in UNACO to interfere with the affair they had both conducted, guiltlessly and joyfully, ever since she had become part of UNACO and of Philpott's life.

"It's very important," Philpott added gravely. "Smith's got out of jail."

"O-h-h," she breathed, "*that* friend."

"*That* friend."

Sonya pondered the news. "He hadn't long to serve, had he?" she said. "I remember he bribed his way to a lenient sentence after the Eiffel Tower snatch.* It could have had only a few more months to run." Philpott nodded his

*Alistair MacLean's *Hostage Tower*

23

agreement. "In which case," Sonya pressed, "wasn't it rather foolish of him to break out now?"

"Maybe," Philpott conceded, "—or maybe not."

"Why 'maybe not'?"

"Because, my pet, it could be he's planning something so important that only he personally can mastermind it. Ergo, he wanted out of Fresnes."

Sonya frowned. "So—we're looking for the big one, are we?" Philpott nodded, and handed her the printout.

"The computer's come up with these," he explained, concern in his voice. "It could be any of them. They're all his style, although a couple are more overtly political than usual for Smith."

A single glance confirmed the impression for Sonya, and she provisionally eliminated the Brussels conference and the Cairo talks. Like Malcolm Philpott, she had become obsessed with Mister Smith when UNACO finally got to grips with him and succeeded in putting him away. Smith was arguably the most enigmatic force in world crime, a rare breed of criminal: dedicated to anarchy, and totally amoral. Perhaps even worse, he was wedded to the abstract concept of crime for its own sake, as a cleansing agent in a second-rate world.

Financial gain seemed hardly to matter to him; he craved solely the power and influence to commit more astounding and more atrocious assaults on people, on governments, institutions, and social systems.

Smith did not seek to become the Napoleon, the Alexander, or the Tamburlane of crime; in his warped mind, he already *was*. No one—not those closest to him, even—knew where he had come from, what he had originally looked like (he altered his appearance like other people changed their clothing), or the precise nature of the obsessional paranoia that drove him. He was fabulously rich, well-connected, young for his age (whatever that was), and a man of almost limitless accomplishment who could have been outstanding in any area of human activity he chose. Yet Mister Smith had chosen one of the lowest forms of human activity and, unfortunately for the world, he had elevated it to an art form.

As Director of UNACO, Philpott had recruited, and still used, international criminals, poachers turned gamekeepers, to fight Smith. They had been successful once, and Philpott was convinced that only UNACO could stop him again.

But if they could not, then whatever the chosen battleground, Philpott had an uneasy foreboding that UNACO, directly or indirectly, would be right in the firing line. Together with its director and assistant director.

"Right," said Philpott, handing the printout back to Swann, "plant agents in sensitive areas of all the operations I've marked—including Cairo and Brussels."

"But not Bahrain?" Basil protested.

Philpott cupped his chin in his hand and pursed his lips. "No," he agreed, "not Bahrain. The transport of the OPEC ministers to Washington at, I believe, the end of next month, is being done in Air Force One, and we already have Joe McCafferty on assignment there as head of security. We couldn't possibly have anyone safer in such a sensitive area."

"Right, sir," said Swann, and was halfway to leaving the room when Sonya called him back. Philpott looked up at her inquiringly.

"I'm not so sure. . . ." she said, appearing deep in thought. Philpott cocked a quizzical eyebrow.

It went back, she explained, to their joint suspicion that Smith could be planning some form of revenge upon UNACO, even if only as a byproduct of the larger operation. If that were so, might he not select the Bahrain gathering and go for Air Force One *because* UNACO's man was assigned to the plane as head of security?

"Deliberately bracket us in the target, you mean," said Philpott pensively.

"Yes, deliberately. After all, what would destroy our credibility more effectively than that something awful should happen to the US president's private aircraft, with one of UNACO's top men in charge?"

Philpott stroked the bridge of his nose, then removed his spectacles and chewed the earpiece reflectively. It was, he thought, a hell of a position to be in, having to compromise one of their own leading field operatives on assignment by planting a check agent on him, but Sonya had advanced a persuasive argument.

25

"He's so unpredictable," she pressed. "The big one could be any of these—or none of them."

"OK, Basil," Philpott conceded, "we'll cover all the options, including Bahrain. I'll contact McCafferty in general terms and warn him to be especially vigilant on the OPEC trip, and you assign an operative to Air Force One."

"With McCafferty's knowledge and permission?" Swann inquired.

"Without it, Basil," Philpott said firmly, "most definitely without it. Clearly, it must be someone Joe hasn't served with previously, has never met, and doesn't even know works for us. We've done it before."

"Not to top cats like McCafferty," Swann persisted. Philpott grinned and said, "There's always a first time for everyone. With Smith, we can't afford to take chances."

Basil left, and Sonya regarded Philpott shrewdly. "Why the anonymous backup?" she inquired. It had not been part of her thinking. She had merely wished to strengthen McCafferty's hand.

Philpott looked back at her levelly, and liked what he saw. He liked her thought processes, too; they had played seven card draw a couple of times in bed, where she had him at a constant and embarrassing disadvantage. "Merely covering the options," he replied.

She grinned. "Or playing both ends against the middle?"

Philpott winked at her. "Yeah, well," he said, "you and Smith aren't the only clever bastards in this little game."

The weather was once again a splendid advertisement for Switzerland, with the air as clear and bracing as Stein's brochure claimed. The Mercedes driver was in excellent humor, too; for once he had a communicative passenger. To Dunkels's astonishment, Smith had insisted on keeping up a flow of spirited conversation throughout the journey to the Edelweiss Clinic. Dunkels guessed that he might be doing no more than testing out his new accent and persona—aristocratic Boston Irish, with long Harvard vowel sounds to match his Ivy League suit. The chauffeur, though, had been impressed, not least by Smith's courtesy in explaining his more obscure witticisms in faultless Swiss patois.

Stein met them at the door and took them straight to the landscaped gardens at the rear of the clinic, which reached back to the sheer wall of the mountain. Jagger sat in a wheelchair in a far corner, talking to a blond nurse, recently hired to replace the previous one who had been fired on Karilian's orders. The fewer people who knew that Jagger and the plastic surgery case from the private wing were one and the same man, the better, Karilian reasoned.

Before Stein could call out to Jagger, Smith shouted, "Colonel McCafferty. Visitors."

The wheelchair swung about, and Jagger, in what even at that early stage was a passable imitation of McCafferty's voice, said, "I don't believe we've met, have we?"

"Good, Jagger, good," Smith exulted. "I have not had the honor of Colonel McCafferty's acquaintance, and it's my intention to keep it that way. You've done well. Already, you've exceeded my expectations."

He turned to Stein and pressed congratulations on him, too, which the little doctor was compelled modestly to accept. The transformation had, in all truth, been a miracle of plastic surgery.

Stein then mentioned that Jagger was curious about the nature of the assignment he was to carry out as McCafferty, but Smith advised Jagger not to worry; he would be told all in a few weeks. Meanwhile, he was to immerse himself in the role, for he would periodically be examined in his mastery of it by Dunkels. "I need hardly have to explain," Smith purred, "that I shall be most displeased if all the hard work and expense I have gone to proves to be wasted. If you are found ultimately incapable of performing this task, I assure you that you will not survive long enough to ponder your failure."

Jagger flushed as far as the stretched pink tissue of McCafferty's face would permit, and made as if to rise from the wheelchair, but Stein and the nurse eased him back down. Stein protested that Smith was being unfair, and could unsettle Jagger's psychological acceptance of the permanent loss of his identity.

Smith dismissed the possibility with an airy wave of his hand, and reassured Jagger of his confidence in the ringer's powers. He repeated that Jagger would learn every-

27

thing he needed to know before long. "You, on the other hand, my dear doctor," Smith said to Stein, "will *not* be told the details of the plan. When it becomes a *fait accompli*, the whole world will know. In the meantime, I am paying as much for your silence as for your undoubted medical skill."

Stein smiled and inclined his head. Smith need have no fears for his discretion, Stein promised, nor would he seek information from Jagger when the ringer was in full possession of the facts. "Then we understand each other, Doctor," Smith replied, a satisfied smile on his face.

Stein beamed back at him. Probably no other man alive, he reflected, had ever doublecrossed Mister Smith and collected a large fee from him at the same time.

No other man, true. But a woman had . . .

. . . and her name was Sabrina Carver.

She had been a member of Smith's Eiffel Tower commando team, but in reality (and undetected by Smith) had helped bring about his destruction there, for she was also a valued agent of UNACO. Sabrina knew the identity of only one other UNACO field operative—and it was not Joe McCafferty.

Philpott had made it a corner of UNACO's game plan to keep his agents anonymous and apart. It protected the agents, and it shielded UNACO, since a captured operative could denounce only himself or herself, or the headquarters staff. And everyone knew who the headquarters staff were; their names were published in official UN documents. Philpott's only truly secret weapons were his agents, which he employed in every UN member state. A full roster of their names would make a priceless intelligence weapon, and surprising reading, especially to the agents themselves.

When circumstances absolutely required it, Philpott paired agents into a team for a "need to know" one-to-one relationship. Sometimes, teams stayed together—if both members survived. Certain operatives were never twinned, either from disinclination, or because they were politically or strategically sensitive. McCafferty was in the strategically sensitive category.

Philpott drew his field staff from all classes, colors, and

creeds, and if he had to pair an agent, he took what sometimes seemed to Sonya Kolchinsky to be an almost perverse delight in matching polar opposites.

For example, Joe McCafferty, who now had to be twinned, was an honest and straightforward career airman, a fiercely patriotic American and a high-ranking officer with an outstanding reputation, both in the Pentagon and in the American Secret Service.

Whereas Sabrina Carver, whom Philpott had selected as McCafferty's partner, was an international jewel thief.

Her fee for the Eiffel Tower job (reluctantly agreed by Philpott) had been the proceeds of an astonishing raid on the Amsterdam Diamond Exchange, which she had carried out to impress Smith into hiring her for his team. Philpott's ruthless efficiency, and proven success with UNACO, frequently collided head-on with his conscience when the delicate question arose of the head of an anti-crime squad actually aiding and abetting his own pet criminals. Luckily, his conscience invariably fell at the first fence.

UNACO's finances, never more than grudgingly yielded by the UN member countries, depended on results, and there was very little that Malcolm Philpott would not do to obtain those results. Particularly when he was forced to deal with criminal monsters like Smith.

Philpott gave Swann his instructions on Sabrina's role of shadow to Joe McCafferty. "There's to be only a one-way 'need to know' this time," he emphasized. "Sabrina must know about McCafferty, but he is not to know about her, unless I expressly order it. Clear?"

Swann left to bring in Sabrina for briefing, and Sonya complained that the situation was still far from clear to her, even if Swann understood it. "He doesn't," Philpott declared, "but he'll do as he's told. The point is that Joe will be a front-line target and won't want to be bothered with looking after a 'twin'. At the same time, he won't appreciate feeling that we've set someone to watch him.

"But I reckon that if Smith does have designs on Air Force One, then Joe will be able to use all the help he can get, and I'll deal with his outraged manhood when the whole thing's over."

Philpott looked gravely at Sonya, and ventured a weary

smile. "It could be bad," he said slowly. "The worse we've ever had to face. If Smith launches an action against Air Force One and half a dozen oil sheiks, I don't have to tell you that there's nothing, absolutely nothing, anyone except our people aboard that Boeing can do about it."

As the long-serving and respected correspondent of the Soviet newspaper *Isvestia* in Central Europe, Axel Karilian enjoyed an enviably high standard of living in a luxury apartment block near the center of Geneva. He had resisted all attempts by the Swiss to plant domestic staff in his flat to spy on him, so it was Karilian himself who answered the imperious ring at his doorbell in the early hours of the morning. He recognised his visitor as medium- to top-ranking in the KGB.

"They did not tell me you were coming," Karilian said in greeting.

"I did not tell them I was going," his visitor said coldly. Karilian revised his estimate; there had clearly been a purge in the Gorski Prospekt, and his uninvited caller, code named Myshkin, was now indisputably top rank. Karilian produced whisky and cigars, vodka and cigarettes being reserved strictly for lower order guests.

"This man Smith," the KGB high-flier said, "interests us. So does his project, whatever it may turn out to be. We will refer to it in vague terms, please, since"—he pantomimed a listening device—"we cannot be too careful."

Karilian protested, in suitably oblique language, that the apartment was "clean," but Myshkin waved him to silence. "It will be as I say," he ordered. Karilian shrugged and nodded.

"We consider the project," Myshkin went on, "to be of the utmost significance to us." Karilian suddenly felt a thrill of unease steal over him. Despite Myshkin's denial, Moscow had obviously penetrated Smith's security; they *knew* his target.

"An international incident of extreme gravity can be created from the Smith project," Myshkin was saying, "one which will cause maximum embarrassment to a certain person who is not precisely our closest friend."

Karilian inclined his head at the blatant clue, while excitement gripped his innards. The reference must be to

Warren G. Wheeler, president of the United States of America—and Karilian had found out sufficient details of Air Force One's future schedule to be certain now that Smith's target was the OPEC ministers. Nothing else fitted the facts. Only by maximizing an incident involving the oil sheiks could Moscow conceivably create an international situation of "extreme gravity" for the USA and UNACO, and cause the American president supreme embarrassment.

"You are with me?" Myshkin inquired. Karilian gravely nodded his head.

"Good. The plan will succeed. It will not be permitted to fail. The *doppelgänger* will be everything he purports to be. Do I make myself clear?"

Without waiting for a reply, Myshkin remarked that if all went well, Moscow would be under a deep obligation to Karilian for involving the KGB in Smith's project. Karilian prayed silently; not pleased enough to bring me back to Moscow.

As if reading his innermost thoughts, Myshkin grinned slyly and sat forward in his chair. The light from the anglepoise lamp illuminated his sharp, knowing features, from the sheen on his dark hair to the point of his pomaded chin.

He made Karilian feel gross. And afraid. "What I mean is that you could be promoted to a posting of your own choice . . . outside Russia."

Karilian tried desperately hard not to show his relief.

"But of course, should Mister Smith's little venture end in failure, there will nonetheless be a welcome awaiting you in Moscow. On the whole, though, I would advise against failure," Myshkin said sympathetically. "You know how—eh—warm our welcomes can sometimes be, my dear Axel, don't you?"

Chapter Four

Hawley Hemmingsway III stretched his big, well-covered frame in the sheik of Bahrain's bath and paddled the foaming water to make the scents rise. The bath had been prepared for him by a maid, but Hemmingsway guessed that at least three exotic oils had been used to perfume his ablutions, one of them attar of roses. "Something about me that even my best Arabian friends won't confide?" he mused.

Hemmingsway chuckled in his deep and melodious voice. Only one aspect of an American secretary of energy could conceivably get up an Arab's nose, and Hawley had no trouble in that direction. He chortled again as he recalled Warren Wheeler's acute embarrassment at the White House luncheon party where Hemmingsway was offered the job.

"You're absolutely certain, now, Hawley," the president had persisted, the anxiety showing in the fork of frown lines etched into the fingertip of flesh between his eyes. "Even three, four generations back—you're sure, are you? Not a single drop of Hebrew blood anywhere? God knows—and I'm sure *you* do—that I'm no racist," Wheeler had interjected quickly, "but I simply cannot afford to annoy these OPEC guys, and one way to get them foaming at the mouth and biting their Persian carpets would be to appoint even a quarter-Jewish secretary of energy."

Hemmingsway had assured the president that he was New England WASP clear back to the Pilgrim Fathers. With a sly grin he added, "As a matter of fact, the Hemmingsways were playing croquet with the Cabots and the Adamses and the Lodges while the Wheelers were still skinning beaver and raccoon to make a dress for Pocahontas."

The jibe had gone unremarked but for a slight lift of the president's eyebrows; Hemmingsway knew his man, however, and had walked away from the West Wing with the energy portfolio safely in his pocket. His credentials duly passed the scrutiny of the Arabs, and when the OPEC ministers met in Bahrain for talks on a possible East-West oil accord, Hemmingsway had been invited to join them as the house guest of the Ruler. One of the sheik's fleet of Cadillacs was put at his disposal, and Hemmingsway derived satisfaction from roaring unnoticed around the island at the sort of gas-gulping speeds that were firmly outlawed in the States by his own energy conservation program.

The talks were going well, too, justifying President Wheeler's decision not only to send Hemmingsway to Bahrain, but also to lay on his personal airplane, Air Force One, for the journey via Geneva to Washington, where the second stage of the negotiations would take place.

Hemmingsway drew himself out of the huge round bath, walked to the shower where he sluiced off the oily water, and from there straight into a toweling robe held aloft by the maid, teeth gleaming beneath her *yashmak,* eyes decorously averted. Hawley grinned and thanked her in Arabic. He was an extremely conscientious secretary of energy.

Strictly speaking, Air Force One is not Air Force One at all unless the president of the United States is on board. Ferrying the secretary of state, for example, it becomes Air Force Two, but it is still the same plane—what the USAF called a VC-137C stratoliner, which is their term for a Boeing 707 commercial long-distance airliner. And if the president chose to loan it out as Air Force One, that was his prerogative. The plane was his, together with the name, current since 1962 but now universally known.

The Boeing was converted to include an office and living suite for the president between the forward and center passenger compartments. Visitors were not invited to occupy the "apartment," but there was plenty of comfortable and roomy seating in the three passenger areas, flanked by front and rear galleys and rest rooms. Externally, Air Force One carried the streaming legend

"United States of America," and the presidential insignia. She was crewed, always, by personnel of the USAF's 89th Military Wing at Andrews Air Force Base, Washington DC.

The sun winked blindingly on her fuselage and gleaming wings as the liner turned on to the heading for Muharraq Airport, Bahrain. Major Patrick Latimer brought the big plane down to skim over the threshold, then he ran it to the taxiway leading to the hardstand. Latimer, though officially designated the pilot, sat in the copilot's seat to the right of the controls. On his left, in the pilot's seat, was the Commander of Air Force One, Colonel Tom Fairman. Behind them sat the navigator, Lieutenant Colonel Paul Kowalski, and next to him crouched one of the flight's two engineers, Master Sergeant Chuck Allen. They completed the closing-down procedures, and Sergeant Allen operated the Boeing's hatch.

Another man—a member of the crew, but with no aeronautical purpose to fulfill—waited for the airport staff to position the moving steps just below the hatch. He was always the first man to leave the plane, the last to board it. He stood by the open hatch, revolver drawn, peering out into the strong, clear sunlight.

Just as it was Colonel Thomas D. Fairman's task to supervise the flight of Air Force One, so the job of guaranteeing the safety of the Boeing, its crew, and occupants, was ultimately the responsibility of only one man: the head of security, Colonel Joe McCafferty.

The entire crew filed to the hatch and waited patiently while McCafferty completed his surveillance. Then Mac holstered his gun and walked down the stairway, followed by Fairman, Latimer, and the other airmen. Last out of the plane was Bert Cooligan, agent of the US Secret Service, and the only other armed man on the flight.

Fairman increased his stride and came abreast of McCafferty. "Seeing the Manama sights before we leave, Mac?" he inquired. McCafferty treated him to a flinty grin. "Your job may be over, Tom," he returned, "but mine's just beginning. Not that the vibrant and sinful capital of Bahrain doesn't hold its attractions for me, but I think I'll check around a bit and then retire to the hotel with a bottle of Jack Daniels and a good security schedule."

Fairman grinned. "Not even a Gideon Bible?"

"Here? No, it's either the Koran or my smuggled copy of *Playboy*—not to be left laying around for the natives to read. Gives them a bad impression of the flower of American womanhood."

Both men laughed, and the Arab watching them from the terminal building's balcony through binoculars minutely adjusted the focus.

Since the age of seven in her native town of Fort Dodge, Iowa, Sabrina Carver had been a thief. She started with a tiny brooch stolen from a fellow passenger on a trip down the Des Moines River. She got two dollars for it, which was a ripoff, for the brooch had three diamonds set into a silver clasp. Sabrina failed to recognize the stones as diamonds; it was a mistake she would not make again.

Ten years later she left her home and Fort Dodge and, as far as she could see, would never need to return to either. She had seventy thousand dollars in a bank account kept for her by an admiring professional fence, and on her eighteenth birthday doubled her nest egg with a hotel raid that the police said could only have been committed by a squad of acrobatic commandos.

For that was Sabrina Carver's forte: she channeled her astonishing physical fitness, her sporting prowess, even her beauty and considerable intellect, into becoming one of the greatest cat burglars ever known. And she used her skill to equip herself, perhaps uniquely, for her ruling passion: not just stealing, but stealing diamonds.

Philpott, who had his finger clamped firmly on the pulse of international crime, became aware of the swiftly rising star (she was still only twenty-seven) and watched her subsequent career with interest and not a little pleasure. He waited for her first mistake, and when she made it in Gstaad, trusting a greedy lover, Philpott had snatched her from the Swiss police and enrolled her as a part-time agent of UNACO.

Philpott paid her lavishly enough for her not to have to steal again, but, as he freely acknowledged, a girl with Sabrina's brains and stunning beauty had never actually *needed* to be a thief; she simply enjoyed it. Stealing was what she did best, and neither Philpott nor her position as a UNACO field operative would prevent her from doing it. That was why she was a part-time agent.

She sat in the foyer of Manama's most splendid hotel and quickly adjusted to the idea that most of the diamonds in Bahrain would be worn by men. She was idly sketching in her mind a plan to penetrate the Sheik's palace when she was forced to relinquish pleasure and get back to reality—Joe McCafferty strode in through the ornate revolving doors.

McCafferty spotted her immediately, for she was wearing the uniform of Airman First Class in the USAF. He had been heading for the reception desk, but changed direction when he saw Sabrina. As he got closer his stride faltered and he blinked. Sabrina Carver had that effect on men; she was breath-catchingly lovely, with a cascade of dark brown hair falling to her shoulders, framing a face elliptical in its contours, from the central hair parting high on her forehead to the dimple in her chin. Her brow was deep, her eyes wide-spaced and large, and her nose and mouth were set in exquisite classical proportion.

McCafferty completed the journey with outstretched hand and slightly glazed eyes. "You're Prewett's replacement, I expect," he said. A flight traffic specialist (the equivalent of a stewardess on a commercial airline) had dropped out at the last moment, and he had been warned by radio that a substitute would meet Air Force One in Bahrain. Fairman was able to make the outward trip with only one stewardess, but he needed two for the passenger run to Washington. As always with the president's jet, all new attachées to the crew reported in the first instance to the head of security. Sabrina stood up, saluted, and handed over her identification documents, as she had been briefed to do by Basil Swann after Philpott had fixed the Pentagon.

She took McCafferty's hand and felt his strong fingers enclose her own. She was careful not to return equal pressure, though her hands were undoubtedly a good deal more adaptable and educated even than his. "AIC Carver, sir," she said, "reporting as directed to Air Force One. You're Colonel McCafferty, sir?" Mac confirmed the introduction; he was still faintly dizzy from the impact she

36

made on him. "Right then, C-Carver," he stammered, "or may I call you whatever it is, since we're off duty?"

She smiled winningly and replied, "It's Sabrina— strictly while we're off duty. Do I keep calling you 'sir,' sir? Only for off duty, that is?"

"Ah—no. My name's Joe, but most of my friends call me Mac."

"Which do you prefer?"

"I'll leave the choice to you."

"Well, since we're apparently going to be friends, perhaps I'd better make it 'Mac,' " Sabrina rejoined with not a trace of coyness. McCafferty smiled a shade awkwardly and she decided that the file photographs of him which Basil Swann had shown her did not do the colonel justice. He was decidedly handsome in an aggressive and somehow unflattering way, with a hint of pugnacity, or perhaps cruelty, in the determined set of his mouth and chin; his nose was long, wide, and straight, and his eyes colored a piercing blue.

She questioned him about their schedule, and McCafferty explained that they intended making a convenience refuelling stop in Geneva while picking up stores which were not easily obtainable in Bahrain. They would stay in Switzerland overnight. Takeoff from Manama (he consulted his watch) was in four hours.

"Do you have a room here?" McCafferty asked innocently, then blushed as he realized how his question could be taken. "I—I didn't mean—for God's sake—well, you know—I'm not *that* fast a worker. Wh—what I meant was—"

"What you meant," Sabrina replied, enjoying his discomfiture and liking him for it, "at least what I hope you meant, was do I, like the rest of the crew, have a room at the hotel where I can freshen up before the trip."

McCafferty breathed a sigh of relief. "Thanks for letting me off so easily. I'm not really that sort of guy—despite anything you may have heard to the contrary."

Mac groaned when he saw how deeply he had landed both feet in it this time, and sent up his hands to cover the flush that threatened to suffuse his entire face. Sabrina burst out laughing, but quickly apologized to save him from even more acute distress. He could not, after all, possibly know that she was able to recite the names of every woman Mac had slept with over the past five years, as well as their assessments of his capabilities—in and out of bed.

"I really *don't* have that sort of reputation," Mac protested earnestly.

"I'm sure you don't colonel—sorry, 'Mac'—but since you've given me the impression that you do, maybe I should think twice about accepting that dinner-date in Geneva you were on the point of offering me."

Mac looked at her in amazement. "How did you know I was planning to buy you dinner in Geneva tonight?" he exploded. "I hadn't even got around to the preliminary—uh—"

"Preliminary seduction moves?" she whispered, wide-eyed and girlish. "Gosh, gee, and golly, I've never been seduced by an expert before, by a famous Lothario like the great Joe McCafferty—"

"Now you're toying with my emotions," Mac protested, drawing himself up sternly. "In my capacity as head of security on Air Force One, and as the first crew member to set eyes on you, I consider it my military duty to protect you from that crowd of rampant wolves by ordering you, AIC Carver, to dine with me this evening in Geneva. Is that understood?"

"Aye, aye, Colonel," she responded, throwing him a second smart salute, "as long as it's purely in the interests of protective discipline, of course."

It was Mac's turn to smile. "I don't normally beat the crew," he said, "but I could always make an exception of you, if that's what turns you on." Sabrina reddened prettily and gulped. "I think we'd better end this conversation and continue our 'on duty' relationship, sir," she said.

"But you'll make it for dinner tonight?" Mac pleaded.

"You bet."

They parted, and the Arab, sipping an ice cream soda in the screened-off bar area to their left, laid his binocular case on the table and jotted an entry in a slim blue notebook.

Sabrina received a message from a man who announced himself as Chief Steward Master Sergeant Pete Wynanski from Air Force One. The commander, he said, had ordered a crew muster in the hotel lobby. She saw the group at the far end away from the bar as she left the elevator. McCafferty was not with them, and she felt unreasonably disappointed. She saluted Colonel Fairman and met the crew, each of whom looked at her perhaps a little too much, to Fairman's evident amusement.

"I can see you're going to enjoy it with us, Carver." He grinned. "Even if *you* don't, the rest of the crew obviously will."

Sabrina smiled back and inquired for McCafferty's whereabouts. "Aah," moaned the delicately structured, poetic-looking Latimer theatrically, "already smitten with our dashing head of security, I can tell. Swashes his buckle at anything female that moves aboard the plane, does Mac, although I have to admit that this time, for once, he has shown excellent taste."

"Stow it, Pat," said Fairman, "AIC Carver's a member of this crew, and I do not want her position made any more—eh—difficult than it is at the moment. She's with Air Force One to *work*, and I want nothing to interfere with that. To answer your question, Carver, Colonel McCafferty's gone out to the airport with Agent Cooligan via the route the OPEC ministers will use. Then, if I know Mac, he'll check, doublecheck and recheck the plane, the police, the airport guards, the luggage hold, and even look for cracks in the runway. Colonel McCafferty's damned good at what he does. I only wish that went for the rest of my so-called crew."

The commander chuckled easily along with the rest of the flight staff, then returned once more to business, asking Sergeant Wynanski if he were all fixed for provisions. Wynanski replied that he had been furnished by the White House with a list of the ministers' dietary requirements, which he had augmented through discreet inquiries at the hotel and at the palace. He still had to pick up a few items from the markets in Manama.

"Good work, Sergeant," Fairman commended him, "you have about an hour. That applies to everyone. I'll want cabin personnel aboard by 1600 hours. Flying crew to Ops by 1650. You'll find minibuses outside this hotel half an hour before reporting times. Boarding's at 1805."

Wynanski and his staff and most of the flying crew

drifted away; Fairman stayed to take Sabrina on one side. As a new crew member, she got the commander's introduction to Air Force One at full strength on the patriotism scale. Fairman also impressed her with the importance of their current assignment.

"This isn't going to be just a milk run," the colonel said gravely. "We're using Air Force One mainly because our own secretary of energy, Mr. Hemmingsway, will be on board—but let me assure you that we do wish to impress the OPEC ministers; we want to make them feel good. I need hardly tell you, if you've been keeping up with the news, that if they don't come in with us on this oil deal, then they're likely to cut back production so far that we'll be riding bicycles and reading by candlelight back in the States for years to come. Nothing, but nothing, must go wrong on this trip, Carver, so—be alert, polite, and efficient at all times. A good stewardess can make the world of difference to a military flight. Chief Steward Wynanski's something of a martinet, but I guess you'll have him eating out of your hand in no time, just like the rest of us."

Sabrina felt herself going hot and was framing a suitably tart reply when Fairman held up a warning hand. "Just teasing, honey, just teasing," he assured her.

"So was Major Latimer, sir," she replied sweetly, "and, as I recall you hauled out his ass for it."

Fairman regarded her appraisingly, and grinned. "Somehow I don't think you really need any advice from me, Carver," he said.

Axel Karilian paced the floor of his Geneva apartment and bayed into the telephone. "It is important—vital—that Jagger contacts me here as soon as possible," he roared. "Do you understand that, Stein?" Karilian sneaked a sideways glance at the menacingly imperturbable Myshkin, lounging on a sofa nursing a generous Chivas Regal.

"It's not long to zero-hour there," Stein protested. "For God's sake, Axel, Jagger will be very busy, with Smith and Dunkels breathing down his neck the whole time. It'll be very difficult to contact him."

"You must!" Karilian insisted. "There has to be a way."

Modesty, a strong suit with Doctor Stein, veiled the slyness with which the little Swiss produced his trump card, mostly for the benefit of Myshkin, whom he correctly guessed was in Karilian's apartment. "Of course," Stein said smoothly, "Jagger *can* be contacted discreetly. I have, as it were, an open channel to him."

"Then *use* it! Jagger *must* call. There are new instructions to be passed to him, which alter the entire picture of the operation. Hot from Moscow, Stein—and they have to be obeyed. Get on with it." He banged the telephone down and was uncomfortably aware of Myshkin's gaze, directed at him through barely raised eyelids.

It took Jagger half an hour from receiving Stein's message before he could elude Dunkels for long enough to make a telephone call. The ringer's blood chilled when the cold, precise voice of Myshkin talked to him first in Russian and then repeated his orders in English to establish absolute clarity.

"As I understand it, Jagger," Myshkin said, "Mister Smith's plan is to—ah—interfere, shall we say, with the operation of Air Force One sufficiently to enable him to make a financial gain from the situation in which the OPEC ministers will consequently be placed. I do not wish to go into further detail on an open line."

Jagger confirmed the details. Karilian nervously pressed together the damp palms of his hands, and Myshkin continued, "Up to a point that is still satisfactory, but we feel that greater advantage can be gained by us if the affair concludes in a more—ah—drastic way. Do you follow me?"

"I—I don't, I'm afraid," Jagger replied uncertainly.

Myshkin gave an exasperated grunt. "I can see I shall have to be more specific," he said caustically. "It is of crucial importance to us, Jagger, that America comes badly out of this episode—as badly as can possibly be imagined. And there is surely one way to persuade the OPEC states not merely to refuse to sign the oil accord, but actually to sever relations of any kind with the United States." Both sides of the conversation were in English now; Myshkin had to make absolutely sure that Jagger understood him.

The ringer gasped in disbelief. "You can't mean—you can't—"

"But I do," Myshkin said. "That is precisely what I mean. You will kill the OPEC ministers, and the surviv-

41

ing crew members of Air Force One. You may leave us to deal with the genuine McCafferty.

"How you do it, Jagger, is your business. But do not fail me. Whatever happens, do not fail. Even if you are the only person alive on Air Force One when it is finished, that will be acceptable. But you must accomplish this task."

Jagger put down the receiver in his Bahrain hotel and took the elevator to the ground floor. As he stepped on to the ground floor, Dunkels hurried forward and grabbed his arm.

"Get into uniform," the German snapped brusquely. "We leave in five minutes. Achmed's reported that the pigeon is sitting up begging to be plucked."

McCafferty and Bert Cooligan came down the steps of Air Force One to meet the advancing posse of uniformed senior Bahraini policemen, all armed to their splendidly white teeth. McCafferty stopped and scuffed one of his shoes over a mark on the hardstand. Cooligan grinned. "That is not, sir," he whispered, "a crack, and even if it were, it's not on the runway."

Mac then met the police—who had tactfully placed themselves under his orders—and handed them copies of the security schedule. After their brief exchange, he and Cooligan walked on to the terminal building, where an Arab toyed with the strap of his binocular case and decided to visit the men's room. McCafferty looked up at the roof of the terminal, and saw three machine gunners placed strategically along the parapet.

"Check those guys out, Bert," he murmured. "Make sure they know that they're to fire *indiscriminately* at any, and I mean any, unauthorized person getting within fifty yards of the Air Force One steps. Give 'em copies of the program, too; I don't want to be shot when I lead in the convoy. I'm going back to the hotel. I need a shower and a drink and another chat with Hemmingsway before we get the motorcade under way. OK?"

Cooligan said *"Ciao,"* and Mac went through the terminal out into the street, in the wake of a tall, well-groomed young Arab in a Savile Row suit, who had a leather binoculars case swinging from his shoulder.

Mac carefully surveyed the front of the airport, where the police detachments were maneuvering into their positions, and so missed the barely perceptible signal which the Arab, known as Achmed Fayeed, made to a cab driver who was separated from the main gossiping bunch at the head of the taxi rank. The driver, who had been leaning casually against the side of a car, arms folded, unwound himself and got into the first cab.

As McCafferty lifted his arm to wave, the cab peeled off the rank and screeched to a halt about six inches from the American's leading foot. Mac yanked open the door, jumped in, and gave the name of his hotel. On the route out of the airport, they passed a byroad leading up to the cargo sheds. A short way along the byroad, its engine revving, sat a shiny black Cadillac. Achmed Fayeed spun the wheel, and cruised out after the cab.

Once he had settled in his seat, Mac returned to his security schedules for Geneva as well as those for Bahrain. Even if he noticed the following Cadillac, it did not register on his mind. Cadillacs—mostly in the Ruler's fleet— were common enough in Bahrain, and throughout the Gulf States. His driver watched the American carefully in the rear-view mirror.

A causeway links the airport at Muharraq with the main island of Bahrain, and when McCafferty glanced up and saw the road stretching out before him and the sunlight glistening on the water to either side, he dropped his eyes once more to the intricate details of his assignment. He was relaxed, and totally unprepared for the savage wrench at the wheel which took the taxi off the tarmac highway and onto a rutted dirt track that veered off to the right just before the watercrossing.

The track led to a cluster of tiny buildings known to the Bahrainis as *borrastis*, mean little huts made from palm fronds and mud into wattle beehives. Mac saw none of this. He went instinctively for his gun, but he was fractionally too late. The driver, a handkerchief clamped to his nose and mouth, aimed an aerosol spray over his shoulder, and it took the American full in the face.

McCafferty actually had his revolver in his hand, but it dropped from his unfeeling fingers. He slumped forward against the back of the driver's seat, and blackness descended on him.

Achmed Fayeed's car pulled up on the rough ground alongside the taxi, and the Arab pointed in the direction of the *borrasti* huts, which were hidden from the main road and the perimeter buildings of the airport by a fringe of palm trees. Both vehicles shot away and were soon lost in the oasis.

Achmed opened the rear door of the taxi and yanked out McCafferty's body. Dunkels strolled from the hut, looking down at the security chief. Then he turned and regarded a second man emerging from the *borrasti*. The likeness between the two was staggering, perfect in every detail.

Dunkels ordered Achmed to retrieve Mac's personal effects, ticking them off on his fingers: wallet, gun, security shield, documents, money, pen, handkerchief, lighter (if any). The Arab ransacked the American's body and handed the articles to Jagger, who stowed them away, checking at the same time that his uniform matched the security chief's exactly. "Take him inside now," Dunkels said, "and bring him round. There are things we need to know that only he can tell us."

"And if he won't?" Jagger asked. Dunkels shrugged. "He's going to die anyway. He might as well make it easy for himself."

"Not too easy," Jagger sneered, and got into the cab. The driver reversed his vehicle in a swirl of dust and took off back down the potholed track towards the causeway. There he turned on to the road-bridge and sped away to Manama.

He was in a hurry but drove with studied care. After all, he carried an important passenger: the head of security of Air Force One.

Chapter Five

Air Force One is a standard-frame Boeing intercontinental jet airliner, 153 feet long and almost as wide with a wingspan of 145 feet, 9 inches. She has four engines—Pratt and Whitney turbojets—which are capable of lifting a maximum takeoff weight of more than 150 tons.

With a range of over seven thousand miles, she can land on less than five thousand feet of runway. No pilot with fewer than four thousand flying hours under his belt can sit at her controls—the motto of the 89th Military Aircraft Wing, Special Missions (MAC), which provides the Boeing's crew, is *"Experto Crede"* (Trust one who has experience). Many times the president and people of the United States of America have had cause to be grateful to the people who fly Air Force One, and doubtless will have cause again.

The plane has a flight ceiling of more than forty thousand feet, and never carries less than ten in her crew. The Boeing's economic cruising speed is 550 mph, and she is unique in American aviation in carrying a lieutenant colonel as navigator. Air Force One flight crewmen wear blue uniforms, and the stewards maroon blazers with blue trousers or skirts, each uniform sporting the coveted presidential service badge.

More by accident than design, the president's aircraft has become something of a cottage industry in its own right. The tableware and accoutrements are custom-made and supplied gratis by manufacturers eager for the first citizen's approval. Since all the articles, from silverware, crystal glasses, dinner plates, cups and saucers, down to ashtrays, matchbooks, and dinner napkins, bear the presidential seal, they are eagerly sought by souvenir hunters.

Given the thriving black market in Air Force One artifacts, it is axiomatic that those who travel on her will yield to temptation and appropriate the portable items among the plane's equipment. These are highly prized, and have even been used as a kind of ersatz currency, rather like schoolboys doing "swaps."

The 89th (located, in fact, in Maryland, though the address of Andrews AFB is always given as Washington DC) would prefer to equip their flagship through the orthodox channels of paying for their own supplies and prosecuting people who steal from the plane, but the traditions of patronage and perks are deeply ingrained into American politics.

She had been cleaned, waxed, and polished in preparation for the OPEC trip, and her tires washed and checked, and she stood now on the runway at Muharraq, proud and gleaming and lovely in the yellowing rays of the sun, waiting for yet another manifest of passengers to board her who would never be charged for their journey.

The starboard engines, three and four, were already running to supply power and air conditioning and to prepare the Boeing for a rapid start. The storage inventory had been minutely examined and approved and, together with the baggage of the OPEC ministers, sent on ahead. On the flight deck the crew were at their posts for the necessary preflight procedures.

Master Sergeant Pete Wynanski, chief steward, handed "Airman" Sabrina Carver a printout of the guest list. "Study it," he snapped, "because this ain't a party for Hollywood moguls. These oil ministers are not just VIPs—they're EDPs."

"They're what?"

"They're what—'sergeant'."

"Sorry. They're what—sergeant?"

"EDPs. Exceptionally Distinguished Passengers. I don't want any of 'em sloshing around in wet socks because you spilled drinks over them. 'Kay?"

"Completely, chief. Uh—sergeant," Sabrina replied. Master Sergeant Wynanski seemed to be the only crew member with an absolute zero-response to her gorgeous body, and he, she reflected ruefully, had to be the one she picked as her boss. "There ain't no justice," she mused.

"Yerright," snapped Wynanski, "there ain't. Now—

dooties. You're drinks. Airman Fenstermaker here"—indicating a honey blonde with tinted glasses and an enormous bosom standing alongside Sabrina—"you're snacks. 'Kay? You may have to swap later. Depends. 'Kay?"

"Right, sergeant," they chorused, though Sabrina's brow was furrowed as her eyes ran down the Arab names. " 'S'matter, Carver?" Wynanski grunted.

"Well, you said I was drinks, but it looks as if most of them will be sticking to tea," Sabrina explained.

"Look, Carver, fer Chrissakes," Wynanski moaned. He had once been a waiter on the Staten Island ferry and had seen life. "You gotta unnerstan'—these guys are Ayrabs. Moslems. Goddit?"

"Uh-uh," she said, shaking her head.

"They ain't supposed to like booze," Wynanski said, patiently, "but from time to time, and especially when they're out or Ayrabia, they—well—indulge, if you get me. But still they can't appear to, and they don't like you to know it, nor anybody else. Right? So. Read down the list again—out loud, so Fenstermaker don't make a tit outa herself as well. Sorry, Fenstermaker. Nothin' personal about yah boobs."

Sabrina spluttered, but regained control and recited from the printout.

"Tea with milk and sugar."

"That's straight tea—real tea, from leaves, with milk and sugar, like it says," Wynanski pronounced.

"Tea with sugar but no milk," Sabrina intoned.

"Scotch," said Wynanski firmly, "on the rocks, no water."

Sabrina's mouth dropped open. "Ohhh," she breathed.

" 'Bout time, too," Wynanski snarled. "Con-tinue."

"Tea with lemon."

"Vodka. Ice. Lime juice." Sabrina made tiny notations.

"Black coffee, no sugar."

"Cognac, neat," Wynanski supplied.

"Tea—no sugar, no milk," Sabrina read. Wynanski looked puzzled. "Gimme that," he ordered, and scanned the list. Then his brow cleared, and a beatific smile illumined his battered face. "How about that?" he whispered, "one o' these guys got the hots for Jack Daniels. Whooppee!"

Through the open hatch of the Boeing, the far-off wail of police car sirens reached Sabrina's ears. The motorcade, she calculated, must be on the causeway by now.

She found herself keenly anticipating the flight, whatever dangers it might hold. Especially, she was looking forward to seeing McCafferty again. He had made, she decided, quite an impression on her.

Philpott gazed meditatively for the umpteenth time at the computer printout, dog-eared now, which was pinned to the front of Smith's UNACO file. "Two down," he said, "three to go." He darted an exasperated glance at the ominous barrage of clocks, adjusted for time zones and the individual preferences of more than a score of countries, sitting atop the electronic mural in the bureau's nerve center, naggingly pushing forward the time for action. "And one just about coming up."

"Sir?" Basil Swann inquired.

"Just thinking out loud," Philpott returned. "All set for Bahrain?"

Swann replied with a trendy "Affirmative." Air Force One, he supplied, would take off inside half an hour, on schedule. Sabrina Carver—"Airman First Class Carver"—was already on board the Boeing, and Colonel Joe McCafferty, according to his invariable procedure, would board last of all, after delivering the OPEC emissaries.

"No gremlins in the tracker bug?" Philpott asked. None, Basil assured him. Philpott chewed his lip, and refused to notice the Gulf time-zone clock, which had advanced by no more than a minute since he had last fixed it with a baleful glare. The tension got straight to his stomach, and he eased out a muted burp. Sonya Kolchinsky, from the neighboring swivel armchair, gave his hand a sympathetic squeeze.

Of the original five events which the UNACO computer had linked to Smith's escape, two were already safely dispatched: the gold bullion run to Moscow, and the Middle East defense talks in Cairo.

The bureau's resident agents—one a Soviet Army physical training instructor, the other *sous-chef* in a Cairo hotel—had slotted into the operations, and both incidents

48

were accomplished interference-free in their varying ways, but assuredly with no sign of criminal activity, from Smith or anyone else. The third event, chronologically speaking, on the master list was the journey Air Force One was about to commence, airlifting the Arabian oil titans to Washington DC via Geneva, Switzerland.

Philpott, for reasons he could not isolate, had a stronger feeling of apprehension about this one than the first two, or even the remaining pair. The fatal joker in the Air Force One pack had always been clear to him: the operation could not be controlled from the ground.

Despite the presence of McCafferty, unknowingly backed up by Sabrina Carver, a swift and audacious strike by Smith at the President's Boeing *could* succeed, immobilizing both agents—or killing them. And Philpott would be powerless to prevent it, or to control the action thereafter. He had insisted as a minimum precaution on a monitoring capacity for UNACO to track the flight. It was impossible, though, to pick up a duplicate radar-trace, so Basil Swann simply arranged a feed of the signal relayed through a communications satellite to the Pentagon.

The signal came from the Boeing's inertial navigation system, and Swann—against the odds, for it was a closely guarded secret—had discovered the frequency on which it was relayed. The signal was then decoded by the bureau's computer, which obligingly translated it into a visual display on the vast wall map.

At present it was no more than a pinpoint, throbbing expectantly on the island of Bahrain like an unleashed terrier.

But when the plane got airborne, the tracker-bug signal would snake out in a green line across the Middle East, the Near East, and the Mediterranean, following whichever course Colonel Tom Fairman had selected to take the Boeing to Geneva.

While the President's plane was in the skies, doing what it was supposed to do, going where it ought to go, the green tracker-line would continue crawling over the map. But should anything happen to the Boeing, the marker trail would vanish.

At all times, Malcolm Philpott would know the exact position and course of the aircraft—unless, by some inconceivable means, Mister Smith launched an attack, over-whelming even UNACO's redoubtable agents, Carver and McCafferty. "And by then, of course," Philpott murmured, "we shan't be able to do a damned thing about it."

"Hi," said the disembodied voice, "finished?"

Cody Jagger stared wildly at the telephone in his hand, and fleetingly cursed himself for not taking it off the hook in his (McCafferty's, rather) bedroom.

Cody had not wanted his first test to come in this fashion. Given an even chance and brought face to face with anybody high enough in McCafferty's circle, he reckoned he was good enough to pass. But trapped on the end of a phone with someone close enough to Mac not to feel it necessary to announce his name . . . the odds were that Jagger would fail. And he had. Stein had played him tapes, over and over again, of the voices of some of the UNACO man's friends, and Jagger had absorbed them. But he had never before heard the voice that had just spoken to him—of that Cody was sure.

He kept silent, seeking a clue, willing the caller to identify himself. Jagger controlled his breathing; his forehead was beaded in sweat. At least he had remembered Stein's instruction for telephone calls: never be the first one to speak; it would give him time to think; it would disconcert the caller, Stein had urged. And it would allow Jagger, in the last eventuality, to feign a wrong number in another assumed voice, and hang up.

He had almost made up his mind to cradle the receiver when the voice said, "That *is* you, Colonel, is it?"

"Colonel"—Jagger's mind raced to cope with the import of the formal address. A friend, but not too close a friend, then. Precise with the use of the title, so more than probably military: Army or Air Force. Possibly a crew member? Not flight crew, though, or engineers; nor maintenance, technicians, or stewards. None of these would have sufficient reason to disturb the security chief in his hotel bedroom.

Only one other man aboard Air Force One would actually have *business* with McCafferty. Jagger decided to take a chance. He could only fail a second time, and he might be able to bluff his way out of trouble.

"Sorry, Bert," he chuckled, "I was miles away."

"You can say that again," Cooligan replied in an aggrieved tone. "Now, to return to the point—have you or have you not finished?"

Once more Jagger waited, but this time deliberately, even allowing himself a small, judicious cough. The sweat was still spangling his eyebrows, yet his confidence was returning; he had, after all, won the first round. He had *deduced* Bert Cooligan—and he had been right.

Now it was Cooligan who was unwilling to break the silence. Could he be getting suspicious? Jagger wondered, the panic raising prickles of fear on his exposed skin.

Finally, Cooligan could stand it no longer. "Look, Colonel," he said patiently, "if you don't want to talk to me, for Christ's sake say so. But do me the favor of coming back from wherever it is that you are, because you sure aren't in your room talking to me on the phone.

"Now just for the record, you told me at the airport—and I say this again—you told me you were coming back to the hotel to shower and have a drink. So—if you haven't finished the shower bit, shall I come up to your room and leer at your magnificent body while you don clean drawers and best Air Force One blues? Or do I wait down here in the bar for you? Or do you wish me to have drinks sent up? Or you want I should go throw myself under a camel? Or like—what?"

Jagger started to say "Sure, Bert" to one of the propositions when Cooligan interrupted him. "Boy, am I dumb, chief! 'Course—you got company. Huh? Tricky bastard."

Cody laughed and assured Cooligan that he was (a) alone, and (b) with him again in body, mind, and spirit. What was he to do now though? Jagger mused. Face the music? He made up his mind.

"Sure, come on up, Bert," he said easily. "Give me five minutes and I'll promise to dress before you get here so's not to put you to shame, on condition that you're accompanied by a bottle of malt Scotch, a crowded ice bucket, four glasses, and—since you've given me the taste—two dusky harlots."

"Tush, Colonel, not while we're on duty," Cooligan admonished.

"You're right, Agent Cooligan," Jagger conceded, "forget the ice." Cooligan chortled and said, "That's better, Mac. You had me worried there for a moment. See you soon."

Jagger mopped his forehead and then snapped his fingers in annoyance. He tore off his uniform and sprinted for the shower, taking the jets of water barely lukewarm. He toweled himself down, slipped on clean underpants, and was lounging on the balcony in a bathrobe when Cooligan appeared.

The Secret Service agent was followed by a waiter pushing a trolley laden in the manner prescribed, and bearing a bonus of sandwiches. There seemed to be a world shortage of harlots, fuliginous or otherwise.

"I checked the airport guards like you said," Bert began when they were settled in easy chairs nursing a double Laphroaig apiece. "Their officers know what they're doing, and the guys themselves seem keen enough, if not a shade trigger happy. No one's been within stone-chucking distance of the Big Bird since the Bahrainis took over. I've briefed them, and I've had a word with the police outside. There'll be no trouble."

"For this relief, much thanks." Jagger sighed, choosing a quotation which he knew McCafferty might employ, "though it wasn't crowd scares I was anxious about."

"Huh?"

Jagger explained that, on the face of it, the trip could present a golden opportunity for Israeli irregulars, or even for a black propaganda PLO coup, zapping the plane and blaming it on Mossad or the Jews in general.

"Cautious old Mac." Bert grinned, lifting his glass in salute. "You don't change, do you?"

"You'd be disappointed if I did, wouldn't you?" Jagger said.

"I would," Cooligan admitted, "and so, no doubt, would that rather gorgeous stewardess Latimer tells me you're dating in Geneva tonight."

Jagger forced a grin as alarms probed sharply at his mind. He nearly bit his tongue to stop himself saying "I am?"

Gradually the rain of stinging blows on his cheeks and the shock of the water dashed into his face from an earthen-

52

ware pitcher brought McCafferty round. Achmed, crouched on his haunches over the American on the mud floor of the *borrasti*, shouted to Dunkels. The German examined their prisoner and complained that Achmed had been unnecessarily rough. A second Arab standing by Achmed grinned and drove his booted foot into Mac's ribs. The breath left the American's body in a rush, and a cry of pain came from his bruised lips.

"Oh, I am sorry," Achmed Fayeed apologized, "his foot slipped." Dunkels laughed, and asked McCafferty if he was feeling cooperative. Mac shook his head to clear away the fog and focus his eyes.

"Does he mean he isn't going to cooperate?" Achmed asked, round-eyed. McCafferty looked at him dully, then, deliberately, he filled his mouth and spat a gobbet of blood-streaked saliva into Achmed's face. Fayeed fastidiously wiped the mess from his chin, studied it on his handkerchief, and nodded casually to the other Arab, his servant, Selim. Selim stepped over the American's body and backheeled him viciously, turning in one fluid movement and crashing his other foot into the side of McCafferty's head, whipping it around to meet Achmed's fist from the other direction. In case the American hadn't got the point, they gave a repeat performance. Then Siegfried Dunkels held up his hand.

"That's enough," he ordered, "I want him to talk. Much more of that and he won't be able to even if he's willing." Achmed leaned forward, grabbed McCafferty by the shirtfront, and hauled him to a sitting position. Dunkels sprayed him with water again, and yanked up his head with a handful of hair. "Well, colonel?" he said pleasantly.

"Whoever you are," Mac replied thickly, his tongue feeling unnaturally big inside his swollen mouth, "whoever you are, you're trying something you can't possibly get away with. Let me go, release me, and I'll see that it goes down as a robbery; the police won't take any action.

"But keep me here, for whatever reason, and I promise you that every soldier in the Bahraini Army and every policeman on this island will be looking for me. Air Force One can't leave without me, and they'll find me—you'd better believe it. They'll have the backing of the president of the United States of America, and I wouldn't want to be where you are when all this blows up."

"What makes you think it isn't just a robbery?"

Mac grinned crookedly and painfully. "No mugger would strip me as clean as you have," he replied. "I don't seem to have a thing on me anywhere now to prove that I even exist. So clearly I was a target—and apart from that, you know who I am."

Dunkels threw back his head and laughed. "We do, colonel," he spluttered. "Oh, we do." Then he stopped, and his mouth set into a sneer. "And we think, too, that you may be, shall we say, overrating your importance? You say that Air Force One couldn't leave without you." He shook his head, bent down and whispered, "On the contrary, colonel, your absence will hardly be noticed.

Mac stared at him. "What the hell d'you mean?" he exploded. "If I'm not on that aircraft—"

"If you're not on the plane," Dunkels interrupted smoothly, "no doubt there would be some speculation for a short while on the flight deck, yes. Colonel—Fairman, is it?—yes, Colonel Fairman, I think . . . he might well express concern to Major Latimer, the pilot is he not? Or Lieutenant Colonel Kowalski, the navigator, could pass some sort of comment to Master Sergeant Allen, the engineer. But I dare say that's as far as it would go. What do *you* think, colonel?"

The cobwebs were still playing paper streamers in the American's mind. He shook his head again, in disbelief. The world was going crazy; this suave European and the murderous Arabs were unbalanced. What they said just didn't make sense. "You have to be joking," he grated. "Washington would hear of it, and when they do—"

"Ah, you mean they'd monitor the flight deck conversation on the open line to Andrews Air Force Base. Of course—"

"That can't be done," Mac flung at him savagely, "as you must know. But it won't take Tom Fairman two seconds to get them on the radio, and Pat Latimer would not, I repeat *not*, take off without me."

Dunkels stood up and roared with delight. "Jeeze, Mac," he said, "that's some bull'seye. That sure is a hole in one. Achmed—see that you-know-who gets the information:

Latimer's known as "Pat," not Patrick or Paddy, and Andrews Base has *no* facility to eavesdrop on the Air Force One flight deck. They can only communicate through the radio. Got that?"

The Arab rose to his feet, smiling broadly. Then he looked at his watch and said, "I'll make the calls on the way back to Manama. I'm overdue already. My master will not be pleased."

"Screw him," Dunkels said shortly.

"Now, now," Achmed chided, "not all we Arabs are pederasts, although they do say—"

Dunkels gestured at him impatiently. "I don't have the time for you to tell me what they say, Achmed. As you mentioned, you're late. On your way."

Fayeed strode from the *borrasti*, but turned at Dunkels's command. "The key," the German said.

Achmed fished in his pocket and tossed Dunkels a small bunch of keys, incongruously suspended on a thin gold chain. "The small one fits the cocktail bar," he said, and waved from the door.

The German turned once more to McCafferty, who was tentatively feeling his battered face and body, the point of Selim's machine gun following every movement, never more than six inches away. Dunkels chuckled and said, "You don't know how helpful you've been to us, colonel . . . or perhaps you do. Anyway," he added briskly, "we must get you looking decent. Selim—" he snapped his fingers at the grinning Arab.

They stripped the American, who was still as weak as a kitten, to his shirt and underclothing. Selim tugged baggy Oriental trousers over his shoes and up to his waist, fastening them with a leather belt. Then Dunkels pulled over Mac's head a full-length, wide-sleeved cloak, and Selim drew up the hood to hide his face.

Mac leaned heavily on Selim as the two men guided him out to another car concealed behind the mud hut, and pushed him into the rear seat. Dunkels got in beside him, and jammed the barrel of a Walther 9mm pistol roughly into McCafferty's injured side. "Just to remind you, colonel," the German said, "no tricks. That would be very foolish."

McCafferty regarded him through puffy eyelids. "I don't

know who you work for, or even what you are trying to do. But I'll tell you once again—you can't get away with it.

"Air Force One is due to take off in less than half an hour. If I'm not on it, there'll be the biggest manhunt in the history of the Persian Gulf."

Dunkels replied with a high-pitched whinny, like a knowing hyena. "But don't you *see*, colonel, you *will* be on the plane."

Mac looked at him blankly. "You—you mean . . . you're going to let me go?"

The German snickered again. "Not precisely, but you'll be there all right. There's no harm in telling you now. As you say, we haven't long to go, and in any case there would seem to be nothing you can do about it.

"You see, it won't be you on board Air Force One as head of security, colonel. But *someone* will be there, somebody remarkably like you. So much so that he'll fool Tom and Pat and Paul and Chuck and Bert, and anyone else who knows you or is likely to meet you in the near future, including Mr. Malcolm Philpott and the president of the United States of America."

The realization sunk slowly into Mac's fuddled brain. He squinted at the jubilant Dunkels and breathed, "You have to be loco if you think you can bring that off. Bananas."

The German shook his blond head vigorously. "No, Mc-Cafferty, we're not," he replied, "neither me nor the man behind me, the man who is going to bring down UNACO, and who doesn't care if the American administration falls with it. It's someone not entirely unknown to you, I believe."

Mac's eyes widened, and he muttered, half to himself, "Of course. Smith. It's got to be. . . ."

Dunkels drove the Walther a second time into the American's ribs. "*Mister* Smith to you, colonel," he replied.

Jagger took Achmed's call in the hotel lobby just as he was leaving the hotel with Cooligan to pick up the EDP convoy. He excused himself and crossed to the reception desk. The clerk handed him the telephone. Jagger digested the information and put the phone down.

Smith received the news thousands of miles to the north

of Bahrain in a darkening room set high up in a once-impregnable fortress. Smith's teeth gleamed and he purred to Achmed, "You have done well, my friend. I'll wish you *'bon voyage,'* and please present my greetings to your esteemed father." He tut-tutted at Fayeed's unfilial reply.

Smith had forsaken his Brooks Brothers shirt and clerical grey suit for a lightweight, stone-colored sweater and dark brown slacks. He picked up a tiny bronze bell and rang it. A girl came in, wearing a dirndl apron over a long green velveteen skirt, and a scarcely opaque blouse, unnecessarily open to the midriff. The blouse was of gossamer-thin, wispy material, and it lay off her shoulders and bisected the mounds of her breasts. In her native tongue, Smith ordered Krug champagne, and invited her to join him.

"But I am your servant," she objected.

"And you will serve me," Smith replied.

Then he, too, made a telephone call and spoke swiftly in yet another language. The man to whom he gave his brief report thanked him courteously and made his farewells. He also accepted a drink—a fine, dry German wine—but not from the hand of the nubile serving girl.

It was given to him by Axel Karilian, who lowered his bulk cautiously on to the sofa next to him and said, "May I take it that all is well?"

Myshkin nodded. "You may."

Chapter Six

The VC-137C stratoliner called Air Force One trembled on the hardstand at Muharraq Airport.

Horns blaring, the motorcade sped into a "no entry" road to the airport—the quickest and, therefore, safest route—and the leading outriders slithered to an unscheduled halt, under the watchful and alarmed eyes of perhaps two hundred Bahraini soldiers and policemen.

Jagger-McCafferty leapt from the last limousine in the convoy while it was still slowing down. He had seen film of an airport arrival by the presidential entourage, and Mac had done the same thing on that occasion. It was now almost a trademark with him—and Jagger didn't want to disappoint any of McCafferty's fans.

On board the Boeing, the crew went through their preflight procedure, Wynanski fussing like a mother hen over canapés, table linen, and sparkling crystal glasses. The commander was tense and edgy, as he always was before a trip. Latimer was his customary debonair and nonchalant self. Kowalski allowed his eyes to flicker across the charted flight plan. Kowalski doubled for the navigation aids, but he was a human being instead of a machine relying on electronics to function. Apart from that, he was a resourceful and experienced navigator—and what the hell, Air Force One carried an inertial guidance system anyway.

Outside the airport, a crowd had gathered to goggle at the flashy black cars and their VIP passengers. They were effectively blocking the route the motorcade was taking—not into the normal departure hall, but through a side road leading straight into the runway area. "Clear the road!" Jagger screamed. "Get those people away!"

Soldiers pressed in upon the spectators and jostled them out of the convoy's path. The access gate barring the road swung open and the cars drove smoothly behind the motorcyclists onto the hardstand, coming to a half directly opposite the steps leading up to the main hatch (or doorway) of Air Force One.

As chief steward, it fell to Wynanski to welcome his eminent guests. He shimmied up to the leading limo and pulled open the door, fixing the oil minister for the Kingdom of Saudi Arabia, Doctor Ibrahim Hamady, with a fierce, toothy grin. Dr. Hamady nodded graciously enough, and climbed the steps to the plane. Hamady would be the only one of the OPEC tycoons to wear, at all time, full Arab dress, beautifully cut for him by a Riyadh tailor of exceptional skill.

The second car flew the Libyan flag, and the routine for

Wynanski was similar. Sheik Mohammed Khalid Dorani, a handsome man in his early forties, with bouffant grey hair and a luxuriant mustache, shook the master sergeant's hand and made for the Boeing, a porter, weighed down with hand luggage, shuffling behind.

The next arrival, the nondescript Sheif Zayed bin Arbeid, of Iraq, was duly decanted, and another limousine left the hardstand. Then came Hemmingsway, who was politely applauded, and in the last car, flying the Bahraini national emblem and getting a special cheer from the home crowd, was a passenger who could have presented Wynanski with logistical problems, if the chief steward had not had the foresight to study his brief with special care.

Sheik Zayed Farouk Zeidan, wearing Western clothes with an Arab headdress, had a proud curving beak of a nose and magnetic black eyes. He was big, with immense shoulders and hands; he was also quite obviously crippled, his left leg hanging useless and wasted. Now sixty-five, Zeidan was accompanied by his twelve-year-old grandson, Feisal, who was on his way back to school in Switzerland. An Arab aide jumped from the other side of the car, jerked open the trunk, and fetched out a collapsible wheelchair. He assembled it swiftly and wheeled it round to Zeidan.

"Thank you, Achmed," Zeidan said, as the man and the boy helped him into the chair. Fayeed bowed, respectfully but not unctuously, and indicated the ramp which Wynanski's ground staff had pushed over to replace the steps. Achmed scorned offers of help, and took the wheelchair backwards up the ramp and into the plane.

Feisal followed his grandfather, and was succeeded by Bert Cooligan. Wynanski ticked off the list on his clipboard: one secretary of energy, American; four ministers, all Ayrab; plus one snot-nosed kid, ditto. Iran and Venezuela, he reflected, would have made a full pack of six for OPEC, but they were unavoidably absent.

Last of all to the airplane came Cody Jagger, looking to neither left nor right, his unholstered gun visible to anyone watching. The hatch closed behind him and the steps were removed.

* * *

Basil Swann handed the receiver to Philpott. "The Pentagon, sir," he intoned gravely, like a restrained *muezzin.* "General Morwood."

"George," Philpott barked, "what reports are you getting from Bahrain?"

"What reports *should* we be getting from Bahrain?" Morwood grumbled. "Weather reports, perhaps?"

"No, damn it," Philpott cursed, "you know what I mean. Is everything all right there? No hitches?"

Morwood sighed and put on an excessively bored and regimental voice. "We're in direct communication with the commander and the pilot of Air Force One, Malcolm. All systems are in order, and all of the personnel are who they're supposed to be and where they're supposed to be. The passengers are even now being conducted to their seats by your agent, Sabrina Carver, masquerading as a member of the United States Air Force, under the impeccable scrutiny of your other agent, Colonel Joe McCafferty. And if UNACO has any more agents aboard, which wouldn't surprise me in the slightest—maybe the entire crew are UNACO staff, *I* don't know, because nobody ever tells the Pentagon any damned thing, you least of all, Philpott—*if,* as I said, you have any residual operatives littered about the place disguised as armchairs or engine cowlings, then I have no doubt that they are also fulfilling their necessary functions, which is what *I'm* trying to do, if only you'd get off the damned line and *stop pestering me.*"

Philpott grinned sympathetically. "Far be it from me to come between a man and his necessary functions, George," he drawled. "Hey—you've got the radar plot, haven't you, as well?" Morwood agreed; they did have the radar-plot. He explained the process with massive patience, as he would to a six-year-old boy young for his age. Philpott held the receiver away from his ear and let the discourse roll. "Satisfied?" the eminent soldier inquired icily.

"Sure," Philpott replied—then confessed, with a shade of genuine contrition, that UNACO, too, had secured an unauthorized trace on the Boeing's course. "Just thought I'd let you know, George," he explained, waiting for the explosion.

But there wasn't one. Morwood chuckled throatily and sneered, "My dear Malcolm, did you really think you'd put one over on us with the tap into the inertial guidance system monitoring? We knew what you were up to, and our boys at Andrews AFB had instructions to look the other way. We weren't born yesterday you know, Sherlock. You keep track, we keep track. That way, everybody's happy."

Philpott gulped, duly chastened. "OK, George, strike one to the Pentagon. But seriously, you will let me know the instant anything goes wrong with the radar-plot, won't you?"

Morwood assured him that nothing *could* go wrong. The Boeing was scheduled to fly at a comfortable height, her range was more than sufficient for the first leg of the journey, she had ample fuel reserves, and she was in excellent working order.

"All the same," Philpott pressed.

Morwood sighed. "Malcolm," he said, "if it makes you happy, I'll give you a progress report on how the toilets are flushing and what goes down them."

He hung up, and Philpott glanced at the Gulf zone block. Take-off in two minutes.

The principal stateroom on Air Force One provided for its guests capacious armchairs built on tracks, with levers for moving or reclining the chairs, like in the better class of car. The chairs were grouped in fours, the pairs facing each other across tables. Sabrina pasted on a brilliant smile and showed the oil moguls to their seats. She warmed to the young Feisal immediately, but drew off when he treated her with something approaching aloof disdain.

On the flight deck the intercom buzzed and Fairman snapped, "Who's that?"

"Wynanski, sir," came the reply, "they're all aboard and settled."

"Strapped in?"

A pause, and Wynanski replied, "Affirmative, colonel."

Fairman grunted, and spoke into a microphone. "Clear to start one and two?" A member of the ground crew checked the area around the port engines. "Clear on both," he replied.

"Start two," the commander ordered. Latimer depressed a switch. "Starting two," he said. The mighty plane shuddered as the engine caught. "Two steady," Latimer added.

"Start one."

"Starting one." Another rumble of elemental power went through the shivering airframe. "One steady. Rotation one and two."

"Move it," the commander said.

Latimer sent the Boeing forward, reported, "Taxiing power," and left the hardstand for the allocated runway at Muharraq Airport. The liner completed a half-turn and sat at the end of the runway. Fairman operated the throttle and the engine noise rose to a banshee whine. "Let's go," he said. The speed of Air Force One increased.

"Rolling," Latimer answered laconically.

Fairman took over the controls at a hundred knots, and when the pilot said "V-one" the commander repeated the code—the fail-safe point for commitment to lifting the plane from the ground. If he accepted it—as he had—there could be no going back on his decision. The plane must take off.

"V-two."

"Rotate."

"Rotating." Fairman eased the control yoke back, and the president's airplane surged into the clear blue sky. . . .

Jagger had gone straight to the rear toilet when he boarded the Boeing, seeing no one but Chuck Allen, whose greeting he acknowledged with a curt nod. Locking the door, he took from the pocket of his flying jacket a smaller version of the aerosol spray can which had been used on McCafferty in the taxi. Jagger opened the door of one of the wall cabinets and placed the can unobtrusively at the back among a selection of toilet articles.

He left the facilities area, and in the rear passenger compartment was confronted by not one, but two, stewardesses. His second test—crisis, perhaps—was unavoidable, staring him in the face. He had reckoned on coping with only one girl at a time, but now he had no choice. So which one was he supposed to have dated?

Cody Jagger may have assumed McCafferty's form and face, but he retained his own taste in women. Not even Stein's genius could erase that. Jagger had rarely enjoyed success with truly beautiful and desirable women. His technique was to grab what he wanted and conquer it by sheer animal force. Of all the women Cody had known, his favorites were blondes built for comfort.

Sabrina Carver was dark, spectacular, and, even in her uniform, expensive. Jeanie Fenstermaker was blonde, and a big, sexy girl behind her tinted shades.

Reverting to type, Cody grinned crookedly at Fenstermaker and said, "Don't forget our dinner-date, Airman."

McCafferty's last conscious impression came at the outskirts of Manama, when Dunkels's free hand advanced towards his face holding the same canister of knockout gas which had been used on him by the cab driver.

The American awoke in a darkened room which, he later discovered, was in a house belonging to Achmed. For the mysterious Fayeed was not merely private secretary and principal aide to the oil minister of his native Bahrain, he was also distantly connected to Zeidan's family, standing high enough in his favor to rate a rent-free villa inside the enormous grounds of the Sheik's home. As Achmed smugly described it to Dunkels, there could be few safer safe-houses throughout the length and breadth of the island.

To Mac's astonishment, he had not been shackled, nor even tied, though he soon learned that this apparent oversight (or contemptuous neglect?) made no difference to his situation. The metal-framed window had been welded shut behind stout iron bars. A small window set high up on the wall had been jammed open to the extent of no more than three-quarters of an inch. There was no other ventilation, and just one entrance to the room; a closet door was set into the wall opposite the bed.

Mac pulled back the heavy curtain and peeped out. Through the violently hued scented blossoms trailing down the wall, a guard grinned up at him and waved a Kalashnikov rifle. McCafferty dropped the curtain back into place, then once more drew it carefully aside. The guard was still there. The gun *was* a Kalashnikov—a Russian infantry weapon, though freely available on the black market. And the man was not an Arab.

He heard the sound of someone opening the doublelocked door. A strong beam of light swept the room, raking the empty bed, locating the only other furniture—a table, chair, and wash basin—and finding the prisoner standing before the window, shielding his eyes against the glare. Dunkels stepped in behind the torch, which Mac could now see was held by another man. The German snapped on the lightswitch and ordered the guard, in a language unfamiliar to the American, to kill the torch. A third guard (armed, like Dunkels and the first man) sidled in and kicked the door shut with his heel.

"We heard you moving," Dunkels said. "I see you're none the worse for your—uh—experience. You may not believe it, but that actually pleases me."

McCafferty spat out a globule of blood and made no reply. Dunkels laughed; and suggested that Mac might get used to the idea that he was worth more alive than dead. He could also speak freely in front of the guards, the German added. They did not understand English.

"Worth more alive to Smith?" Mac sneered. "If I am, you sure had a funny way of showing it back in the hut."

Dunkels spread his hands wide in an elaborate shrug. "You're still here, aren't you? In one piece? Doesn't that speak for itself?"

Mac grinned painfully. "It tells me only that you're keeping me intact for reasons that suit you rather than me."

"Such as?"

To learn more from him about his role with UNACO, or on Air Force One, Mac hazarded. Or until whatever mad scheme Smith had hatched up for the president's plane had come to its logical end—disaster. Or just to prolong the agony because Smith and Dunkels were grade A bastards. "Any one of those reasons," Mac added, "or all three."

Dunkels chuckled again. "Normally I'd agree," he countered, "because normally you'd be right."

"Not this time?"

The German shook his leonine head. "No, somebody else wants you alive. They'd like a chat with you, too. In fact, they asked me to tell you."

"Did they? And afterwards? After they've finished their—chat?"

Dunkels shrugged again. "Who knows? You're obviously valuable to them. They might get to like you."

McCafferty looked long and hard at the sentries. He had been covertly observing them during his exchange with the German. He thought Dunkels might be telling the truth; they appeared to follow nothing that was being said. True, they had both laughed at times—but only when Dunkels laughed, and, comparatively speaking, a long time after they should have.

He returned his gaze to Dunkels. "So who are my newfound friends," he inquired acidly, "the ones who want so badly to chat to me?"

The German smirked. "Would you believe—the Soviets?"

Mac blinked and raised an eyebrow. Dunkels nodded enthusiastically. "Does Smith know?" Mac asked. Dunkels smiled, very slowly. Obviously not, Mac thought. "And what's in it for you?" he pressed. Dunkels opened a hand and made scratching motions across the palm with his fingernails.

"So you deliver me to them and cheat on Smith and they pay you lots of lovely dough?"

Dunkels nodded again. "You catch on, buddy," he grinned. He explained that, totally unexpectedly, the Russians had contacted him through an emissary at his hotel. He had already been paid sufficient money—in dollars—to persuade him that the Soviet offer was genuine.

"It's *they* who want to interrogate you, not me or Smith," he stressed. "You want to stay alive—play ball. You don't have a choice, McCafferty. Get wise."

He spun on his heel and left the room, the two armed men backing out after him. As the door was relocked, Mac reflected on the two pieces of important knowledge he had gained . . . one of them horrifying in its implications.

If the false McCafferty was now controlled not by Smith but by the KGB, were they planning to use the ringer to doublecross Smith? And if so, could they then afford to leave the hostages alive?

McCafferty bit his lip and shook his head angrily at the sheer impotence of his position. He had priceless information within his grasp—yet he was locked up as tight as he would be if he'd been court-martialed and pulled five to ten in Fort Leavenworth.

That brought him to consideration of the second piece of intelligence Dunkels had unwittingly shown him. Not only could his guards speak no English; but, like the man he had seen outside his window, they were not Arabs.

What nationality were they, then? Mac wondered. And if he found out where they came from, could he use the knowledge?

Once again Jagger was helped by a twist of fate which he had first diagnosed as malign, yet the fact that he had encountered both stewardesses together, so forcing his hand, had actually saved him. They were standing close to each other, and as soon as the words were out and he saw Jeanie Fenstermaker's generous mouth start to open in perplexity, Jagger switched his gaze to Sabrina Carver and repeated the injunction, "As I said, don't forget our dinner-date, Airman."

Now it was Sabrina's turn to look bewildered. "You may have *said* it to me," she pointed out, "but you were *looking* at Jeanie. At least, the first time you were."

Jagger stared at her. "I was?" he queried incredulously. "Are you sure? Gee, I'm sorry—eh—Airman. It's the tension of the job—you know? The spy business gets to you in funny ways. Sometimes it just doesn't pay to be straightforward."

Sabrina gave him a doubtful look and asked him if he would be fully recovered by the evening, just so that she could be sure she was still supposed to be going out with him. Jagger grinned easily and affirmed that he would be his old self again by the time they got to Geneva. He smiled even more broadly as he appreciated what he had said. "See you both later, then," he added, ending the encounter as speedily as politeness would permit.

He walked quickly towards the front of the plane, still in something of a quandary. Since meeting Sabrina, he had re-run the McCafferty *amours* through his finely trained mind, and he was certain that her face had not appeared among the thumbnail sketches. So she must be someone McCafferty had literally only just met—and for whom he had formed an instant attraction. The trouble with that was that Jagger didn't even know her name.

He reached the flight deck and casually leafed through his own security files until he came to the copy of Wynanski's crew and passengers manifest. If the big blonde, whom the other had referred to as "Jeanie," was Airman First Class Fenstermaker, Jean, then his date—less desirable because more inaccessible—must be Airman First Class Carver, Sabrina. Problem solved.

Not that it mattered, Jagger thought with a fleeting sneer. Neither of the girls would reach Geneva alive. Pity to waste Fenstermaker, though, he grinned to himself. She showed promise.

"Private joke, chief?" Cooligan inquired, spotting the sly smile.

Jagger pulled himself together. "Sorry again, Bert," he said, "I was looking forward to my date tonight."

"Ah, *la belle* Carver," Cooligan replied with relish. "You'll give me a full report, of course."

"If you don't see me at breakfast," he rejoined, "you won't need a report. You can just use your imagination."

Sabrina and Fenstermaker passed through to the stateroom at the exact moment that Sonya Kolchinsky, in the UNACO control room, saw the green dot of Air Force One shoot out a hesitant tendril on the wall map. "She's away, sir," Sonya sang out to Philpott, nudging him gently. Philpott raised his eyes and heaved a hugh sigh of relief.

"Then drinks are in order, Sonya, my dear," he declared, "because for the moment we're safe. Smith didn't make his strike on the ground, where I expected him to, and if he's going to do it while she's airborne it'll have to be *some* plan to beat the team *we've* on board. So, for a while—let's relax, shall we?"

He stood up and led the way into his office, turning only to remind Basil Swann that the inertial navigation system trace on the Boeing must be monitored at all times. "And keep in touch with General Morwood at the Pentagon," Philpott continued. "He's cued into the actual radar-track through the radio link to Naples. That's our doublecheck. Call me the moment you have even the slightest feeling of unease about anything. I don't care if it turns out to be wrong. We have to watch this one like the proverbial hawk; there's a great deal riding on it for UNACO."

He and Sonya sank into deep armchairs, hers in the far corner of the room by the window, Philpott's midway along the wall facing his desk. He sipped a Plymouth gin, with ice and water and a tiny white cocktail onion bobbing on the surface; it was an affectation he had borrowed from a very senior British sailor. Sonya drank a dry martini.

"I wonder if we've been worrying too much about this one," Philpott mused. Sonya wrinkled her brow and made a fetching *moue*. "No," she decided, and took a longish pull at her drink. "As we agreed at the beginning, it's got all the hallmarks of the big one for Smith. Unlike you, though, I didn't favor a strike at Bahrain."

Philpott stretched out his legs, regarded his gleaming black shoes, and saluted her with his glass. "Geneva?" Sonya nodded.

"Well, we've taken every precaution," Philpott contended. "McCafferty's been instructed to exercise special care right from the very instant of the approach to touchdown. The Swiss, like good little UNACO members, have been exceptionally cooperative, both in allowing our people access and giving them effective backup—the airport, the drive to town, the hotel, the private dinner party—everything's covered.

"Every inch of the way has been vetted and will be under surveillance. Anyone scheduled to come into contact with our guests at any level has been scrutinized and passed—or otherwise, in which case they've been replaced. I honestly believe we have Geneva wrapped up," he ended, a complacent smile on his lips. He raised his glass again and toasted her impishly.

"Always provided," Sonya said, "that Air Force One ever gets to Geneva."

Philpott chuckled. "God damn it, Kolchinsky," he exclaimed, "I was just about feeling good on this one, and now you go and spoil things." He helped himself to another long gin, and flashed her a broad wink.

In the Boeing's stateroom, Stewardess Carver made clear notes on her pad of the precise form of drink requested by each passenger. She ended up with Scotch narrowly win-

68

ning over vodka, plus a pair of Jack Daniels and a genuine tea without milk or sugar. This would normally have represented another Jack Daniels, but Sheik Zeidan ordered it for the twelve-year-old Feisal, so it really had to be tea.

"OK," she said, smiling at the boy. As an afterthought she fished from her pocket a bar of chocolate which she offered to Feisal. "Helps to pass the time," she said brightly. The slim brown fingers of the solemn-faced little Arab boy remained daintily laced in his lap, and he looked neither at her nor at the chocolate. Then he said, "I regret that my medical advisers do not permit me to eat such things. But you could not have known that. You may leave." He spoke in perfect Oxford English, like a candidate for a job as a radio announcer for the BBC.

His grandfather, who was playing chess with Hemmingsway, leaned over and spoke softly to the boy in Arabic. Then he smiled apologetically at Sabrina. "At his age, young lady," he said in his rich, dark voice, "life is earnest indeed, not to be frittered away in mere living. Dignity is all when you are twelve. Nonetheless, what he said is true, though I cannot defend the way he said it. But my grandson does have a diabetic condition and so, naturally, cannot enjoy chocolate as other children do. It is a cross—if you'll forgive the Christian allusion—which he has to bear."

Sabrina flushed, momentarily unsettled. "I-I'm so sorry," she stammered. "Naturally I wouldn't have suggested—"

Zeidan waved his hand in a gesture of tolerance and forgiveness, spiced with a soupçon of deprecation. "Please, of course not. But as Feisal said, you could not have been aware of his condition." He hesitated, and then ventured, "There is something, however, that you might be able to do for me."

Sabrina assured him of her willingness, and Zeidan inquired if the aircraft carried a physician. Sabrina shook her head. "When the president's on board, his doctor would normally travel with him, but this is a relatively short flight—so . . . Anyway, don't worry about it. I am a qualified paramedic. If Feisal should need something, I'll be glad to help."

Zeidan smiled his thanks and said, "Perhaps, then, you

would care to take charge of this." He picked up from the table before him a small tooled leather case and handed it to her. Sabrina opened its clasp, and saw the hypodermic syringes and insulin capsules. "I'll be glad to, sir," she replied.

The "tea" was served from genuine Chinese teapots—for appearances, as Wynanski explained—which were part of a set taken on at Bahrain. The ministers, Hemmingsway included, drank from delicate, paper-thin china cups, rattling now with unaccustomed chunks of ice, which had been diced into smaller, more manageable lumps by the acute chief steward.

The moguls, supplied with acceptable snacks by Airman Fenstermaker, whose superstructure earned admiring glances, settled down to talk oil. Jagger walked through the stateroom on one of his seemingly compulsive tours of the plane, and Sabrina gazed thoughtfully after him.

Unlike her colleague, she had not been wholly convinced by the attempts of the man whom she unhesitatingly accepted as Joe McCafferty to cover up his memory lapse in the rear passenger area. His explanation—the tension of the flight, the pressures of security—*might* excuse the faulty recognition, but Sabrina did not altogether accept it. She was not extraordinarily vain but, try as she might, she could not for the life of her see how anyone could confuse Jeanie Fenstermaker with Sabrina Carver.

She had casually quizzed Wynanski about McCafferty, asking if the security chief was normally moody at takeoff times. "No more than most," Wynanski replied, "but one thing's for sure: when he's on duty, Mac's all business. No time for women—even one like you, the sap."

Sabrina stood in a corner of the stateroom, a puzzled frown still clouding her face. She did not hear the soft step on the carpeted floor. Then a hand fell upon her shoulder. She jumped and wheeled round. "Penny for them," Cooligan said. She stammered an apology and confessed that she had been miles away.

Bert looked at her curiously, rubbing his chin. "Yeah," he drawled, "there's a lot of it around. Seems to be an occupational hazard on this trip especially."

"What on earth d'you mean?" Sabrina asked. Cooligan gave an embarrassed chuckle; it was nothing really, he

70

muttered, trying to play it down. Sabrina persisted, sensing something that could be important to her. Finally Bert confessed, "It's just that I had much the same sort of trouble with my boss, Colonel McCafferty, on the telephone back in Manama."

Sabrina felt the skin of her cheeks and forehead tighten. "On the phone? What—eh—what kind of trouble?" Cooligan replied that it had not been anything serious. "I feel kind of silly talking about it now, but at the time it seemed, well, strange. He was so immersed in his thoughts that I might just as well have been talking to a brick wall."

Sabrina weighed her words carefully. "Did he, by any chance, not quite—sort of—recognize you?"

Cooligan looked at her in surprise, then nodded. "That's right. For a moment, it was like he didn't know who he was talking to. . . ."

On the flight deck, Colonel Fairman sat back in his seat and ordered Latimer to radio Naples for a position. The pilot spoke into his microphone. "Naples Control. Air Force One calling Naples Control. We are crossing 24 degrees east at flight level 280 and estimating 22 degrees east at 31."

The voice of the controller at the Naples base came cradling back to them in measured, stilted English. "Rover, Air Force One, I have you on my screen. Call at 22 degrees east."

A few hundred miles away, another airplane sat at the furthest edge of a runway which pointed like a finger at the Adriatic Sea.

All was dark around the unlit bulk of the plane, made darker by lowering clouds. The aircraft was little more than the suggestion of a shadow on the ground.

Suddenly the lights of a dozen motor vehicles—cars, jeeps, and a small pick-up truck—flooded the scarred runway with radiance, picking out the gravel and dust motes dancing lightly among the weeds in the stiff breeze.

The aircraft's engines boomed into life, and the Boeing taxied out into the pool of illumination.

71

Chapter Seven

There could be no mistaking the size, the conformation, the livery of the plane—the stars and stripes on the flag, the presidential insignia, the United States of America legend—nor the white fuselage, the blue black nose, and pale blue underbelly and engine cowlings, perched on the silver wings.

It *was* Air Force One. Or at least, as with Jagger's resemblance to Joe McCafferty, to all intents and purposes it was Air Force One.

Which was good enough for Mister Smith, seated in his car at the seaward end of the runway, watching the mighty liner speed towards him preparing to take off.

Finding the airstrip—miraculously built in 1944 to a length of 4500-plus feet for the newly launched German ME262 jet fighters—had been the first vital contribution of the Russians when Smith had invited the KGB into a tenuous partnership. For the airstrip—long since abandoned and overgrown—was on the flat, low-lying Dalmatian coast of Yugoslavia between Zadar and Sibenik, and Smith had become convinced early on in his planning that the theft of the president's Boeing could only be achieved from an Eastern bloc state. And even post-Tito Yugoslavia was closed territory to Smith.

But not to the Russians. They had been able both to locate the sort of runway he needed, and to provide the help he would require to clear it and man it. The vehicles on the runway and the men in their driving seats, plus the sentries who even now guarded the real Joe McCafferty in Bahrain—they were all recruited from the same ultra-left partisan group whose headquarters were in the nearby mountains.

Set up and funded by the KGB, they were pledged to return Yugoslavia to the orthodox Communist fold. By infiltration, acts of terrorism and agit-prop, and intimidation in the classic pattern, they were some way along the road to success. They would also provide the troops Mister Smith would use to keep authority at bay while he carried out the final phase of his plan—the collection of the ransom for the OPEC ministers. Though there had been precious few signs of interference from the authorities so far, Smith thought. The KGB again?

The aircraft had been obtained by Smith legally. It was indeed a Boeing 707, but not what the USAF would call a stratoliner. Instead, he had searched for, and found, an old cargo freighter, its useful life now almost at an end. She suited Smith's purpose to perfection; he had bought the plane cheaply, and had her resprayed and painted, though not restructured.

The Boeing passed Smith's car, dragging its gigantic shadow in its wake. The noise was horrendous, starting as a raucous whine and rising through a crescendo to a staccato rattle, then dying out over the water in a series of massive, reverberant booms as the liner left the ground and soared into the night.

Mister Smith stroked the knee of the girl beside him, his willing servant from the castle. "Now," he said in English, "it's up to the Russians and their clever little friends in Italy. Why don't we return and await developments, my sweet Branka?"

Apart from her name, the girl hadn't understood a single word, but she smiled and covered his hand with hers. His intentions were plain enough, anyway. . . .

The man codenamed Myshkin paced the radio room in the Soviet Union's Zurich embassy, listening intently to the running commentary from the operator, headphones clasped to his ears, who was translating from the Serbo-Croat of his informant in Belgrade.

Myshkin looked at his watch, and then met the eye of Axel Karilian, who had been bending over the radio operator, making noted on a pad. Karilian's thick lips parted in a vulpine smile. "Congratulations, comrade," he said, "everything is going according to plan . . . *our* plan, that is, though Mister Smith is still convinced it's his."

Myshkin's eyelids in their slightly epicanthic folds quivered in agreement. It was a gesture, Karilian had noted, that often passed for extreme enthusiasm in Myshkin. Where other men might practically dislocate their necks in nodding vigorous approval, Myshkin would merely compress his prissy lips and flutter his eyelids. It was an oddly menacing habit; not feminine, as it might sound, but serpentine and secretive.

"I must confess," Karilian admitted, "that I don't much relish the idea of McCafferty being around a minute longer than is necessary for our purposes. He's a constant threat to us. His capacity for danger will cease only when he is dead."

Myshkin frowned. "I'm half inclined to agree with you," he said, "but McCafferty knows things which are important to us, both about UNACO, whom we can never really trust though we help support them, and most of all concerning the USAF, the Pentagon, and Air Force One.

"Do you realize what we have done, Axel?" Myshkin said, his voice rising by a carefully adjusted semitone in something dangerously close to excitement. "We have captured a full colonel of the United States Air Force without their actually realizing it. We can hold him and milk him dry, *and they may never even know we have had him.*

"After all, why should they? He'll still be with them, effectively, as the sole survivor and undoubted hero of the Air Force One hijack—the man who defeated the master criminal that UNACO couldn't catch."

Karilian raised his bushy eyebrows at this. "Huh?" he grunted. "Since when did that become part of the plan?"

Myshkin smiled, and not for the first time Karilian felt prickles of fear probing his body like acupuncture needles.

"Moscow considers it advisable," he replied. "And why not? Should Smith get in our way, or prove to be an embarrassment, who says he necessarily has to survive? We don't need him," Myshkin went on softly.

"Jagger will have plenty of assistance, provided by us and responsive to our direction, so that when Smith least expects treachery—at the moment of his seemingly complete triumph—how easy it will be for Jagger to—um—dispose of him, and hand over the ransom to us. I'm sure

74

the KGB will find equally practical uses for it—wouldn't you say, Axel?"

Axel would. He chuckled warmly. Not because he wanted to, but because he felt he had to.

During the hours he spent in the darkened room, McCafferty had been allowed out only twice: once to relieve himself and again, as night fell, to walk in the garden, always under heavy escort. Not just human escort, either: the Arab Selim kept an unkempt, savage Alsatian on a thick chain, long enough to wind several times around the man's waist before clipping on to the collar of the fierce dog.

The villa, Mac saw, was a two-story house set in its own defined plot of land within the palace grounds. Traffic noise indicated that it must be near a road, and he calculated that the high wall at the end of the garden formed the perimeter both of the villa and of the royal residence. His room—the only one with a barred window—was on the first floor, facing front.

McCafferty had spotted three other bedrooms and two bathrooms, and imagined the usual reception suite on the ground floor. The accommodation fitted the number of men guarding him: one on patrol in the garden, one outside his door—these were both as yet unidentified foreigners—plus Selim and his evil dog, and Dunkels. The guards, Mac thought, probably bunked together.

However hard he tried, the American could see no way of escape. There were no unplugged loopholes, no weak links. Wearily, despondently, still nursing his cuts and bruises, Mac returned from his second excursion and heard the door of his room doublelocked behind him.

Then came another sound—a familiar one but not, he was positive, previously heard by him since his arrival at the villa. The telephone rang in the hall downstairs.

After a few moments, the key grated in the lock and the door swung open. Dunkels followed the same routine as before, allowing the guard's torch to locate McCafferty, and then turning on the shaded lightbulb from the wall switch. Mac, for what the Germans called "security reasons," was forbidden to touch the switch. He deduced that the house could be seen from the road, and Dunkels would not risk the chance that the American could use the light to flash an appeal in Morse.

Dunkels seemed in good fettle. "I have news for you, Mc-Cafferty," he announced. "You'll be getting out of here shortly. Some—uh—'friends' of mine will come to take you away, by sea I gather, to a place which is, shall we say, more compatible to their interests. Also you're to lose a couple of your faithful attendants. I'm told by Mister Smith that they're needed back in—eh—back at our operational base, where someone's shorthanded."

With a sweep of his hand, Dunkels indicated the two guards, who grinned uncomprehendingly. McCafferty replied, in Russian, that he would be glad to see the last of them, since they stank like pigs and put him off his food.

Before Dunkels could stop him, the younger of the two guards sprang forward, bawled obscenities at Mac in his native tongue, and crashed his rifle butt into the American's face.

Dunkels grabbed the man's arm and pulled him away roughly. Mac had swiveled his head at the last moment and the Kalashnikov caught him only a glancing blow, but it was enough to raise fresh blood from an old wound and set his head ringing with pain. Stars exploded before his eyes, and he dabbed at his raw cheek with a soiled handkerchief.

He grinned crookedly but triumphantly behind the rag, though, for his gamble had paid off. He had banked on the sentries understanding either Russian or German since, from their speech and appearance, they seemed more likely to be Central European than to belong to any more remote ethnic group. And while McCafferty was nowhere near even Dunkels's class as a linguist, he had long ago learned to swear succinctly in something like fifteen languages. For a constant world traveler, it was convenient to know when foreigners were displeased with you.

The guard had played straight into his hands: the richly obscene oaths hurled at Mac were the only half-dozen words of Serbo-Croat the American knew, but now he could be certain of a Yugoslav connection.

Yugoslavia fitted the Boeing's schedule, too, lying just off course of the safest route Fairman would choose for Switzerland: overflying the friendlier states of Arabia into the Mediterranean, and up one side or the other of Italy to cross the Alps. If Smith wanted to snatch the President's plane, McCafferty reasoned, then Yugoslavia, with its crypto-Soviet presence, would make an ideal launchpad for the hijack.

Dunkels smoothed the ruffled feelings of the guards and turned back to the American, his face a mask of barely controlled anger. "That was smart, McCafferty," he hissed, "but whatever you've learned, the knowledge will do you no good. There's still no escape from here and, as I said, you'll be gone before long in any case.

"However, since you appear to want to play games, we'll leave you someone to play with. He's very friendly, I'm told—as long as you don't upset him."

While Selim slowly unwound the heavy chain from his waist, one of the guards hammered a six-inch staple into the jamb of the door. Selim clipped the Alsatian's collar to the hook, and leered at McCafferty. "The chain's long enough for him to reach all over the room," the Arab said. "I wouldn't move, if I were you. It's long past his dinnertime, and we don't seem to have any dog food left. I'll leave the light on; then at least you'll be able to see him coming."

He slammed the door and locked it. The dog stood glowering at Mac, who lay rigid on his bed, fixing the animal with an unwavering stare. Finally the dog gave in, yawned prodigiously, and settled down on its stomach, chin resting on paws. Its eyes stayed open, and its tongue roamed over its sharp white teeth.

Mac heard the front door shut and a car start up. Dunkels's voice came to him through the little fanlight. "Keep an eye on him, Selim," the German said, "I'll take these two to the airport, and be back in half an hour or so."

One guard remained, then, Mac reflected: the Arab. And his friend the Alsatian. He stirred restlessly, and the dog was on its feet in a flash, baring its teeth in a warning snarl.

If Mac were going to make a bid for freedom, he had half an hour—no more. And first he must deal with Selim's dog.

Fairman fussed and fumed as the aircraft wound its undulating route to the west, following a wiggling snake

77

trail which was anything but the arrow-straight path the commander would have wished.

The Boeing was never forced to deviate outrageously, but when Fairman filed the flight plan he had been uncomfortably aware that he was permitted to overfly certain territories solely because of the passengers he carried, and denied others because of the plane he was flying. Indeed, if it had been merely the president of the United States on board, Air Force One would have had to follow a vastly different and even more complicated course.

The Boeing's commander swore mildly in sheer relief as the plane crossed the frontier into friendly Egypt. Latimer, the pilot, let the sardonic smile which had been marring his Italian Renaissance good looks since takeoff stay on his face. He adjusted course for Suez, spanned the Canal keeping Port Said to starboard and Cairo to port, and sailed out into the Mediterranean over Alexandria.

He saw the waters gleaming darkly below him, and heard Fairman broadcast a brief description to the EDPs in the stateroom, who seemed to be drinking tea like it was going out of fashion.

Latimer spotted Crete looming up to starboard, and altered direction to follow the flight plan: proceeding not up the Adriatic past the Balkan states, but flying over Sicily and taking the Mediterranean searoute all the way up the coast of Italy, entering Italian air space at Genoa and traversing Piedmont to begin the descent to Geneva.

The "identikit" Air Force One, meanwhile, also had the hazy blur of Crete roughly in its sights to port as it sped down the Adriatic below the radar screen, on a course which would only briefly parallel that of the president's Boeing—but it would be long enough for Smith's master plan to work.

In a rest room cabin behind the flight deck of the genuine AF One, next to the forward galley on the starboard side of the plane, Cooligan, a brace of engineers, and Jagger played five-card draw for modest stakes. It was not something which McCafferty normally encouraged, yet—as Cooligan noted with surprise—the security chief himself had suggested the game. Another instance of untypical procedure by the colonel to nag at the Secret Service agent's mind . . . still, what the hell, he thought; anyone can have an off day.

Jagger got to his feet on a winning streak, and excused himself from the next hand. "Problems?" Bert asked sympathetically. "Want me to join you?"

Jagger shook his head. "No," he replied, "just count me out. I don't feel too easy about this one. . . ."—a ploy which he hoped would cover up what he knew had been erratic behavior on his part—"I know nothing can go wrong, but I think I'll take a walk around, just to check."

"Looking for stowaways, colonel?" ventured one of the engineers. The other comedian added, "Perhaps somebody got on while we were over Saudi Arabia—or was it Syria? They all look the same to me."

The four men laughed, and Jagger easily strolled out, not quickening his pace when he reached the stateroom, nodding affably to an aide, and arriving at the rest room complex at the rear of the Boeing without encountering any other crew member except Jeanie Fenstermaker. She was *en route* for the EDP lounge with smoked salmon and asparagus twists, encased in thinly sliced overcoats of fresh brown bread and butter. Jagger took one and ate it.

He locked himself in the tailend toilet and stayed for five minutes for the sake of appearances, should he encounter Fenstermaker again too quickly. He slid the aerosol can into his pocket, flushed the toiletbowl, washed his hands, and stepped out through the door, almost cannoning off the busty blonde as she was making her way back to the rear galley, her tray empty.

"Big appetites, huh?" he grunted.

"Seems so, colonel," she responded. "Mind you"—blushing becomingly—"I think they also like sort of seeing Sabrina and me as well. And there's an awful lot of "tea" being served, Colonel. Sergeant Wynanski can hardly keep up with demand."

"Where's Wynanski?" Jagger asked casually.

Jeanie pointed behind her at the galley. "In back, as always, slaving over a hot canapé."

Jagger grinned, glanced at his watch, and said, "Off you go then, Airman. Won't do to keep the Ayrabs waiting, will it? Could flunk your chance of marrying a sheik—or at least of joining a harem."

"Huh," Fenstermaker pouted, adding a disapproving sniff. Jagger waited for her to close the door, then tapped on it and said in a loud voice, "Pete! You in there?"

"Who's that?" Wynanski queried. He shuffled over to the door and jerked it open, Jeanie at his elbow.

Jagger smiled with his teeth and said, "Got a present for you." Fenstermaker's mouth was already opening in anticipation, so she collected a deep lungful of the knockout gas spray, and slumped to join Master Sergeant Pete Wynanski on the floor.

McCafferty moved his head to steal a glance at his watch, and the dog squirmed threateningly on its belly. Eight minutes had passed. Mac could wait no longer; if he were to act at all, it must be soon.

He sat up on the bed, and the dog rose with him, neck hair bristling, mouth open, wet lips pressed back over its teeth.

Mac swung his legs to the floor and, in one continuous movement, stood with his back to the closet door, fingers groping behind him for the handle. The Alsatian padded noiselessly towards him, trailing its chain. The powerful body swayed fractionally from side to side like a suspension bridge in a high wind. Its flecked eyes never left the man's face.

McCafferty found the knob handle of the closet and yanked hard on it. The door shot open and struck him on the shoulder blade. His fingers traced the fastening: it was a ball catch connecting to a socket in the jamb, and disuse had made it a pretty stiff fit.

He stepped aside and pulled the door ajar, praying that the closet was big enough to enter. His luck held: it was a walk-in, lined with empty shelves.

The dog followed him into the closet.

Mac stepped out again, more quickly. The Alsatian came after him, chain rattling, the dog panting, exuding a strong odor.

McCafferty backed once more into the closet, the dog at his heels.

The American jumped out this time. So did the dog, but

turning in its own length, whereas Mac used one long stride, backwards and forwards.

In again. The dog spun around, brushing his leg.

And Mac leapt clear over its body, slamming the door on its muzzle just as the dog turned to follow him.

The Alsatian threw itself in fury against the door, but the rusty catch held. McCafferty dragged the bed in front of the closet and jammed it close to the wall.

Then he raced to the locked door of the room, and jerked frantically at the chain embedded in the woodwork. Already he could hear Selim pounding up the stairs to the landing and along the corridor, attracted by the hysterical baying of the Alsatian from its dark prison.

Sweat poured from Mac's brow as he leaned his muscles against the chain. With a rending screech the staple came loose. He wrenched out the collar fastener, tore over the closet and stabbed the hook into the door over the catch, lifting his bunk and using the bed end to hammer the metal into the wood.

Selim was already at the door. Mac snapped off the lightswitch and stood behind the door, holding the slack length of chain in his hands.

Expecting the light to still be on, Selim switched his gun to his left hand and jabbed the button of his torch with his thumb, directing the beam towards the source of the noise.

McCafferty's vicious kick broke Selim's wrist. He dropped the gun and howled in a discordant counterpoint to the ululation of the dog. Mac jumped him and looped the chain around his neck. Gradually the American brought the Arab to his knees, trapping the man's body with his legs. Selim coughed and gagged, and the scream died in his throat as McCafferty choked his life away.

Unbelievably, the dog had forced the closet door, and Mac saw the bed slide out into the room as the huge brute urged its body into the widening gap.

Then the Alsatian was clear, and its desperate barking changed to a snarl of rage. In the light of the torch, still incongruously gripped in Selim's dead hand, McCafferty saw the dog spring, streamers of foam hanging from its extended jaws.

He dropped to the floor, rolled over, grabbed Selim's Walther pistol and poured shot after shot into the flying

81

body of the killer Alsatian. The dog crashed into the partly open door, whinnied, then lay still beside him, panting. Mac turned his head and forced himself to look into its dying eyes. The saliva congealed on its tongue and the rasping breath stopped.

He was free.

He staggered down the stairs and out into the night, dragging in great gulps of cool air. Then he collected his wits and searched for a second car.

He found one at the rear of the villa, but the vehicle was locked and there was no key in the ignition. Mac ran into the house and up the stairs. He kicked Selim's corpse on to its back, and snatched a bunch of keys from the trousers pocket.

It was only when he was well on his way to the American consulate at the wheel of the car that he fully appreciated the difficulties that still confronted him.

As he had half-jokingly reminded Dunkels an eternity ago, McCafferty had no means of proving his identity. He had been stripped of everything—wallet, credit cards, security passes, money. He owned nothing more than the clothes he stood up in: a pair of baggy pantaloons and a torn, soiled, blood-soaked *djellaba.*

Worse even than that, he must now try to convince a skeptical consul that he was in reality a man whom the consul himself had seen with his own eyes boarding the personal aircraft of the president of the United States not three hours before.

Chapter Eight

The three-handed draw game was still in progress when Jagger returned to the rest-room cabin. He bent over the table and said to Cooligan, "How's it going, Bert?"

Jagger drew out a handkerchief to dab at his face as

Cooligan replied, "Fine—since you left. Your going brought me luck."

"Yeah?" Jagger queried. "Is that a fact? Well, see what this brings you, then." He clamped the linen square over his nose and mouth and sprayed all three men. One by one, the cards fell from their nerveless fingers and their heads slumped on to the green baize. The flimsy little table almost overturned, but Jagger caught it in time, steadying it and holding it upright. He could not afford too much noise penetrating in either direction.

Jagger relieved Cooligan of his gun and murmured, "Sweet dreams."

Next, the flight deck. Kowalski was saying to the Commander, "There's a hell of a lot of mush up ahead on the screen. Think we ought to contact Naples?" Fairman turned to view the radar, and grunted noncommittally. Then he ordered Latimer to make the link with the control station.

"Naples Control, Air Force One to Naples Control," the pilot intoned. Naples replied; still the same formal, robotic voice. "There's a heavy radar return building up ahead, Naples," Latimer continued. "Request change in routing to Geneva."

Naples considered the question, and radioed back, "Roger, Air Force One. Change to a heading of two-seven-six. Do you copy?"

Naples got an affirmative, and Latimer signed off.

Bartolomeo Volpe had tucked his student books into his battered document case in the social sciences lecture theater at the University of Bologna and left early with the permission of his tutor who, like Bartolomeo, was a cadre chieftain in the Red Brigades. At about the same time, Christina Patakeminos leaned back in her chair in the social sciences lecture theater at the University of Athens, closed her eyes, and waited impatiently for the mid-morning break.

Bartolomeo boarded a plane heading south, and arrived in Naples at the precise scheduled time passed on to him in the instructions from his local Communist cell. He waited for a bus to take him out of the city, and checked his watch and grinned as he imagined the dark-eyed

83

Christina doing much the same thing from Athens's Egypt Square.

Neither the boy nor the girl—who had become lovers at a youth seminar in Sofia a bare six weeks earlier—knew from whom the Athens and Bologna Communists received *their* orders. The ignorance did not bother them: they bombed when and where they were told to bomb; killed whomever they were told to kill. They were admirable products of international terrorism.

No killing on this one, the Italian thought regretfully as the bus dropped him at the appointed spot on the coast road. Important, though, the cell had said: a strike at the very roots of capitalism.

The electricity cables feeding Naples Control radar station skirted the sea cliffs in a dark gully away from the main road. The supply to Athens Control was also strategically hidden near the cliffs dropping down to the Aegean Sea from the Plain of Marathon. Bartolomeo checked the time again, his eyes almost crossing on the second hand as it swept round to zero-minute.

He levered the lid off a junction box and clamped a small magnetic timing device to its metal side. Then he clipped through a pair of wires laid bare in the cable, and twisted their ends on to the twin terminals of the timer. The clock hands were set for thirty-five minutes.

Hundreds of miles away, Christina Patakeminos followed the same drill sequence down to the last letter, smiling to herself as she thought of Bartolomeo duplicating her movements south of Naples. They pressed the switches on their timers barely half a second apart.

Bartolomeo screwed down the lid of the junction box, shinned off the pylon, and walked away into the night, whistling an aria from Verdi's *Luisa Miller*. Christina hummed a catchy little number by Theodorakis and hitched a lift back to Athens. . . .

Jagger was surprised to meet Sabrina Carver on his way to the flight deck of Air Force One. "Trouble, Airman?" he queried.

Sabrina shook her head, and her mane of dark hair lifted off her shoulders and settled again. "Just being diplomatic," she replied. "Feisal—you know, the Arab boy—

wanted to see the works. Colonel Fairman said it'd be all right."

Jagger nodded and brushed past her, scarcely noticing the contact, fingering the strap on the holster of his gun. Sabrina shrugged and murmured, "Mac, you sure are one businesslike fella."

Jagger rapped on the locked door of the flight deck and was admitted at the same instant as the Naples controller said "Christ Almighty!" when his radar screen blanked out.

"Hey, what the—?" exclaimed an operator.

"Where's everything gone?" screeched a supervisor.

"Everything including us, Athens, and Air Force One," the controller returned grimly. He blinked rapidly and shorted his disbelief.

"Tried the hot line?" the supervisor asked.

"Dead."

"Shee-it."

"Quite."

General Morwood, in the Pentagon operations room, was almost as tersely expressive when he took the call from Naples. "Lost them?" His eyes went to the wall map, smaller than UNACO's but still showing the Boeing's tracer. "How *can* you have lost them?" he demanded. "We still have them on the inertial guidance track."

"I mean we've lost all our radar, sir," the Naples controller said a shade desperately, "and so has Athens. As far as we know, Air Force One is still there. And of course, general, if *you* say it is . . . well, that's good enough for me."

Morwood motioned to his closest aide, a full colonel. "Tell Philpott at UNACO what's happening," he whispered, covering the mouthpiece, "then listen in here. I'm gonna tear the heads off Naples and Athens."

"Hi there, Mac," caroled Latimer as Jagger climbed into the flight deck, "getting bored back there?" Fairman added a greeting and Kowalski gave the security chief a wry grin. Feisal's eyes were widening as he studied the instrumentation.

"Yeah," Jagger returned, "I thought you guys might

85

need livening up a bit. Eh, sonny," he drawled to the Arab boy, "maybe you'd better get back to your seat, huh? You can come up here again later."

Jagger's tone was light and casual, but Fairman looked at the security man's eyes and whispered, "Something up?" Jagger nodded. Feisal hesitated, and appealed mutely to the commander. Fairman patted his shoulder and said, "Scoot, kid. Like the colonel says, you can be our guest another time." Reluctantly, the boy edged out through the door.

Fairman waited until the door closed, and then inquired, "What the hell's wrong, Mac? Do you have problems we don't know about?"

Jagger grinned crookedly, shaking his head. "Not exactly, Tom," he said, "it's *you* who have the problems."

"Like what?"

"Like this." Jagger pulled out his gun and rammed it into the back of the first flight engineer's neck. "All of you," he commanded, "freeze."

Basil Swann stuttered out the news that Morwood's operations room had reported radar blackouts from Naples and Athens.

Philpott slammed down his glass on the table, rose to his feet, and crossed to the office door, Sonya just behind him. He strode into the UNACO ops center and stared at the map. The green snake was still inching across the Mediterranean.

"I was about to add, sir," Swann said, "that General Morwood said not to panic, because his trace still shows AF One, and so does ours. He says it must be purely a localized fault."

Philpott stared at him in amazement. "*Two* localized faults?" he inquired acidly. "Naples *and* Athens going out at the same time is sheer coincidence? Nothing to worry about?" His face started to go red until Sonya squeezed his arm.

"We are *not* panicking, Basil," she said, "but we *are* concerned."

"Too damned right we are." Philpott snorted. "Even if Morwood can convince himself that something like a widespread electrical storm can simultaneously knock out a pair of radar dishes hundreds of miles apart, he can't convince *me.*"

Swann gulped with difficulty and asked for instructions. Philpott pounded his fist with his palm, and his brow creased in concentration. "It's got to be Smith," he muttered, "and even then he'd need some help."

"Sir?" Swann inquired.

"Get this, Basil," Philpott replied, pointing a rock-steady finger. "I want a squadron of fighters from Naples Command scrambled. Do it now—and I mean NOW—and.tell them to stand by. I want no questions from them, no arguments, just action."

Swann nodded. "And their orders, sir?"

"No direct orders yet. Get them on standby; instant readiness. Use my Red Priority; that should persuade them I'm serious." He swore and slumped into a monitor's chair.

Basil Swann blinked behind the lenses of his horn-rimmed glasses and took small, neat steps to the console of UNACO's master computer. . . .

Fairman's iron control stilled all thoughts of panic among the Air Force One flight crew. "If this is a joke, colonel," he said slowly to Jagger, "I'll have your ass for it."

"No joke, colonel," Cody replied. "It's a stickup—for real."

Fairman looked steadily at him, but could see no humor in his eyes, no smile on his lips. Nothing but the ugly snout of the gun denting the flesh of the engineer's shaven neck. "You've been . . . *you* have been *bought?*" he asked, soft-voiced, incredulously.

"Sort of," Jagger gritted, "but don't let it worry you. Just bear in mind that I'm a qualified and experienced pilot, that I know every alarm system and button in the plane. Reach for one and I blow Chuck's head off. And that's for real, too: soft-coned bullets, low-calibre, dumdum variants. Used like this at close range, there's no damage to the fabric, no depressurizing. No damage to anything or anyone but Chuck. And he'll be dead. You're next, Tom. So behave."

The stunned crew heard another voice filtered through Latimer's headphones. "Naples Control calling Air Force

One! Report your position! Report your position! Do you read?"

"No," Jagger ordered, reaching out and jerking off the headset, "you don't copy, Pat. Everybody, unplug." They remained mute, not moving. Jagger pressed the muzzle of his gun more firmly still into the engineer's flesh and said quietly, "Unplug, guys. Don't play heroes—just do it."

Tom Fairman's unwavering stare met Jagger's cold, flinty eyes. The commander reached forward and ripped the plug of his headset from the control panel. Numbly, the other crew members followed suit. . . .

Although Fairman had initially cursed his flight plan because of the need to avoid sensitive air space, he had in fact been permitted to take the orthodox "Great Circle" route from the Persian Gulf to Switzerland, overflying Saudi Arabia and Egypt to emerge from Africa over the Mediterranean, and leaving Sicily to his left and the Italian coast to starboard as he made his way up to Genoa and across the Alps. That, anyway, was the original plan. It would have covered a distance of about 2,600 miles in a flying time in the order of five hours, which was less than half of the Boeing 707's full endurance.

Air Force One had flown 1,950 miles in three hours, forty-five minutes when Jagger entered the flight deck just as Fairman was pointing out to Feisal the retreating blob of Crete and the still-distant coast of Greece.

Mister Smith's "identikit" Boeing freighter, now wearing the livery of the president's plane, had taken off from its abandoned wartime airstrip on the coastal belt of Yugoslavia. Its target—the rendezvous point with the real Air Force One—lay four hundred miles to the south at latitude 37 degrees north and 19 degrees 15 minutes east, on the lower fringe of the Ionian Sea. Gradually, the two great aircraft began to converge. . . .

The Air Force One navigator, Kowalski, studied the new course ordered by Jagger with an amused sneer on his lips. "I see it," he murmured, "but I don't believe it. Where the hell are we supposed to be going? And why, for the love of God, do we have do go down from 28,000 feet to 250 feet in what I reckon to be no more than, say, ten minutes? It sure is going to stir things up behind."

Jagger leaned forward and transferred the gun to a point somewhere between Kowalski's eyes. "Then the quicker you set about it," he whispered, "the sooner their discomfort will be over."

He straightened up. Latimer mouthed an obscenity and fiddled moodily with the controls just as the crew of the fake Boeing—pilot and copilot, mercenary fliers fresh out of Mozambique—started climbing at the rate of 2,900 feet a minute. . . .

"Repeat your new projected course," Jagger ordered, and Latimer intoned, "We'll be heading 350 degrees, diving to 250 feet. Bang up the middle of the Strait of Otranto, as requested, *sir.*"

Jagger ignored the sarcasm and turned his attention to the bank of circuit breakers controling the wireless and navigation aids of the airplane. "Take 'em out—all of 'em," he rapped to the flight engineer, who glanced at Fairman for approval.

The Commander pursed his lips and sighed. "He's got the gun," Fairman snarled, "so do as he says."

Jagger congratulated him on his common sense. Fairman looked balefully at the man he supposed to be his friend Joe McCafferty. "I hope to Christ you know what you're doing, Mister," he said, "because when you wipe out that lot you leave us about as well equipped as the Wright brothers were on their first flight, and they weren't flying over water in darkness. You might as well ask me to crash this bird into the sea right now."

Jagger switched the point of the gun to Fairman, but the commander didn't flinch. "I mean it, Mac . . ." he added. "*You* know that, for God's sake. I don't have to tell you. You're a pilot yourself. We have to have eyes. Don't leave us blind, or we won't make it."

"So you need . . . what?" Jagger asked, unsure of himself now. The sketchy introduction to basic flying in his briefing had in no sense prepared him for this; Smith's orders had been to take off McCafferty, not match his knowledge built from a lifetime's career.

"You know damned well what I need!" Fairman exploded. "I want the radio altimeters, the weather radar, and the flight system. That way we might just—and I mean just—get wherever you want to go, though landing will be something else—but something else, I promise you. Keep the communications locked up, OK, but give me eyes."

Jagger's gaze ranged from face to face as though seeking confirmation of Fairman's words. The flight engineer—they were all now under the spell of the weaving gun—had paused within range of the circuit breakers which would cut the liner's communications—or most of them. But now he tripped the switches, and then made the mistake of letting his eyes flicker nervously to a metal box fixed to the bulkhead.

"What's in there?" Jagger rapped, following the man's eyeline. "Just some more circuit breakers," the engineer replied in a tone which was a little too casual to be credible.

"Open it," Jagger commanded, and the engineer rummaged in his bag for a screwdriver. "You, colonel," Cody said turning to Fairman, "can have your eyes, but get this aircraft down to sea level."

Fairman ordered Latimer to illuminate the "fasten seat belts" sign, and then he set the new heading. Latimer confirmed that he had carried out the necessary checklist of procedures for the descent, and the flight system put the Boeing into a slow right-hand turn on to the course Jagger had directed.

Cody kept an eye on Latimer until his attention was distracted by a screw falling from the cover plate of the mysterious box on the bulkhead. The engineer lifted the plate off to reveal more circuit breakers.

The hijacker gestured with his revolver. "Those too," he said, "trip them."

The flight engineer looked helplessly in Fairman's direction, but Jagger transferred the gun to within six inches of his face and said, "Now!"

Reaching up with a trembling hand, the engineer obeyed. The green light on Philpott's wall display twinkled out.

Philpott rubbed his eyes. He turned to Sonya, who said, "My God, it's gone."

The green snake was still somehow imprinted on Philpott's retina. He closed his eyes and creases gathered at

90

the bridge of his nose. "It was—turning," he said slowly. "Just before the track went out, the plane was definitely turning." He opened his eyelids and glared at the wall map, as if willing the green trace to return. "It was turning maybe forty-five degress."

Swann's voice, small but oddly consoling, came from the computer console. "I can confirm that, sir," he said, "it appeared to be changing course to take it up the Adriatic Sea instead of the Mediterranean and Tyrrhenian Sea."

"But why?" Philpott murmured. "And why have we lost the trace? Or is this just another 'localized difficulty'?"

The telephone rang, and Sonya, who was nearest the receiver, snatched it from its cradle. She identified herself and listened in silence, then said to Philpott, "It's General Morwood, Malcolm. They've lost the trace as well."

Philpott jumped to his feet. "Tell him I'll be back to him shortly," he said brusquely. "Basil—those fighters. I want them airborne like thirty seconds ago, and out on the track of Air Force One." Swann bent his head to the console and flexed his fingers. Then Sonya Kolchinsky shouted, "Wait."

Philpott turned to see her with a hand raised, listening intently to Morwood's operations center. She covered the mouthpiece and said quickly, "Morwood says Gibraltar Radar reports that AF One is still, repeat still, on track. They've picked her up on the fringe of their area, and they're certain of their identification. There's no other comparable traffic."

The UNACO director cursed under his breath, and snapped, "Basil, do as I said. Get the fighters off. I don't care what the Pentagon says, or Gibraltar Radar. Something's wrong out there, and it's not happening by accident. It's Smith. I know it's Smith."

Sonya waved at him and pointed to the telephone. "General Morwood," she whispered, handing him the receiver.

"What the blue bloody blazes is happening, Philpott?" Morwood shouted. "First we lost the track and then Gibraltar say they've got her all safe and sound. What does it mean, for God's sake?"

"It means that I've requisitioned an Eagle flight from Naples Command," Philpott replied tersely. "It means that I'm convinced something has gone wrong with the president's plane, and I'm not taking any chances."

91

"You've done WHAT?" the General roared.

"You heard."

Silence reigned in the Pentagon operations room. Then, from Morwood, "Good thinking, Malcolm. I should have done it myself. Keep me posted. I'll call you if anything comes up at this end."

"There is, of course, one thing you can do, George," Philpott continued airily. "Raise Air Force One through Andrews and get them to check that everything's A-OK on board. Tell them to confirm without any possibility of doubt that things are absolutely normal there, and as they should be."

Morwood grunted, and snarled an order to his aide. The Air Force One had long since finished her steep climb and was giving a passable imitation of an on-course flight to Gibraltar Radar when Andrews AFB finally raised the flight deck. Her speed had dropped to barely 150 miles per hour, and she was stealthily losing altitude as well.

"What's going on there?" Andrews demanded. "Naples and Athens said they lost you, and your own communications are on the blink. The inertial guidance track has gone, too. Do you read?"

"Systems malfunctions at both ends, I suppose," the skipper replied in a more than adequate imitation of Latimer's languid drawl, filtered to an indistinguishable metallic rasp by the communications equipment.

"Is that you, Pat?" Andrews asked.

"Who else?"

"Is Tom there?" Andrews pressed.

"Fairman here," the copilot replied. "What's all this about? We are on schedule and raring to make Geneva. McCafferty sends his love. Got something special lined up for tonight, I think."

Andrews probed gently at other openings, but eventually retired satisfied. They passed the good news to Morwood, and Morwood informed Philpott, whose Eagle flight was by now airborne and beyond recall . . . even if Philpott had any intention of summoning them back to base, which he hadn't.

The skipper of the "identikit" Boeing checked his precisely calculated schedule and suggested to his copilot that it was time they were gone. They strapped on parachutes

92

and made for the emergency exit. The plane was on autopilot, and at their greatly reduced speed and height, the two men would easily clear the freighter's slip stream.

The skipper kept an ear cocked to the radio desk, waiting for a particular signal to pierce the fuzzy sound. It came, transmitted from a ship in the Mediterranean two miles below them. He turned to his colleague with a "thumbs up" sign, and crossed to join him at the exit door.

Then he reached up a hand, slid off the top of a black plastic box wired to the emergency exit sign, and pressed a switch.

The aircraft was plunged into darkness, and the two men jumped out into the swirling breeze. . . .

In the stateroom of the real Air Force One, Sabrina saw the "fasten seat belts" sign flash on, and felt the liner dip as it banked to starboard. "Gentlemen," she said, and then gave an experimental cough and tried again, a little more loudly. Heads turned and inquiring eyes fastened on her.

Sabrina indicated the sign and said, "The commander requests you to put on your seat belts, please." Hemmingsway looked at the electric wall clock and pointed out that they were still the better part of a thousand miles short of their destination.

"Probably a little turbulence?" Sheik Dorani, the Libyan, asked.

"Something of the sort," Sabrina replied.

"We appear to be going downwards," Sheik Zayed Farouk Zeidan observed.

"We are," his grandson Feisal confirmed, "at a rate of perhaps fifty feet a second, or thereabout." The news, coming as it did from a boy of twelve in precise and clipped Oxford English, sounded so incongruous that Hemmingsway started giggling.

He fell silent when the Iraqi, Sheik Arbeid, addressing the room at large for the first time, since he was not gifted with the capacity for small talk, said, "The young one is correct. We are diving."

Eyes turned again on Sabrina, who flushed and said, "I'll—uh—I'll try to find out what's happening. No doubt we're just getting under some bad weather or something."

"No doubt," Sheik Zeidan commented urbanely.

93

"Unlikely, though," Feisal ventured.

"Why?" Hemmingsway asked, curious, and then cursing himself for seeking an opinion on aeronautical practice from a lad younger than his own children, whose knowledge of anything beyond sex and pop music could be safely abandoned to the back of a small postage stamp.

"We would not need to dive as steeply," Feisal replied, "and we do not seem to be encountering turbulence or an air pocket. We are, simply, descending."

Hemmingsway pulled himself together. "Now look here," he said, "I am your host aboard this aircraft in the absence of the president of the United States, and while I'm sure the opinions of our young friend are of consuming interest, I see no reason why we should not be *told* what is occurring, rather than having to *guess.* Airman," he said to Sabrina, "we will follow the commander's orders and keep our seat belts fastened. *You* will get a member of the flight crew to come out here *now,* and give us an explanation."

Sabrina started to obey when the Boeing gave a sudden, violent lurch. Sheik Dorani clutched the arms of his seat. Doctor Ibrahim Hamady, of Saudi Arabia, leaned forward to rescue a cup that was skating off the table, and Sabrina heard a noise from the rear of the plane, which she correctly identified as kettles and pots crashing to the floor. Sheik Zeidan's imposing face registered startled apprehension when a gasping, retching sound came from the seat beside him. He bent over the boy, who was battling for breath, taking in huge gulps of air.

The Bahraini turned to Sabrina and snapped his fingers imperiously. "His medication. Quickly, young lady," he urged.

Fighting the angle of the aircraft to stay upright, Sabrina started for the rear galley where she had left the syringe and insulin capsules.

She encountered no one else along the route, which for some reason that she could not pinpoint worried her more than it should have done, and reached the galley. She jerked open the door, and her astonished gaze fell on the bodies of Master Sergeant Pete Wynanski and Airman Jeanie Fenstermaker. . . .

* * *

One at each side, the two leading fighters in the Eagle flight drew abreast of the dark and sinister shape of the Boeing. The Eagle leader called the plane, but his only reply was an impenetrable buzz of static.

"There's not a single light showing on her," the pilot of the second fighter reported. "Anything visible your side?"

"Nothing," Eagle leader replied. "Drop back a bit, will you? Get as close in as you can. See if you can spot anything—anything. A movement, the flicker of a match. Any Goddamned thing you can see to convince me and Naples Control and UNACO that this isn't just a ghost, because that's how it looks to me, and I can't make a report like that without getting a free pass to the funny farm."

The second plane peeled away and came up behind the Boeing again, adjusting his speed to that of the huge grey shape. The pilot, insofar as he was able, examined every inch of the liner, checking the external markings and scrutinizing each window along the fuselage as the moonlight briefly caught her. He speeded up and peered into the darkened, empty flight deck.

The pilot dived and resumed a course parallel with his leader. "Nothing," he confirmed, "absolutely one big fat zero. Not a sign of life anywhere. Something God-awful, unimaginable, must have happened. She's just been abandoned—crew, passengers, everybody."

"Zilch!" his leader retorted, and then, more graphically, "Balls! That's Air Force One there, baby, not some mystery joy-rider—and not the *Marie Celeste,* either. The crew of AF One don't just chuck the passengers overboard and jump out of a ship that's to all intents and purposes flying perfectly normally. Are you sure you didn't spot something, overlook something? It could have seemed unimportant, but it may be the clue we're after."

There was silence, except for the crackle of static, and then the second pilot's voice, hesitant and confused, came over again. "There was something—yeah . . . you know, that didn't seem quite, sort of, right, kosher. But I thought I was just seeing things—or not seeing them, even."

"What was it?" Eagle leader demanded. "For Christ's sake, tell me!"

"Well, it was the—"

The sky was lit by a blinding flash and a glare of orange, then crimson light, shading to a fierce yellow. The shock wave reached the two fighters fractionally before the huge blast of sound boomed in their ears. The two little planes bucked and leapt through the wispy clouds and screamed away to right and left, each performing tight circles to come around again and dive towards the wreckage of the Boeing as it dropped from the night sky.

The fiery cigar shape of the Boeing's fuselage was now starkly illuminated as the fighters chased it down to the sea. Eagle leader made his panic-stricken report to Naples base, where it was received with uncomprehending horror.

"Shot down?" Naples queried.

"No!" Eagle leader roared, "*not* shot down. It just— exploded. There was *no missile*. It must have been a bomb. A bomb—on an empty aircraft."

"Empty?" from Naples.

"Positive. Empty, and in total darkness."

"And it *was* Air Force One," Naples pressed.

"Affirmative."

"You're sure?"

"Affirmative."

"No."

There was silence from Naples, then the robot voice said, "Who was that?"

"Eagle Two," the pilot of the second fighter confirmed.

"And you're saying—" the controller left the question hanging in the air.

"I'm saying I don't think it was Air Force One," the airman rejoined.

This time Naples refused to break the silence, and the USAF pilot said, "First, some information. What kind of main hatch, you know, the actual door, did Air Force One have?"

"What kind of door?" Naples echoed in bafflement. "An ordinary one, as far as we know."

"Dimension, say, four feet?"

A busy, almost frenetic, silence occupied Naples now. Then the controller came back. "We have the specification of the Boeing in front of us. It had a normal-sized hatch, built for average height and weight passengers. Why do you ask, Eagle Two?"

"Because *this* bird *didn't*," the fighter pilot crowed triumphantly. "I checked it in the air on the level, and again on the way down. *This* Air Force One's door measured all of seven feet wide."

"Then it was—" began Eagle leader.

"Then it *couldn't* have—" put in Naples Control.

"No," replied Eagle Two, "it wasn't a VC-137C stratoliner nor any other kind of Boeing 707-320B airliner. My guess is that it was some old freighter tarted up to look like Air Force One. . . ."

". . . my guess, too," murmured Malcolm Philpott, who had been patched through to the three-way conversation. "And what's more, I know who did it."

Sonya Kolchinsky burst into his office, her face alive with strain and concern. "It is true?" she asked. "General Morwood says Air Force One has been shot down or bombed. Is it true?"

Philpott turned in his chair and chuckled up at her. "Oh yes, it's true, my pet. But tell General Morwood not to worry: we've got another one."

Chapter Nine

A crumbling outcrop of wartime ruins framed against the night sky above the remains of a concrete bunker lay just to the right of the runway where it ended in a sudden crevice. Dirt ramps had been banked up to mark the very limit of usable track, but they would be frighteningly ineffective against the weight of a plunging jet.

Paraffin lamps, spluttering noisily, their flames dancing and weaving, paralleled each other down the entire length of the runway, with a battery of them at the end, but there was no disguising the fact that Mister Smith's Kosgo airstrip had not been designed to take a Boeing 707.

Smith lounged against a low concrete wall, directing the placement of the forty-strong reception committee—all in rough battle fatigues, all heavily armed.

"Why are we here?" the girl asked. Her elfin face peeped out from the hood of a sable fur coat; her hands were encased in a matching muff, and her feet in sable-lined grey leather boots.

"We wait," Smith replied in Serbo-Croat.

"For what?"

Smith raised a finger to her lips and said, "Hush, little one." She followed his gaze as he peered into the sky.

Barely audible on the breeze, the throaty growl of a jet engine cut like an idling bandsaw through the thick, low cloud. Smith ran his fingers over the girl's lips and she licked the tip of each one.

"How long?" Fairman rasped.

"Most of five thousand feet," Jagger confirmed.

"Most?"

"Uh-huh. The strip was built for jets, but not very big ones."

"It's impossible," Fairman protested.

Jagger shook his head. "Good, old-fashioned airmanship, Tom. But mind the gully at the far end."

"Gully!"

"Yeah. The runway sort of—well, peters out. It's quite a deep drop."

"Jesus Christ."

Jagger smiled and said, "Maybe a prayer would help."

Kowalski remarked that there was an island coming up to port.

"Well don't tell us," Latimer remarked peevishly, "you're the navigator. What is it?"

If they were on course, Kowalski explained, it would be the island of Vis. "See any others?" he asked.

"To where?"

"Starboard."

Latimer probed the blackness, and identified two shapes looming on the right. He passed the news to the navigator.

98

"Spot on," Kowalski said, "the first one's Hvar and the second Brac. It's dead straight now until landfall."

"Gee, thanks," Fairman said.

The commander requested further details from Jagger of the landing strip. The runway itself, the ringer told him, would be marked by paraffin flares. Fairman's jaw dropped. "You did say paraffin flares?"

"Sure. They're very effective in fog."

"It isn't foggy," Latimer pointed out.

"Don't bet on it," Jagger replied, "they get funny weather around here."

Fairman sighed and said, "Go on."

Jagger grinned and assured the commander that the worst of the bad news was over. "That was the primitive aspect," he added. "Beyond that they're quite well equipped. They have a transponder there which operates on your radar frequency, so you'll be able to pinpoint the exact position.

"They've also got VHF radio—battery powered, naturally—and they'll use that to keep you abreast of conditions on the ground."

"They speak English, then," Fairman inquired acidly, "not ancient Sumerian or Stone Age grunt language?"

"One of them almost certainly speaks all three."

Latimer asked if, assuming they were almost there, the plane could have back its VHF radio for tuning to the correct frequency. "Sure, Pat," Jagger replied, "you can have the radio, but I'll do the tuning. The less you know the better."

Holding a headset to his ear with his free hand, Jagger adjusted the frequency to 118.1 and made contact with the Kosgo base. He handed the communicator to Fairman. The commander heard a precise and cultured English voice recite all the details he needed to know: the runway heading, atmospheric pressure reading at aerodrome level, and the wind speed and direction.

"Do call again," Smith added, "when the transponder blip indicating the exact position of the airfield appears on your screen." Fairman grunted and surrendered the headphones to Jagger, who signed off.

"Happier?" the ringer said.

Fairman ignored him and told Latimer, "We'll drag her

99

in low and slow. When the blip comes on I'll take the controls and try it at about 110 knots. Then we'll coast in and snatch it back to manual if—or, I hope, when—we spot the lights."

The Boeing ran for a further twenty miles at 250 feet, straight as a die to Kowalski's immense satisfaction, when the green spot started glowing on the weather radar screen.

"Tell your friends we have them on visual," Fairman instructed Jagger, unconsciously treating him as part of the normal complement of Air Force One—which indeed, as far as Fairman was concerned, he was, although not on the flight deck. When Jagger had passed on the intelligence, Fairman added, without turning to look at the ringer, "If you know what you're doing, you'll keep out of the way for the next ten, fifteen minutes."

Jagger held on to the back of Fairman's seat as the plane bucked, and moved the point of his gun until the short hairs on the back of the commander's neck erected of their own volition, though the metal had not touched him. "Listen, Tom," Jagger purred, "if you don't land this aircraft, I will."

"That," said Latimer, "I should like to see."

"But you wouldn't see it, Pat, that's the point," Jagger replied smoothly. "You'd all be dead."

Silence fell on the crew and they concentrated perhaps too minutely on the task in hand. Jagger had rammed the message home, and not one among them doubted that he meant what he said. . . .

Sabrina closed the door of the galley after slipping the catch of the lock. At least Wynanski and Jeanie were still alive, though she calculated they would not regain consciousness for some time. But who had done it? And why? And what could she do about it?

Clutching every support — walls, furniture — that came to hand, she struggled back to the stateroom with the tooled leather first-aid kit in her hand. Dr. Hamady, who had unbuckled his seatbelt and was crouching solicitously over the crippled Zeidan and his grandson, leapt to help her as she lost her balance and crashed against a table. They remained precariously rooted to the floor, until

Hamady realized that they were no longer bending over to compensate for the steeply inclined angle of the plane.

Sabrina straightened and gasped with relief. "So," said Dorani from his seat "we have ceased to dive."

Sheik Arbeid, the taciturn Iraqi, placed a cup on the polished surface of the table before him. It rattled slightly, but stayed in position. He grunted confirmation.

Sabrina hurried to Sheik Zeidan and gently released his hold on the boy, who was now almost unconscious. She loosened his seatbelt, then unzipped the trousers of Feisal's immaculate grey suit. Zeidan gripped the arm of his wheelchair with his left hand, and with the other took the boy's legs on his lap until he was fully stretched. Sabrina pulled down his trousers and underpants, pinched and swabbed a patch of flesh on the boy's small, taut buttock, and injected a dose of insulin.

Almost immediately, Feisal's feverish mutterings ceased and his breathing became calmer. Zeidan carefully patted the beads of perspiration from his grandson's face, and whispered in Arabic "Sleep, my jewel, my prince."

All the OPEC ministers and their aides had now resumed their seats, and Hamady, who had courteously waited for the medication to be finished, fixed Hawley Hemmingsway with an angry glare.

"You mentioned some time ago, sir," he said, "that you would endeavor to discover why we have been put to this considerable danger, let alone discomfort. If you do not accept that we have been placed in peril, I would urge you to consider that His Excellency Sheik Zeidan's grandson could still become gravely ill. I think you owe us an apology and a full explanation.

"I can speak only for the monarch and government of Saudi Arabia, but for my part I assure you that we shall feel inclined to accept neither the apology nor the explanation unless they are completely satisfactory, and the situation is restored immediately to normality. As for the oil accord, in the service of which we have undergone this humiliating experience . . . well, I leave that to your imagination, Mr. Hemmingsway."

The American secretary of energy sat stunned and silent. Then he breathed a sigh and nodded his head slowly. "Clearly, Dr. Hamady, gentlemen," he said, "I have no more idea than you do what is going on. I now propose to find out."

He rose from the seat, and his eyes met Sabrina Carver's. He read in them the clear message of warning and danger, reserved at the moment for him alone, though Zeidan, watchful as ever, had caught the interchange. "Come with me, young lady," Hemmingsway growled, and led the way towards the flight deck. . . .

"Lights up ahead, I think," Latimer exclaimed.

"Coastal lights," Kowalski cautioned. "We're approaching land now. Could be anything."

The commander called for flaps, and Latimer reached out his left hand to operate the lever mounted in the center console. Position indicators on the right of the instrument panel registered his actions, which were monitored by Fairman and Kowalski—and, above all, by Jagger.

The aircraft's speed died rapidly and Fairman demanded more. Then he ordered the landing gear to be lowered. Latimer obeyed like an automaton, the tension and strain mirrored on his handsome face. A distant rumbling beneath the aircraft signaled the dropping of the landing gear. With the mild thump that always accompanies the final locking of the undercarriage, the jarring motion communicating itself through the floor to the soles of Jagger's feet, three green lights flashed on above the operating lever on Latimer's side of the flight deck.

The flight system was still controlling the aircraft, but the Boeing showed a tendency now to pitch and wallow, as all airliners do when they are operating close to their stalling speed. The eddies and currents and warm air thermals coming from the sea and the liberal scattering of tiny islands did nothing to help steady her progress. . . .

With the stateroom door firmly closed behind them, Hemmingsway grabbed Sabrina's arm and whispered hoarsely, "What the hell's going on here, airman? You know something, don't you? Well, tell me!"

Sabrina wrenched her arm away and said, "You're hurting me, sir. You have no need to. I'll tell you what I know—and I'd better warn you, it's all bad."

The color left Hemmingsway's big, florid face as Sabrina filled him in on the scene in the rear galley. He wanted to speak, but the words refused to come.

"If you're trying to ask me if we've been hijacked, sir," Sabrina said, "the answer is yes, I believe we have. Whatever's happening to us is being masterminded from the flight deck, which I'm sure will be locked against us. But I think there's a way to get more evidence that should convince everyone back there."

She led the way to the rest room cabin, and pushed at the door. It met an immediate obstacle, giving them no more than a two-inch-wide aperture into the room. Hemmingsway lent his weight to hers, and the body of the fallen engineer rolled across the carpeted floor and folded itself around a leg of the cardtable.

Sabrina's mouth set into a grim line. "I was afraid of this most of all," she said, indicating one of the three men.

"Who's that?" Hemmingsway asked.

"The Secret Service agent, Bert Cooligan. And his gun's been taken," she replied.

"And that means what?"

"It means," Sabrina said, "that the security chief, Colonel McCafferty, must be up there"—jerking her head towards the nose of the plane—"under arrest like the flight deck crew. We don't have anybody else who can help."

Hemmingsway looked shrewdly into her eyes. "Not even you, I suspect, young lady, because you're no ordinary stewardess, are you?"

Sabrina smiled and said, "No, I'm not, but I'm on your side, like Joe McCafferty. But the point is—I'm not armed, so we're still back where we were."

Hemmingsway's tall frame had slumped as he realized the gravity of their position, then he pulled himself up with a visible effort. "I'm not taking this lying down, airman," he snapped. "I'm going up front now. I'm going to find out who's kidnapped us, why, and where they're taking us."

"I wouldn't advise that, sir," Sabrina returned anxiously. Hemmingsway fixed her with a fierce, but controlled stare. "In a real sense, airman," he continued, "it's my plane, my responsibility, my job to do something about it. And I don't shirk my responsibilities. Ever."

He led the way from the rest room cabin and halted before the flight deck, Sabrina at his elbow. Hemmingsway

103

raised his hand to rap on the locked door, but a voice, sharp and incisive, came behind them.

"Freeze," said Achmed Fayeed. They turned and saw the gun, pointing at the left lapel of Sabrina's blazer. Achmed stepped backwards and motioned them to follow. Hemmingsway opened the door and let Sabrina precede him into the stateroom, then stumbled through himself as the Arab brutally shoulder-charged him. Hemmingsway lurched into a table and fell to the floor, his head resting against the base of Zeidan's wheelchair.

Zeidan's piercing eyes fixed on the face of his aide, and he said, "What is the meaning of this outrage, Achmed?"

Fayeed straightened up and sneered, "Surely, you can see for yourself, cousin. This aircraft has been commandeered under my orders, and is now being flown to a place designated by myself and my friends."

"And what happens next?" Dorani inquired, completely unruffled, like the other Arabs.

"You will be told that at the right time," Achmed returned. "For the moment, you are my prisoners. Remain in your seats, and fasten the belts."

Hemmingsway climbed to his feet, breathing almost as heavily as Feisal had been a few moments before. "You won't get away with it, damn you," he hissed, "this plane belongs to the presid—"

"I am aware," Achmed cut in, "who the aircraft belongs to. That is why we have stolen it. And you are wrong, Mr. Hemmingsway, in any case. We have already got away with it. You are powerless to prevent us from accomplishing our purpose, and your people back in Washington, and yours, and yours"—ranging around the room—"do not, in fact, know what is happening, and would not believe it if they did."

"Why not?" Zeidan asked curiously.

"Because they think you are dead," Achmed replied.

Sabrina paled and clutched at the head of Arbeid's seat. Achmed said to her, "Your assistance as a stewardess is no longer needed, and your function as a secret agent has been nullified. Sit down with the rest, and fasten your seat belt."

Dumbly, Sabrina complied. Philpott's worst fears had

been realized: a strike in the air had been launched at the president's Boeing.

And his words came back to her. "If that happens, nobody can help you. You're on your own. . . ."

Fairman was sweating, and he knew Latimer had spotted it. The commander was finding it difficult to do no more than rest his hands and feet lightly on the controls, following the effect of the pulses sent out from the computer brain that was really flying the machine. His eyes kept flickering to the airspeed indicator, resolutely steady at 110 knots.

"Three miles or so, I reckon," Latimer said. "See anything?"

"Not a thing," Fairman replied. His next words were cut short by Jagger.

"There!" Cody yelled, pointing ahead. They strained their eyes through the clouded night and saw, dimly, a signaling light a short distance away.

"Altimeter setting," Fairman snapped.

"One-zero-zero-nine," Jagger answered. "Wind, three-seven-oh degrees at one-six."

"Right on the nose baby," Fairman continued. "OK, I have control." As he spoke, he flicked the switch on the left of his control column to cancel the automatic system, and settled down to pilot the Boeing manually.

The aircraft juddered as they hit a patch of turbulence, and the starboard wing dropped sharply. Fairman righted it again in what was really a reflex action. The runway, picked out by the flickering dots of the paraffin lamps, was in sight. Fairman eased his hands forward to start the landing.

He muttered to himself, not caring whether anyone else heard, that it was like being back at flying school. When the end of the runway slid down the windshield, you were too high. When it slid up, too damned low. So far it remained dead center, and Fairman hoped, prayed, that it would stay there.

It was a long, dangerously slow, descent. Air Force One shot out the searching beams of its own landing lights, and a hundred tons of airplane followed the twin rays as they raked the pitted track between the smoking paraffin lamps.

Fairman completed the run in, and the great silver airliner burst onto the runway in a squeal of tires. Fairman's knuckles whitened as he gripped the steering column and fought to keep it under control.

"Reverse thrust!" he yelled. Latimer obeyed. The noise of the jets rose in an ear-splitting boom to a crescendo as all seventy-six thousand pounds of thrust were diverted to slow the liner's progress along the absurdly short landing strip.

Air Force One rattled and shook, and the plane's speed fell dramatically, throwing the stateroom passengers violently against their restraining belts. Crockery, personal articles, document cases, all flew off the tables and smashed against the bulkhead.

Outside, the girl's hand flew to her mouth and cut off a shriek of terror as the huge shape bore down on them. She pulled at Smith's arm, and he allowed himself to be dragged back behind the low wall, as if that afforded any ultimate protection from the racing jetliner.

Fairman watched the faint, flickering bank of lights at the end of the strip draw closer and closer. Then, suddenly, there was nothing in the windscreen but blackness.

Latimer, Kowalski, and Jagger held on to anything that wouldn't move, and the Boeing slewed into a hard right turn, its tires smoking. It came to rest nearly at a right angle to the gully, its port wing hanging out over the deep gash of the crevice.

Latimer licked his dry lips and said, "Hairy."

"Cut engines," Fairman breathed. The pilot chopped the switches and the whining jets died to a whimper.

"Excellent," Smith purred. "You see, my lovely Branka," he said to the girl, "you can always rely on the United States Air Force in an emergency."

Two Air Force Ones? Morwood queried. Definitely, Philpott explained: one hijacked and diverted, the other taking its place until the radar picked up the scent again. Then it would be seen cruising along the correct course at the correct altitude, and its crew would bail out at the appropriate time, probably when a ship was waiting at a prearranged signal to pick them up. The bomb on board the plane would throw the Pentagon and UNACO into total confusion while the real AF One was spirited away.

"Like where?" Morwood demanded.

The angle of turn before the liner disappeared from the inertial guidance system trace would indicate Greece or Yugoslavia, Philpott surmised.

"No closer than that?" Morwood persisted.

"If you want me to guess," Philpott replied, "I'd say Yugoslavia. If it's Smith and he has help, which I believe he may, then it'll be Yugoslavia, because he could not operate with complete freedom in Greece, and neither could the sort of assistance I think he's getting."

"Which is?"

"The KGB."

Morwood digested this information, and was tempted metaphorically to spit it out as inedible. Philpott broke the ensuing silence to round out the picture of Smith which was already forming in the general's shrewd mind. In the end, the catalogue of Smith's known previous crimes against humanity, against social systems and conventions, against established order and security, convinced the Pentagon that Smith must indeed be the man behind the hijack of the president's plane. And if Philpott said the criminal must have Soviet help, then Morwood accepted that as a running hypothesis.

"Makes it difficult for us, though, Malcolm," he added.

"I get the point," Philpott conceded. "It's impossible for the USA to act in any role on Yugoslav soil. You might have got away with a presence in Greece, but not in Yugoslavia. I accept that. I also accept the unstated corollary to your premise: it's UNACO's baby. It can't be anyone else's."

Morwood chuckled drily. So America was, for once, on the sidelines—and the opposition already had a head start on UNACO.

"How so?" Philpott asked.

Morwood's chuckle deepened to a belly laugh. "Haven't you seen the latest tape from the United Nations? There's a special emergency debate on the assumed hijack, and the Russians are already stirring it for you to the limit of their capacity for troublemaking, which I assure you is considerable. You're practically on a no-win streak even before you get your first shots off, old boy. Let's see you wriggle out of this one."

Philpott cursed his own forgetfulness in failing to keep a weather eye on his employers, and ordered Swann to cue in the General Assembly on the video. It became speedily apparent that, if anything, Morwood had understated the seriousness of UNACO's position.

Saudi Arabia had followed Iraq, Bahrain, Iran, and every other combination of outraged OPEC dignity in attacking first the Americans, and then UNACO, for allowing terrorism to erupt under their very noses in the US president's personal and supposedly ultra-secure airplane.

"Are the lives of our leading citizens of so little consequence to our supposed allies that they are unable to ensure their safety on a five-hour plane trip?" thundered Libya.

"Never before have even the imperialist bandits of the Western world manifested so patent and brutal a contempt for the servants of Islam," Iran echoed. "Are we such dirt beneath their feet that we are to be trussed up and handed to the first criminal dog that comes along, yapping to do his masters' bidding and lining his pockets with a ransom which the Americans are clearly confident they will not have to furnish?"

Philpott winced before the TV monitors, knowing that worse was to come.

"And this pallid lackey of the United States, this 'UNACO' "—the Bahraini ambassador invested the acronym with such withering scorn that Philpott feared the characters would melt on his office door—"this cryptocapitalist sore in the UN body politic, whose salaries we pay, whose staff we keep in sybaritic idleness, who actually made the security of this flight their particular responsibility . . . is it too invidious to suggest that doors may have been left open for this aerial highwayman, that palms were greased, souls corrupted—that Malcolm Gregory Philpott, defender of our freedoms, pillar of international rectitude, doughty champion of the oppressed and opponent of the malefactor . . . is it so unimaginable that Philpott himself might have a share in the complicity of this foul and dastardly act?"

Philpott reached for the switch, and before the monitor pictures faded he saw the Russian delegation unravel their folded arms and bang the table in cynical approbation.

Smith's guerillas coupled a tractor to Air Force One and towed her to the shelter of a dilapidated but roomy hangar. There, a busy little crane covered every visible inch of the Boeing in tarpaulin sheets, leaving only the main hatch uncovered. A flight of steps was wheeled up and Achmed Fayeed opened the door. Smith stalked into the building and stood at the foot of the stairway tapping a gloved hand with a silver-topped ebony stick. He was ringed by swarthy lieutenants, submachine guns at the port.

Achmed led the way, and stood before Smith, grinning widely, twirling the pistol on his finger, cowboy-style. Smith said nothing, but reached out his hand and placed it on the young Arab's left shoulder in an unmistakable gesture of approval and comradeship.

The hostages and crew members filed or were carried down the steps, Hemmingsway following the OPEC ministers, with Sabrina Carver behind him. To Sabrina's bewilderment, there was no sign of McCafferty, and hope sprang in her breast that even now he might still be at liberty, waiting for the right moment to gain the upper hand and free the prisoners. She also calculated that her Air Force One uniform and obvious anonymity would conceal her own identify, but she was wrong.

Smith's face now wore a smile of clear amusement as she tried to use Hemmingsway as a shield. "I must admit," he said slowly, "that I did not expect to find *you* on board this aircraft. But why play the shrinking violet, my dear Sabrina? Modesty never suited you, as I recall from our brief sojourn at my château before the ill-fated venture on the Eiffel Tower.

"Can you conceivably, I wonder, have changed your vocation after—what is it—three and a half years? No longer the international jewel thief extraordinary, but abandoned to the monastic womb of service life? It seems unlikely. Perhaps you would care to offer an explanation of your presence here."

109

Achmed cut in, "No need, Mister Smith. I can tell you about her. She's with UNACO."

"Aaah," Smith drawled, "so . . . one of Mr. Philpott's eager little beaveresses. Doubtless you were prostituting yourself for him on our previous encounter, too? Yes, your silence and evident shame indicate that to be the case, Well, now, Miss Sabrina Carver, clearly I underestimated you then. Be assured that I shall not make the same mistake again. Achmed, I give her into your personal and special care. Do what you will with her—only make sure that she suffers. . . . Make very sure of that, Achmed."

Fayeed caught her wrist and pulled her to him, and Sabrina had to restrain herself from retaliation, but now was not the time, she told herself; she had to learn their location and get word to Philpott. And look after the boy, Feisal. Achmed could wait.

Smith continued, "And one still not with us? Could he also be suffering from unaccustomed shyness?"

"No chance, Mister Smith," Jagger called from the doorway of the plane.

"My dear colonel," Smith crowed, "join us, please, and complete our pleasure."

All eyes were on him as he descended the steps—on him, and on the gun which he still carried in his hand.

"Oh, my God, no," Sabrina breathed, "not you, Mac. Not you."

"Oh, yes," Mister Smith sneered. "Indeed, I don't know how we should have managed without Colonel McCafferty's all-too-willing assistance."

Chapter Ten

The US consul in Bahrain was neat, pedantic, and obstinate, and called Mackie-Belton. He had been immediately prejudiced against the grimy, blood-streaked figure who

110

had forcibly invaded his privacy and interrupted his dinner with an Arabian lady of enormous discretion but small reserves of patience. Now Mackie-Belton's own tolerance was approaching the end of its tether.

"Put yourself in my position," he insisted, not for the first time, "and give me one reason—not half a dozen or twenty—just one reason why I should believe you. You come bursting in here uninvited, wearing filthy Arab clothing and a USAF shirt, underwear, and socks, obviously having fought your way out of some seedy drinking party, and without a shred of either evidence or identification to back you up, you insist you're someone whom I know from my own experience you cannot possibly be.

"When I clearly do not accept your story, you insult me, threaten me, bully me, try to cajole me into telephoning the Director of UNACO and the operations room at the Pentagon—and then you are outraged when I propose calling the police. Let me tell you—and do not come any closer, please—let me tell you that the only reason you are still here and the police are not, is that your story is so incredible, so fantastic, that it just might have a grain of truth in it."

Mac sighed and slumped into a lumpy armchair, his legs outstretched, his fingers plucking disconsolately at the beading on the upholstery. He lifted his eyes wearily to Mackie-Belton, and saw scarcely a chink in the implacable hostility of the plump little man in the white tuxedo, thinning brown hair plastered down to cover his scalp, buck teeth gleaming in the tight mouth. The consul's bifocals were suspended by the earpieces from a thin gold chain looped around the back of his neck, and falling to rest on his pleated white dinner shirt like some extravagant order from a Middle Eastern potentate.

"So what will you do, Mr. Belton?" he muttered.

"Mackie-Belton, if you don't mind. Well, for a start, I will not contact either the Pentagon or UNACO, but I will endeavor to find someone on this island who might know you and could confirm that you bear at least a passing resemblance to Colonel Joseph McCafferty whom we know to be aboard Air Force One—which, by the way, in my opinion, you do not, although I have met the gentleman only once."

111

Mac groaned and passed his hand over his face—then snatched it away and sat bolt upright in the chair, his blazing eyes and harsh breathing unsettling Mackie-Belton even more.

"Of course!" he hooted triumphantly, and Mackie-Belton winced anew, "you're right, of course! Now shut up and listen, because I'm going to tell you something which you *will* believe!

"Ankara, wasn't it? Don't interrupt, don't move, don't even breathe . . . Ankara, yeah, three—no, four—years ago. I'd had my wallet stolen and I was strapped for money. I came to you"—his brow furrowed with the effort of remembrance—"I came to you in a little green office"—he shut his eyes and clenched his fists—"with a damned great palm tree in the corner. The door was marked Consulate: Documentation and Credit,' or something like that.

"You let me have five hundred dollars, didn't you? Reluctantly, as I recall, but you were able to check my papers and everything figured. I sent it back by money order as soon as I got to London. For Christ's sake, there were only two of us in the room, Mr. Mackie-Belton. No secretary, no aide. I couldn't possibly know this unless I'd been there. I even remember your last words: you said 'Give my respects to Fortnum and Mason,' and I replied that Selfridge's Food Hall was nearer my mark, which didn't seem to please you at all.

"Now then. God damn it—am I right? And if so, who am I?"

Mackie-Belton frowned, lifted the gold-rimmed bifocals on their slim chain, breathed first on one lens, then the other, extracted a crisply folded white handkerchief from his top pocket, and polished the glass with fastidious deliberation, then replied slowly, "You are Colonel Joseph McCafferty."

Mac leaned back in the chair, crossed his legs, grinned, and said, "*Olé* and yippee. So—can we go to work? Because time, Mr. Mackie-Belton, is of the essence. It's Air Force One I'm talking about—a hijack plot, OK? It's happening, consul." He rose to his feet, towering over his unwilling but benign host. "Even now, it could be happening."

For the next half-hour, McCafferty fretted, fumed, and

112

boiled while Mackie-Belton contacted the American embassies in Ankara and London, then Andrews Air Force Base, then his brother at Princeton University, and finally, when he was convinced that he had enough personal cover to preserve his own career if Mac turned out to be an extremely gifted lunatic, slotted through a call to Basil Swann—who didn't believe him.

Mackie-Belton chewed his lip, hummed offkey and raised his plucked eyebrows as he handed the receiver to McCafferty, making a careful note of the duration of each call for the telephone bill which he would inevitably pass to UNACO. But if Mac had found the consul stubborn, the diplomat wasn't even in the same league as Basil Swann. He struggled in vain against Basil's adamantine logic, then changed his tack and switched to the form of personal recollection which had eventually persuaded Mackie-Belton.

Gradually, the doubt crept into Swann's voice, and Mac seized the opportunity to demand—in tones which Basil (who had had brushes with McCafferty before) could not fail to recognize—that he should be connected to Philpott.

An hour and fifty minutes after barging into the consul's thankfully secluded villa, where the Arabian lady's unstoical forbearance had passed breaking point, Mac talked at last to his chief. They pieced the story together from fragments of each other's intelligence or inspired guesswork: Mac had no direct knowledge of Smith's involvement, but was able to supply Dunkels, Achmed, and the Yugoslav connection; Philpott knew nothing of the Bahrainian assault, but papered over the cracks with the radar incidents and the elimination of AF One's inertial guidance track, together with the explosion of the fake Boeing.

Philpott, at least, made his decision swiftly. While acknowledging that McCafferty's tale verged on the unbelievable, the two men were agreed that (a) the President's plane had been hijacked with the real or false McCafferty on board; and (b) that Smith was behind it, luring the aircraft by some means and for some as yet undisclosed purpose to Yugoslavia, where a Russian (almost certainly KGB) nexus had been established.

"Right," Philpott said, "we move—though not, I fear, to

113

Yugoslavia. We have to play our cards very cleverly, Mac. Anything to do with that place, or any other member of the Red camp, is such sensitive territory it's just not true. UNACO members they may be, but they spit like tigers if I suggest one of them may be directly implicated in something, even if it's unintentional."

"So where do we go, and what do we do?" McCafferty asked.

"We go to Rome," Philpott replied, "and start from there. It's the best staging post in Europe, as you know. They're a joy to work with, the Italians; they're so used to duplicity they regularly doublecross themselves."

"And what shall we do when we get there?"

"With any luck, we'll pick up this guy Dunkels and hope he'll lead us to Air Force One."

"Which is in Yugoslavia," Mac pointed out reasonably.

"By then," Philpott said warily, "I'll have persuaded the Yugoslav Government to offer strictly limited cooperation to a strictly limited UNACO force."

"You and me?"

"Right. Oh, eh, plus Sabrina Carver, who's on the plane."

There was a pregnant silence from McCafferty's end. Then, with suspicion and something like anger slowly rising in him, he said, "I didn't know Sabrina Carver was one of us, sir."

"No," Philpott agree, "you didn't, did you?"

To the right of the stone doorframe a tapestry dropped fully six feet to the floor. Like the dark, richly-colored oil painting next to it, starting level with its top and running for about the same distance along the wall, the tapestry portrayed a hunting scene. Its frayed canvas showed, in dull browns, greens, and blues, the sticking of a wild boar by a small army of hunters; it was an unequal battle, though the boar had matched tusk for spear to some effect. The oil painting was of a more usual scenario, a stag at bay in a glen, standing off the snarling dogs who were being encouraged by mounted huntsmen, bloodlust contorting their features. Only the stag retained a shred of dignity, its great brown eyes registering bewilderment rather than fear.

114

From the picture, the eye traveled almost by compulsion to the set piece which dominated the long, white-walled room: the head of a "royal" or "imperial" stag, mirror image of the doomed giant in the oil painting, its twelve-point antlers casting shifting, spiky shadows on the wall in the lamplight. Below the deer king, but still above the door, processing around the room in a mournful frieze of sudden death, were smaller stags, an eagle or two, a peregrine falcon, a grimacing boar, some barn owls, a brace of obligatory foxes, and a few pet hounds, interspersed with the brass funnels of hunting horns and nonfunctional guns by the rackful.

The furniture was of heavy, pitted wood, and the windows were cross-hatched with ironwork. The light, from two oil lanterns, was feeble, creating pools of shade, recesses, and places of uncertain passage. Sabrina thought it fitting that Mister Smith should immure his hostages in his trophy room. So, too, as it happened, did Smith.

The terror and desperation reflected by the mounted heads and corpses communicated themselves to Smith's captives. The crew members talked, aimlessly for the most part, in whispers, Jeanie Fenstermaker holding a handkerchief to her eyes and being comforted by the diminutive Wynanski; Cooligan lolling against a table apart from the engineers, tight-lipped and coldly enraged by McCafferty's treachery; Fairman, Kowalski, and Latimer conversed in low tones about likely locations, for although they knew roughly whereabouts in Yugoslavia the airstrip lay, they had been blindfolded for the trip to the castle. Of the oil titans, Dorani endlessly smoked cheroots, to the disapproval of Hamady, who was discussing ransoms with him; and Hemmingsway poured words into the uncaring ear of Sheik Arbeid. Only Zeidan, like the mighty stag, was impassive and alert, his smouldering eyes probing the furthest reaches of the room, seeking weaknesses, disadvantages . . .

The minibus, its windows darkened, had driven to a halt outside the hangar at Kosgo where Sheik Zeidan asked the one question which Smith had permitted the hostages.

"Who are you, dog?" said the old Arab. Smith's fingers caressed the silver point of his cane, and he took three steps to stand over the crippled sheik, his eyes narrowed, his mouth like a closed man-trap. Zeidan had not troubled even to meet his gaze.

"You may call me Mister Smith."

"May I—Smith?"

Achmed bounded to the wheelchair and turned it roughly so that Zeidan faced him. "*Mister* Smith, cousin," he grated, "do not forget that."

Zeidan regarded him with intense distaste. "I speak with the master, scum," he replied contemptuously, "not to his lick-spittle hyena."

Achmed wrenched the chair around again, and Feisal leaped in to catch it. The boy steadied the chair, and said, low-voiced so that no one but Achmed and Zeidan could hear, "You *serpent.* All of these curs will die, but for you I will reserve a death so terrible that the maggot you call your brain will be unable to encompass it."

Achmed started to laugh, but then his lips stretched into a snarl and he backhanded Feisal across the face into Sabrina's waiting arms. "What have I to fear from a senile cripple and a diabetic brat?" he yelled. "It is *you* who will—"

"Shut your mouth!" Smith commanded, his voice ripping through the young Arab's bravado like a chain saw. "All of you—keep silent! *I* will tell you when you can speak, and it is not now! You"—he gestured to the man in battle fatigues who had descended from the minibus—"get them under way. No more delays!"

Smith grasped Branka's arm and yanked her off towards his car. Fayeed, still furious, mimed to the guerillas to bind and blindfold the captives, and the hostages were pushed, reeling and helpless, to their transport.

The bus cut inland on the main road from Zadar on the coast as far as Masienica, then turned off on a minor route for Knin, and started the steep climb into the Dinaric Alps. The captives, frustrated in their blindness, could not see the countryside getting wilder and more rugged in the bright moonlight. The road wound up into the mountains, then gave way to a rougher track until they reached a stretch of level ground where the surface improved.

Flanked by a low, thick stone wall, the route hugged the side of a hill, which gradually fell away and flattened into

116

a crater, a sculpted bowl in the ribs of the mountain. And in that hollow lay the castle of Windischgraetz.

It was an extraordinary sight by day, the road twisting and turning until the final lap, and suddenly the castle was there, grafted on to the mountainside like a lump of coal in a snowman's face. The narrow track widened to form a quadrangle and parking area, and facing Smith's visitors was a drawbridge over a leafy chasm. This led to a corridor and entrance hall, shut off from the world outside by a huge, arched doorway and carved double doors. The drawbridge and entrance portal occupied much of the width of that end-facing wall, for Castle Windischgraetz was long but slim of girth, bent round to fit the contours of the cliff.

The lofty walls supported peaked slate roofs, also built on to the rock face. The wooded cliff towered above the castle and, most impressive of all, outlined it against the gaping maw of a cave reaching into the heart of the mountain, its mouth curving like a black halo over the tallest point of the building. The roof slates rose in pyramid turrets, and under them sat rows of darkened windows in the rough-weathered stone of the walls.

The castle of Windischgraetz stood fifteen hundred feet above sea level, the eyrie of an eagle, impregnable, almost unapproachable, since the days of Charlemagne.

Smith's hostages were marshaled across the drawbridge and into an interior courtyard where twin cannon guarded another stone entranceway. There Smith ordered the blindfords and bonds removed, and the captives taken to the trophy room. Sheik Zeidan was carried up the stairs by two burly crewmen, and his wheelchair slung in after him.

Smith stood outside with the big iron key in his hand. "Go to the radio room," he instructed Fayeed, "and wait for a contact from Dunkels. He should be on his way by now. I'll entertain our guests for a while, but let me know as soon as you hear word of his movements."

Achmed hurried away and Smith turned the key noiselessly in the lock. Two guards came up behind him, submachine guns once more at the port.

Hemmingsway remarked sourly that he hoped Smith had come to state his terms. Assuredly, Smith said, he had. Fairman asked how long Smith planned to hold

117

them, and Smith assumed they would be freed once the ransom for their release was in his hands.

"Ah," Hamady breathed, "so it is a ransom."

"Naturally," Smith said, "Did you think I had you kidnapped merely for the pleasure of sharing your company?"

"We were wondering, perhaps," Zeidan observed heavily, "whether it might not have something to do with our status as OPEC emissaries. That your motives could be, shall I say, more overtly political than merely mercenary."

Smith, who was enjoying himself, took the insult without flinching. "Your exalted positions, sheik, bear only commercial value for me," he sneered. "In some ways I detest what you stand for, your stranglehold over our Western oil supplies, your greed and primitive cruelty to your peoples . . . but I am neither politician nor moralist, Your Excellency. I regard you as medieval robber barons, ripe for plucking. That you should be relieved of some of your enormous wealth is, I suggest, long overdue. I regret the presence of a blameless American among you, and I regard the crew members of the president's toy as no more than passing nuisances. I have other plans for Miss Carver. From you gentlemen,"—indicating the seated Arabs—"I require nothing but money—in kind."

"What kind of money in what kind of kind?" Hemmingsway demanded.

Smith studied him in surprise. "Perhaps you *do* wish to speak for them—haggle for them, Mr. Hemmingsway. So be it. The ransom is fifty million dollars."

Hemmingsway swallowed with difficulty and licked his dry lips. "And in what form?"

"In cut diamonds," Smith replied firmly. "They are so pretty—and so eminently negotiable, don't you think?"

Mackie-Belton prevailed upon a high-ranking and discreet Bahraini police officer to provide McCafferty with clothing suitable for what the American would only describe as "a somewhat colder climate." Swann phoned with the message that a jet was already *en route* for the Gulf island to pick him up and take him to Rome. "With a few extras," Basil explained. "Passport, documentation;

arms for you and Miss Carver and the agent, Coloigan; field glasses, communicators—that sort of thing. Everything'll be stowed in a knapsack on board the plane. All you have to do is walk off with it at Leonardo da Vinci, Rome. The jet'll be in Bahrain well before dawn. Good luck, Mac."

"Thanks, Basil," McCafferty replied, and before Swann could hang up slipped in a request for money. "Cleaned out, you see," he explained.

Rarely for him, Swann chuckled. "Why not try the consul?" he suggested, and broke the connection.

"This," said Mackie-Belton later, returning from another ego-bruising session with the Arabian lady and brandishing five hundred dollars, "is getting to be a nasty habit."

At three in the morning, the consul ruefully said goodbye to the Arabian lady, and at three-thirty McCafferty received a call from the Bahraini police captain telling him that Siegfried Dunkels had left the island.

"Going where?" Mac asked hopefully.

He could almost hear the policeman smirk. "First stop Athens—then Zagreb."

Just at that time, Philpott was unavailable to give instructions, having received a summons to a distinctly acid meeting with the UN's dour and heavy-humored secretary general, so Mac was airborne when the order came from UNACO to divert his aircraft to Yugoslavia and lie in wait for the German. . . .

When Smith next visited the hostages, he brought armed guards with him again, and three more guerillas hauling tripods and a large electric battery. "I thought you needed a little more illumination," he said cheerfully, "and even if you don't, I do."

The men rigged up the equipment, and poured photo floodlight into the room. Fayeed sidled in behind them with a Polaroid camera, and Smith posed the hostages, OPEC men in front, crew members behind, against a totally neutral section of wall, removing trophies, pictures, furniture . . . anything which could lead to an identification of the location.

After checking that no member of the group was making

an unauthorized signal with fingers or eyes, Smith nodded to Achmed, who clicked away and produced several reasonable prints. Smith approved four pictures, and instructed Achmed to sent them immediately by courier to Trieste and Dubrovnik. "They must catch the first editions of the morning newspapers," he emphasized, "together with details of the ransom demands. And don't forget—one to the Associated Press agency as well. I want this to hit the States, too. It is, after all, their airplane."

Fairman muttered something at this sally, and Smith inclined his ear with a sympathetic smile. "If I caught what you said correctly, colonel," he said pleasantly, "you were offering your opinion that Air Force One could be located by satellite sensing devices. Am I right?" Fairman nodded grudgingly.

"I thought so," Smith continued, "and I'm sorry to disappoint you. The engines were covered in dry ice as soon as the tarpaulins were laid. They cooled off within a few moments. The aircraft cannot, I regret to say, be detected. Now"—addressing all of them—"you will doubtless be relieved to hear that I have no intention of compelling you to spend the night in these uncomfortable surroundings.

"Achmed will show you to the quarters which have been prepared for you. I am afraid some of you will be doubling up; I can only hope that the partners allocated to you are acceptable. Achmed?"

Once more the hostages were led out, and the only trouble Achmed encountered was when he tried to separate Sabrina and Feisal. He had wanted her for himself; the fate of the boy did not concern him.

"I must stay with him," Sabrina appealed to Smith. "He's ill. You surely can't want anything to happen to him. He isn't even on the ransom list."

Zeidan reinforced her plea by pointing out that if Feisal suffered another attack, Sabrina alone could administer his medication. To Achmed's evident annoyance, Smith agreed, and Sabrina and Feisal were led up another flight of steps to a room which looked as if it had been hastily adapted for accommodation, containing as it did nothing but two beds, a table, and a washbasin, with an adjoining toilet. Its most conspicuous feature, however, was the long slit running the full length of the external wall, protected from the worst effects of the weather by an overhanging eave, jutting out like a peaked cap.

The vent was paneled in glass now, but Sabrina guessed that it had once been a lookout position, a sentry room, affording as it must a panorama of the entire area, assuming they were up as high as the definite chill in the room suggested. There was no lighting in their cell, so they undressed, and Sabrina had just snuggled down into her bed when they heard the sound of a motorcycle starting up in the courtyard below.

Pulling the bedspread off to wrap around her nakedness, Sabrina hurried to the slit window, and was joined by Feisal. A loud "clunk" came from somewhere to their left, and Fiesal whispered, "Must be a drawbridge."

"Good thinking," Sabrina said, shivering as the cold nipped at her body. The motorcyclist roared away, and from their perch they were able to follow his lights for what seemed miles down the twisting road.

"That was a Honda," Sabrina said smugly. She knew motorcycles almost as well as she knew cars, and was adept at driving both.

Feisal nodded in agreement. "Hondamatic 400," he confirmed. Sabrina stared at him. "How could you tell that?" she asked.

This time Feisal snickered. "He went for at least two hundred yards without changing gear. On a Hondamatic 400 you don't have to change up until you hit 55 mph."

Sabrina's eyes widened. "I didn't know that," she ventured.

"I am not at all surprised," Feisal remarked. "There would be no reason for a woman to possess such knowledge."

Sabrina tried to hide her grin. "Listen, you smart-aleck, know-it-all kid—" she began, but Feisal cut her off.

"That's what everyone says," he assured her airily. "And incidentally, your somewhat inadequate garment has slipped. May I be permitted to congratulate you on your magnificent breasts?"

He jumped back into bed and was fast asleep almost as soon as his head touched the pillow.

* * *

121

McCafferty's executive jet streamed through the night sky and deposited him at Zagreb well before the sun was high in the east. He passed easily enough through customs with his backpack, which had been covered by UNACO's diplomatic immunity on a hastily forged *laissez-passer* that Mac had found, on Swann's instructions, among the aircraft's store of useful documents. The Yugoslav guards examined the form and cast suspicious eyes at the pack, but waved him on.

He used his newly acquired credit cards to hire a car, a small but powerful Polski Fiat with a formidable top speed on the speedometer. He didn't have long to wait. Dunkels's flight arrived on time and Mac, huddled down in the rear seat of his car, saw the German enact the same performance at the Avis desk. Just as Dunkels was completing the formalities, however, he was hailed from the roadside.

He turned, and both he and McCafferty saw a black Mercedes—with Swiss plates—moored at the curb. Dr. Stein's talkative chauffeur grinning at Dunkels's evident surprise. The German jumped into the front seat and the Mercedes pulled away—with the Fiat following at a discreet distance. McCafferty gritted his teeth as he stamped on the car's accelerator. He had a score to settle with Dunkels. And with Smith. He sensed that their chase marked the start of the last lap.

Chapter Eleven

Dunkels headed south from Zagreb on the M12a, which was signposted for Busevec, Lekenik, and Zazina. The road was fairly deserted, and Mac had to keep the little Fiat well back to escape detection. After about nineteen miles, Dunkels's car swung to the right for Gora, and then turned left into a small private airfield. It was hardly more than a large stretch of grass, permitting a clear run of barely fifteen hundred feet in any direction. Standing near the group of rusty, corrugated iron sheds which passed for hangars was a Russian-built Kamov helicopter.

The helicopter's contra-rotating blades were already revolving for takeoff, and the Mercedes drive straight up to it. Moments later McCafferty caught sight of Dunkels running crouched beneath the rotors to get on board. The door had not even closed when the engine revolutions started to rise, and a low, loud pulsating roar of sound heralded the Kamov's departure.

Mac cursed under his breath. He should have foreseen something of the kind, or waited for backup. Now he was powerless to keep on the German's tail. He parked the Fiat on a grass verge behind a rubbish-filled metal skip as the Mercedes shot out of the airfield and skidded into a turn. Mac pulled up the hood of his parka to hide his face but the chauffeur passed him without even a first look.

Then the Kamov's engine noise rose to a howl, and the helicopter passed over his head, its down-draft tearing the leaves from the trees and flattening the grass.

The American moodily started his own engine and drove up the narrow road just past the field, intending to reverse into its entrance for the trip back to Zagreb. He was looking over his shoulder to get the proper sighting when his eye fell on a small gaggle of light aircraft parked near the sheds. He whistled and said, "Hey. Suddenly it's Christmas."

Mac reversed all the way into the airfield and put the Fiat in the space between two of the sheds, then he got out to examine his unexpected presents. There was a twin-engined Cessna, an old Piper Tripacer, an Italian Marchetti, and what appeared to be several versions of the Yugoslav UTVA. He checked that no one else was about, and inspected the three leading Yugoslavian planes. He had never flown one, but he kept up to date with the technical journals, and knew that the UTVA had a low stalling speed, good short-field performance and, unusually, a surprising amount of speed.

McCafferty rubbed his chin and slipped a stick of chewing gum into his mouth. "I'd say, at a rough guess, forty . . . forty-five miles an hour faster than the Kamov," he mused. Another thought struck him: the UTVA could probably fly at least seven thousand feet higher than the helicopter. A grin split his face and he said, out loud, "Now then. Let's see if someone has been careless enough to leave the keys in one of these babies."

He chose the aircraft parked alongside the end of the first hangar, and immediately struck gold: the keys were there. He strolled casually back to the Fiat, still keeping his eyes peeled for signs of life. Mac took his knapsack out of the car and locked the door. Then he scuttled back to the UTVA and threw himself into the cockpit, keeping his body below the window line while he carried out the pre-takeoff checks.

Mac tested the master switch, and the indicator showed he had a full tank of fuel. He checked that the electrical system was functioning, and then moved the stick and rudder pedals to ensure that there were no control locks on. Whispering a "good luck" message to himself, he operated the start control.

This was the most crucial stage of the operation, because the engine noise would be a dead giveaway—though with any luck it would be too late by then to stop him. The engine fired at once, and his luck held: he looked out of the window, careless now whether anyone saw him or not. Mac had a gun in his hand and was prepared to make an issue of it . . . but still he had the field to himself. He shrugged, took a chance in opening the throttle wide (which was far from standard practice), and pointed the nose in the direction which seemed to give him the longest takeoff run.

Within a hundred yards the tail had responded to the gentle forward pressure on the stick. Mac's view improved as the nose of the rather old-fashioned aircraft leveled, and fifty yards further on the airspeed indicator was showing forty-five knots. He wound the elevator trim to prepare for flight, and found himself smoothly airborne and climbing steeply, without any conscious effort.

When he crossed the perimeter of the little airfield, the altimeter was already showing two hundred feet. He breathed a sigh of relief and turned back over the field to fly south after Dunkels. As he passed the group of rusting sheds, he peered out and again saw no one moving around.

"Where the hell's the resident mechanic?" he thought. "There must be one. You can't leave the entire place unattended with all these planes lying about." Then the penny dropped: Smith must have bribed the mechanic to leave Dunkels a clear field for takeoff.

McCafferty turned his attention back to Dunkels, estimating the Kamov's course at about 190 degrees. Setting the same course for himself, he climbed four thousand feet to enlarge his view and compensate for the start the German had on him. He figured he could make up the leeway with the superior performance of the UTVA—particularly if he pushed it slightly beyond the recommended limit. He scanned the area below him on both sides, every inch of land and sky, not seeing the beauty of the rolling countryside, nor the sunlit, tree-lined slopes . . . he looked only for the telltale signs which would betray the elusive helicopter: the glint of reflected light from the whirring blades, the fly-sized black speck against the bright blue, the dark shadow stealing across a green meadow.

A road, a river, and a railway line passed beneath his gaze. To his left a small town nestled in a fold of the gentle hills. Mac fumbled for a crumpled, dog-eared chart left in the cockpit, and identified the town as Glina. He peered more closely at the chart: next stop, Topusko—to starboard.

He leaned to his right, looking out, searching for Topusko, and there was the Kamov, flying so low that it appeared for one ludicrous moment to be covering the ground like a car. McCafferty chuckled and spat out the chewing gum, which in any case had lost its flavor.

While rerouting McCafferty to Yugoslavia, Philpott decided that Sonya and he should stick to their original plan and make for Rome. Whisked through customs at Fiumicino as VIPs, they left the airport with their minimal luggage untouched, ignored the thieving conmen operating as unlicensed taxi drivers and the yellow cabs themselves, and made for a NATO staff car sitting by the "No Parking" sign. The jaded high-ranking officer in British Army uniform standing by the car unlaced his arms and pasted on a welcoming beam.

The officer—tall, greying, and keen-eyed, with a toothbrush mostache that ended precisely at the corners of his mouth—threw up a salute that was somewhere between a wave and a semaphore signal. "Morning. Tomlin. Brigadier."

Philpott replied, "Morning. Philpott. UNACO."

Tomlin said, "I'm NATO. Naples. In charge of the local end."

Philpott said, "My associate, Mrs. Kolchinsky. We're in charge of both ends." He nodded towards Sonya and then they both shook hands with the soldier.

"We don't usually meet—ah—visiting firemen," Tomlin continued earnestly, ignoring Philpott's darkening brow. "However, I've been ordered to this time, so you must be pretty important."

"Not really," Philpott responded offhandedly, "just an ordinary chap with some ordinary questions, brigadier."

"Oh, splendid," Tomlin said, conducting them into the car and seating himself in a jumpseat. "Jolly good show. Well then, fire away."

Sonya's firm grip on his wrist was helping Philpott control his rising temper, though he found it difficult to fuel his anger in the face of Tomlin's complete insouciance. "Well, to start with, is there any word on the wreckage of Air Force One?" he inquired.

"Ah," Tomlin said, leaning forward conspiratorially, "yes, there is." He instructed the corporal at the wheel of the car to drive them away, then confided to Philpott that the wreckage of the plane had been located.

"But—" he added, and gaped when Philpott supplied, "But it's not Air Force One."

"Quite right," Tomlin confirmed. "But how on earth did you know?"

Philpott tapped the side of his nose. "Fireman's secret," he whispered. "It was a Boeing 707, I take it?"

It was, Tomlin conceded, though as far as they could make out from the debris, it was a freighter, not an airliner. There was no registration mark, so the plane could take days to trace.

Philpott digested the news; he had hoped to link Smith definitively with the hijack through an instant identification of the "lookalike" Boeing, but it seemed he would have to wait for his affirmative evidence. Not, though, for long.

A squawk from the front of the vehicle announced a radio message. Tomlin shot back the dividing partition and rapped, "What did they say, corporal?"

"Headquarters, sir," the NCO replied. "Ransom demand for the OPEC ministers received in Trieste and, I think, Dubrovnik. Something's gone out on one of the American news agencies, too."

The brigadier was all business now. "HQ then, and step on it." He preened himself as though he had been personally responsible for the invention of radio, and said to Philpott, "Bit of a turnup, no?"

"No," Philpott said, "I was expecting it." The soldier arched an expressive eyebrow, but said nothing. Philpott moved in smoothly for the kill. "What's more, brigadier," he said slyly, "one gets you ten that the guy behind the ransom demand is called Smith."

Tomlin sniffed. "Bit, eh, sort of—commonplace, isn't it?"
Philpott chuckled. "The name, maybe; not the man."

In the operations room at NATO HQ, Philpott and Sonya studied blowups of the Polaroid pictures wired over on request from Trieste and from the AP bureau in Belgrade. Tomlin shot one of the prints under a desk magnifier and the image was thrown on to a wall screen. "All present and correct, sir?" he inquired, suitably chastened since his discovery that the hijacker was indeed named as Mister Smith.

Philpott and Sonya mentally ticked off ministers and crew members, all of whose faces were on record at UNACO. Unobtrusively, they were intently scanning just one among the dozen or so faces—for Jagger, naturally, was in the group of captives.

"Unbelievable," Philpott murmured. "Uncanny," Sonya said. "It's the greatest surgery I've ever seen. Everything . . . even Mac's mother would swear—"

"Brigadier—" Philpott cut her off with a peremptory, though not unkind, gesture, "have you formed any opinion about the background to the snapshot?"

The brigadier said without hesitation that it was a castle. "Flagstone floor," he explained airily, "roughcast walls. We've got a few of 'em in England, you know."

"No, I didn't," said Philpott interestedly, "you must tell me some time."

The sarcasm was lost on Tomlin, who merely nodded sagely and repeated, "No doubt of it. A castle."

Philpott agreed, and asked the brigadier if he knew of any castles in Yugoslavia.

"Is that where it's supposed to be?" Tomlin bleated. Philpott nodded. The brigadier shrugged. "Hundreds?"

"Probably not," Philpott said. "But there are certainly enough to make the right one difficult to find without any other identification."

A clerk brought in copies of the ransom note and, like Hemmingsway had done, Philpott whistled when he saw Smith's demand for fifty million dollars' worth of cut diamonds. "It's a helluva lot of money," he mused.

"What about the rest?" Tomlin said shakily.

"Rest?" Philpott echoed.

Tomlin flourished the Associated Press tape, giving the full story, unlike the UNACO report, which had been split up into paragraphs with analysis, of which Philpott had only the first.

Tomlin paraphrased, "Unless the Arab nations—or someone . . . UNACO's mentioned—meet Smith's demands, he'll kill one minister every three hours.

"My God," Tomlin whispered, "he must be mad. Do you think he means it?"

Philpott looked up from the UNACO report. "Oh, he's serious all right," he said gravely. "And he may also be mad enough to carry it out."

Sonya Kolchinsky compressed her lips into a line. "Is there a deadline, brigadier?"

Tomlin glanced back down at the paper in his hand. "There is," he verified. "It's one hour from"—he looked at his watch—"about now. UNACO's acceptance of Smith's terms must be broadcast on the American Forces' Network from Rome at precisely 1000 hours, local time." He looked levelly at Philpott. "Over to you, sir," he added.

Philpott drew a large breath and vented it as a sigh compounded as much of resignation as of frustration. "An hour . . ." he muttered, ". . . just one hour and we could lose Hawley Hemmingsway."

"Why Hemmingsway?" Sonya inquired.

Philpott smiled. "Can you see Smith executing a valuable Arab before a nonnegotiable American?"

A stiff breeze ruffled Philpott's hair, and the warm sunlight filling the Piazza Barberini caused him to shade his eyes and squint up at the waiter.

"*Signore?*" the waiter asked.

"*Eh—capuccino,*" Philpott replied. Then he caught sight of the figure of a man crossing the road from the subway station.

"*Signore!*" he called after the retreating waiter. The waiter turned, his newly pressed white smock bristling with anticipation. "*Due capuccine,*" Philpott ordered. The waiter echoed "*Due. Prego, Signore,*" and scuttled off. The man from the subway advanced and sat, uninvited and unsmiling, at Philpott's table.

UNACO's first priority after examining every aspect of the ransom demand had been to plan how to stall for time. Secondly, the ransom must be assembled. This had been the easier option. Sonya put through telephone calls at Philpott's direction to the Johannesburg and Amsterdam Diamond Exchanges and to the chief executive of De Beers. On UNACO's credit the sum was promised. Delivery of the equivalent in cut diamonds would be made from Amsterdam by the next flight from Schipol to Fiumicino.

Meanwhile, Philpott had anxiously probed the situation from every angle. "I must have time to find Smith," Philpott demanded, slapping the table in the NATO ops room with his open palm. "He cannot be allowed to take command. Once we broadcast our agreement to his terms, he'll follow up with the location of the ransom dropping point in a real hurry, and before we know it he'll have gotten away with it."

"But you will make the broadcast?" Tomlin asked cautiously. "I know it goes against the grain, sir, but I think you'll agree that we dare not risk the lives of any of the OPEC ministers. Unless you feel Smith is simply bluffing."

Philpott slowly passed a hand across his forehead and allowed the fingers to slide down his face. He looked out of the window and stared at the silent maelstrom of Rome's

129

traffic far below. "He may be bluffing in the sense that I don't believe he will *himself* kill a minister." he finally replied. "Killing's not Smith's style. On the other hand, there will be by the nature of things unstable people with him . . . I have a sketchy outline of two of them. And apart from that, Smith is certainly not above staging an execution convincingly enough to persuade one of the other hostages to pass it on to us as a fact. I've no doubt Smith has radio facilities—and will use them to blackmail us, broadcasting in short bursts so that we are unable to track down the frequency."

Tomlin nodded gloomily. "We wouldn't know whether it was true or not," he agreed. "We would have to assume it had actually happened. It would be a bluff we could not call."

The two men sat for a minute immersed in their separate thoughts, and then Philpott jerkily shifted to the front of his seat and scribbled on the notepad before him. He tore off the first page and handed it to Tomlin.

The brigadier studied it and smiled bemusedly. "As easy as that?" he inquired. Philpott shrugged. "We have to buy time."

"But you have no idea how to contact Smith because we don't know where he is," the brigadier objected.

"That's what I'm trying to do," Philpott replied. "I must smoke him out. Have that message broadcast on AFN at nine-thirty, and again at ten, and Smith, I guarantee, will be in touch. By then, I'll have found out the way to get through to him."

"And if you don't?"

"If I don't, we lose Hemmingsway."

Tomlin pursed his lips ruefully and said, "I'm glad it's not me taking that kind of chance. Your president would not be best pleased at losing a friend as well as an airplane, if you'll excuse the levity, sir."

Philpott inclined his head. "We have to grab our chances where we can with Smith, brigadier," he continued. "And rest easy," he assured Tomlin, "I have no intention of needlessly sacrificing Hawley Hemmingsway or any other oil minister, as President Wheeler knows full well. I think I can pull this off, but it'll take time—and

130

time is something we don't have. Now if you could give me a couple of minutes?"

Tomlin nodded and walked to the far end of the operations center. Philpott picked up the telephone and replied in Russian when the man at the embassy of the Union of Soviet Socialist Republics said, *"Buon giorno, Signore."*

Philpott was playing a hunch which, if he was wrong, not only would put them completely at Smith's mercy, but also could lead to the murder of an American secretary of energy. He swallowed the touch of bile which had risen to his mouth, and said, "I wish to speak to General Alexis Nesterenko."

There was the expected silence before the man gave the expected answer: there was no General Alexis Nesterenko at the embassy. Philpott continued smoothly, "You may know him better by his codename: Myshkin." He could hear the click as the resident KGB station commander cued in to the call.

"We know of no one of that name, and we do not understand what you mean when you refer to a codename," the operator said stolidly.

"Very well," Philpott said, "I will have to assume that you do not wish to communicate to your superiors some information which it is crucial to their plans that they should receive. I will bid you goodbye, then."

"Eh, wait for just one moment, *Signore,*" the operator broke in, switching to Italian. "You—you did not"—he was obviously trying to interpret instructions whispered to him across another line—"you did not give us your name."

"My name is Malcolm Philpott, and I am the director of the United Nations Anti-Crime Organization. I fail to see how that can interest you, since you claim to have no knowledge of the man to whom I wish to pass this information."

Another delay, and Philpott could hear clicks multiplying on the line like mating grasshoppers. Then the operator came back on. "It is as you say, Mr. Philpott, we do not know the man you have spoken of, nor indeed the other name which you used. It might, however, be helpful if you could tell us your immediate movements."

"For what purpose?" Philpott inquired innocently.

131

The operator had stumbled again over his words, then managed to get out the lame excuse that it could be of assistance to the matter in hand.

Philpott toyed with him for another minute, then said, with a touch of asperity, "Oh, very well. I shall be in the Ristorante Aurelio in Piazza Barberini in precisely ten minutes from now. I'll be drinking coffee at a sidewalk table. I may well enjoy a cigar as well. No doubt I shall insult the waiter and refuse to pay the bill. Piazza Barberini, as you may know, is quite close to the American Embassy in the Via Veneto."

"We know where the American Embassy is, *Signore,*" the operator replied stiffly, and broke the connection.

"You must have been expecting my call," Philpott observed pleasantly as the coffee arrived. Myshkin sniffed disapprovingly and changed the order for himself to *caffè negro.* Philpott apologized and slid the second cup of *capuccino* to his own side of the table.

"Say what you have to say, and please be quick about it," Myshkin pronounced tartly.

"Aren't you interested in learning how I knew you were involved, or even that you were in Rome?" Philpott asked.

"You didn't," Myshkin rejoined. "It was a blind guess. You can also have no certain knowledge of any implication of myself or my country in the affair which at present occupies your attention."

"Then why are you here?" Philpott pressed gently. He could not risk frightening off the Russian, though he surmised correctly that Myshkin had no intention of being intimidated.

Myshkin allowed an inchoate smile to illumine his wintry face. "Curiosity, Mr Philpott, nothing more. Clearly my—eh—swift accession to a position of power in the Politburo has interested not merely the Western secret services but also UNACO, otherwise you would not be familiar with even my real name, let alone my codename. Also, there"—he hesitated as if reluctant to admit a weakness—"there may be ways in which we can help each other."

"In too deep, Myshkin?" Philpott inquired ironically.

"By no means," Myshkin protested. He lit a vile-

132

smelling cigarette with a Dupont lighter and sipped his coffee. Then he examined his fingernails and glanced out appreciatively into the square; a party of four girls, beautiful and freshly groomed, young and enticing, was bound for the Via Veneto. "An illicit rendezvous?" he whispered to Philpott. "Meeting sugar daddies at one of those ruinously expensive hotels?"

"At this time of day?" Philpott queried, enjoying the Russian's dilemma. Then he glanced at his watch and realized that the charade must soon end. The KGB clearly could not take the initiative, so UNACO must.

He began slowly, after lighting a cigar and breathing a speculative wreath of smoke Myshkin's way, "Since you mentioned the matter which is at present occupying my attention, as I believe you phrased it, would you consider it discourteous or *outré* if I referred to it directly?" Myshkin affected not to have heard him. Philpott grinned and tapped a corrosion of ash on to the pavement.

"UNACO's involvement is obvious," Philpott went on. "An attack on the personal aircraft of the US president is bad enough, but when the passengers include the leading lights of OPEC, this is something which surely the whole world must deprecate—or at least which it cannot ignore. The criminal Smith, whose name may not be unknown to you"—Myshkin considered the point, then shook his head—"this man Smith stands vilified at the bar of global opinion, from every quarter. It is an act of cynical brigandry, and must be condemned with all the force at the command of right-thinking nations with the security of civilized behavior at heart."

Myshkin nodded gravely and methodically stubbed out his cigarette. He looked inquiringly at Philpott and accepted a cigar from the American's handsome leather case, inscribed in ornate gold letters: "With affection and respect, Leonid Brezhnev."

"Naturally," Philpott said, "Smith must be acting alone, since it would be unthinkable that any nation— even more so, should that state happen to be a client of UNACO's—might offer such a creature solace, let alone help."

"Naturally," Myshkin agreed.

"Such a nation, if it exists, would earn the enmity of

133

every member of the UN, especially those countries with influence in sensitive areas such as the Middle East, places which could be crucially important to the state which was unwise enough to support a pirate like Smith, who has no political affiliation nor any conscience."

"Indeed," Myshkin commented, reading the bill for the coffee with studied concern. "These fashionable *ristoranti* are not cheap, Mr. Philpott."

"Neither is international respect, General Nesterenko," Philpott rejoined. "To return to the subject under discussion—such a nation could be gravely mistaken if it assumed that America would take the entire blame for this unfortunate incident, which may well result in the deaths of one or more of the OPEC ministers."

Myshkin looked sharply at him. "What makes you say that?" he inquired brusquely. Philpott explained the terms of Smith's ransom demand and the threat that accompanied it.

"It looks very much as though America, at the moment anyway, is bearing the brunt of international excoriation," the Russian observed.

"But that," Philpott replied earnestly, "will last only as long as the world doesn't know the identity of the nation which helped Smith to set up this hijacking. And once it is established that Smith has received active encouragement and assistance, even down to providing men and arms for him and smoothing his passage in a hostile environment, the contempt of the injured nations will, without a shadow of doubt, be turned on the country which has made all this possible.

The Russian grinned, almost admiringly. "Your diet must be exclusively founded on carrots and fish, Mr. Philpott," he said dryly. "You are consummately adept at shooting in the dark."

Philpott called the waiter over and paid the bill with a five thousand lire note, neither expecting nor receiving the change due to him. He laid a copy of the newspaper *Il Messaggero* carefully on the table between himself and the Russian.

"I know your countrymen pride themselves in keeping up to date with political thought in Italy, " he said. "Tucked into the leader page is the text of a message which will be broadcast on the American Forces' Network in roughly three minutes from now. It will be repeated at 1000 hours. It is not the news Smith was expecting.

"It asks for a two-hour delay. As Director of UNACO I shall appreciate it, indeed I would consider it a favor, if some pressure can be brought upon Smith to accede to this request. Obviously, should any harm befall a minister, Smith will be hunted to the ends of the earth. Perhaps you would care to ponder, my dear Myshkin, as to how best this information can be passed to Mister Smith."

Myshkin looked up at him benignly. "I, Mr. Philpott? What could conceivably persuade you that I might have some channel of contact with this monster?"

Philpott bowed his head. "If I have conveyed that impression to you, general, you have my deepest apologies. No doubt we shall meet again soon."

He stepped out into the Piazza Barberini, and a long, dark blue NATO staff car, a flag fluttering from the apex of its bonnet, drew up alongside him. Philpott got in, and the car pulled away.

Myshkin took another careful pull at the Cuban cigar, deprived it of its nosecone of ash, then dropped the still-light butt to the ground and stepped on it as he walked out into the square. A black Zil limousine, Soviet flag fluttering at the apex of its bonnet, purred at his heels. He turned, and the door swung open. . . .

At five minutes after ten, the telephone rang in the NATO ops room, and Smith said, "Two hours, Mr. Philpott, not a second more."

"You have my word," Philpott replied, careful not to identify the caller with Tomlin at his shoulder. "It merely allows for certain formalities to be completed."

"No tricks, Philpott," Smith warned. "Not only the Americans and Arabs, but your estimable Sabrina Carver are at my mercy, remember."

"True," Philpott conceded, "though I am confident you will not harm them. You must know by now—from Dunkels, I imagine—that my friend the erstwhile security chief of Air Force One has escaped from custody in Bahrain. He was the only card in your hand in which the Russians could be remotely interested. They will not, I know, look with any enthusiasm on your failure to hold him for their interrogators. No doubt you have concocted some story to mollify them in the meantime, but they would believe me if I told them he had escaped, Smith. I don't think you would wish them to know that."

"Hence my agreement to your request for a delay," Smith answered. "Use the time wisely, Mr. Director."

"I intend to," Philpott said, glancing up at Tomlin.

Chapter Twelve

As far as McCafferty could judge, the Kamov pilot must be following orders in flying low to escape radar detection. Mac throttled back so he could more sensibly use his high vantage point to monitor Dunkels's progress. Clearly, the helicopter was also intent on avoiding even the smallest village, let alone any larger center of human habitation.

The American decided that, given all the precautions the Kamov pilot was taking, he would also be aware that the only source of danger to him must come from above, and would be keeping his eyes peeled. The place for anyone intent on secret pursuit was behind and below the helicopter, Mac thought.

Chopping the power in his own machine, Mac put on a bootful of rudder, pulled the stick over, and side-slipped towards the ground. He took up straight and level flight again at about fifty feet, and some quarter of a mile behind the little Kamov, which was literally skimming the tree-tops.

For the next hundred miles or so, McCafferty effectively saw nothing save the series of greens and browns which flashed across the periphery of his vision. He was concentrating on the steel grey body of the Kamov as it flew up shallow valleys, danced over hilltops, flirted with the crests of tall forest trees, and buzzed the surfaces of a dozen sapphire blue lakes.

An hour and a half went by with McCafferty fighting to balance elevator, rudder, and aileron, opening and closing the throttle a thousand times in an effort to stay hidden while keeping contact with a target whose speed fluctuated between ninety miles per hour (which was easy for Mac to parallel) right down to under fifty miles per hour. This was a trickier proposition, for it brought the UTVA to the point of stall, where she wallowed with slack controls and insufficient height to recover from the effect of even a slight mistake by her pilot. The sweat coursed down his face, and his language matched the blue of the sky and waters.

Suddenly the ground started to rise steeply. Mac's altimeter showed twelve hundred feet more than the zero which he had set before his departure from the low-lying airfield near Gora. He looked anxiously ahead. Still in front of him were mountain peaks that seemed fifteen or sixteen hundred feet higher. He snatched a quick peep at the map crumpled over in front of him and identified the Dinaric Alps.

When he looked back the Kamov had vanished.

McCafferty fought his momentary panic and quelled it. The helicopter, he reasoned, couldn't simply have disappeared from view, or sunk out of sight into the ground. His first instinct was to slam the throttle open and surge forward as fast as possible, but instinct and caution held him back. The Kamov was still there somewhere, he told himself; Mac's problem was that he couldn't see it.

He wound the UTVA into a steep, spiraling climb to overfly the ground before him without attracting attention. Four thousand feet of extra height registered on the dial in a little over three minutes, and then Mac resumed his original course. He peered to starboard, his eyes exploring the rocky terrain. Then he grinned and said, "Hot diggety."

The mystery was solved. The helicopter had vaulted the edge of a natural glacier formation and slipped into the steep valley below it. The valley was a thumbprint amid the sharp, pointed mountains, and there was a grassy tree-fringed platform set into the hillside at the top of a winding road.

Facing this natural ledge, which started off as barely a

smudge but grew to respectable proportions in Mac's view, was a castle, perched precariously against a dent in the mountain.

At a slightly lower level, a flat area had been gouged out of the rock and smoothed over. The Kamov rested on it, the rotor blades turning at no more than walking pace.

Siegfried Dunkels had arrived at his destination.

An aide bustled into the NATO computer complex and asked for Philpott. Directed with an irritable wave by a red-haired American major, the courier whispered to the UNACO chief that transport was waiting to take him to Leonardo da Vinci for the Zabreb flight. Philpott was busy receiving Sonya's assurances that the diamonds were being assembled and dispatched in the care of a leading member of the Amsterdam Diamond Exchange, and at the same time coping with Tomlin's obvious keen desire to impress UNACO with *his* obvious keen desire.

"I've also scrambled a squadron of P-90s to square-search beaches, salt flats—any open ground that could take a 707," the brigadier expatiated.

"Yugoslavian beaches?" Philpott asked in astonishment. "She's not a member of NATO, you know, brigadier."

Tomlin glared like a cornered schoolboy coming out of a strip joint. "I am aware of that, sir," he snapped, "and although we appear merely to be including Yugoslavia in the search area on a casual basis—taking it in along with Italy, Sicily, Greece and the islands, Corfu, and the Albanian Coast—I have at least established contact with the Yugoslav authorities and explained the problem, of which, naturally, they are aware since the news broke in their own country. They *also* suspect that Air Force One and its captives are in Yugoslavia, and—"

"And so they think you're just wasting aviation fuel looking anywhere else, but at the same time they're not inviting you in. That it, brigadier?"

"Something like that, sir," Tomlin mumbled.

"So that's why I'm going to Zagreb," Philpott supplied, "because whereas they don't want NATO trampling all over their beautiful country, they'll accept—they're bound to, by their membership—a small UNACO contingent."

Tomlin then confessed, with a sheepish grin, that his pilots had been instructed not to be overconscientious in their search of areas outside Yugoslav air space. "We shan't be wasting too much fuel, sir," he added, "if only because we've no real idea where you could hide an aircraft that big."

Philpott stopped putting papers into a briefcase and favored the soldier with a sympathetic but knowing look. "You won't find it, brigadier. It can't be camouflaged, so Smith will have hidden it, and removed any possibility of tracing it with heat sensors by cooling it down, or something like that. If I know him, the plane'll be under cover and wrapped in tarpaulins by now."

Tomlin nodded. "I suppose you're right," he sighed. "I'll call off the hounds. Incidentally," he added, "there's something else that's been bothering me." He waited for an encouraging inclination of the head from the UNACO man, then said, "It's just that Trieste is well outside our radius. Why do you suppose Smith sent the ransom demand there?"

Philpott considered the question. "You have a point there, brigadier, a good point." Tomlin flushed with gratification. "I can only assume," Philpott went on, "that it was intended to throw us off the scent. Now that you mention it, I'm inclined more and more to the opinion that Dubrovnik is nearer to our presumed center of activity, so Zabreb will be a good place to start from. Keep thinking. You're actually very good at it, brigadier."

With that, Philpott leaned over to kiss Sonya, causing Tomlin's blush to deepen, and left the room trailing a covey of uniformed acolytes.

Three minutes after his flight was airborne, the telephone rang on Sonya Kolchinsky's desk, and a breathless voice said, "Is the chief there, Sonya? I've got to speak to him. It's Joe McCafferty. I've found Smith."

Sonya crooked her finger at the red-haired major, who bounced over and skidded to a halt in front of her chair. "I don't care what it costs or how difficult it is," she said, "But I want the call on this line"—she pointed at the receiver in her hand—"patched through to Mr. Philpott's plane. And I want it done *now*."

"Yes, ma'am," the major replied, "oh yes, ma'am." He

139

shot off to the communications room as though preventing World War Three depended on it.

Sabrina and Feisal had refused breakfast, but Feisal had to have food at stated times, so they started toying with a mid-morning snack that Smith sent up to the attic room. It was a gruel of some kind, larded with greasy croutons, and they quickly found it unpalatable. "I had no idea Yugoslav food was so bad," Sabrina began, regretting it when Feisal launched into a dissertation on Central European culinary traditions.

Feisal dropped the subject when she raised her eyes to heaven in mock horror, and he followed her gaze when it stayed up, instead of coming back down. She had spotted something they had not noticed before—a small opening in the ceiling where it joined the bare rock of the mountain wall. Sabrina crossed to the corner and squinted into the hole. "Hey," she exclaimed, "I can see daylight, Feisal."

The Arab boy joined her and they ran their fingers over the rock wall. The junction was in fact a shallow fissure, going beyond the ceiling and showing, as Sabrina had remarked, a small chink of light at its very top.

"I don't think it's wide enough for me," Sabrina said doubtfully, measuring the fissure against her body.

"All right for me, though," Feisal insisted. "We Arabs look after our bodies. It's our diet, you see."

"Yeah, I get it," Sabrina said hurriedly. "Look, I know you mean well, Feisal, but I'm not sure I ought to let you take risks like going up that hole. Your grandfather would be furious with me if—"

"And he would be furious with *me* if I did *not* go," Feisal bristled, "so that is settled. Now if you would be so kind as to hoist me up there . . ."

As Sabrina stooped for him to climb on her back, they heard the scrape of the iron key in the lock. They were seated at the table when the door was flung open and Bert Cooligan stumbled into the room.

"He was foolish enough to make a run for it," Achmed Fayeed, who appeared behind the agent, said. "As you must all be aware, escape from the castle of Windischgraetz is not possible. For his pains, Mr. Cooligan will join you up here."

140

Cooligan sat on the bed and rubbed his bruised limbs. He had slipped his guard on a toilet visit, he told them, and managed to get as far as the courtyard, but Fayeed had raised the drawbridge in his face.

"It was brave of you, Bert," Sabrina consoled him, "but I think it really is useless, like that man said."

Cooligan looked at them slyly. "Don't you believe it, honey," he whispered. "Having tried to escape once and been recaptured, I'm the last guy they'd expect to try again. And that's exactly what I'm going to do: try again."

"Well done," Feisal commended him, "be assured that I shall offer you every assistance."

Cooligan goggled at the boy and gasped, "You don't say."

Sabrina grinned. "He does say, I'm afraid," she remarked, "over and over again, all the time. But he has a point." And she indicated the gap in the corner of the room.

The agent joined them, nodding approvingly and picking up Feisal all in one movement. At the full extent of his reach, he pushed the boy up into the hole. "Room enough?" he called out.

"More than sufficient," Feisal called back and squirmed up the fissure until he blotted out the tiny patch of light . . .

Mac sheered off and gave the castle a wide berth. He flew on down the valley, noting the rough, unmade track which served as a road. There didn't seem to be any other inhabited area, as the valley, deceptively small from the air, wound through a gorge and meandered out into a flat plain. From his new high altitude, the American could see as far as the Adriatic, with its shoals of tiny islands swimming off the coast.

His plan of action was comfortably clear: he must land the aircraft and make contact with Philpott, for he had no doubt whatsoever that he had located Smith's headquarters and the hostages' prison. The frying-pan-shaped area, Mac realized, was the valley's mouth, and he spotted just the sort of situation he had been seeking: a ruined house, the traces of its once fine and spacious formal gardens still visible from the air. Sheep and goats grazed where the great lawn had been, but it would suit his purpose, for it looked reasonably flat and smooth, and was all of three hundred yards long.

Mac completed his descent and made one quick pass at low level to check the surface and frighten the animals up to one end of the pasture. Then he turned tightly and prepared to land. The UTVA slipped over the crumbling stone boundary-wall at exactly forty-five knots, and the pilot made a perfect three-point touchdown, braking gently to a halt after using only two-thirds of the available space.

Seeing a large open barn next to a clump of tall trees near the ruin of the house, the American opened his throttle again and taxied towards it. The barn, though it looked dilapidated and sported a few holes in its roof, swallowed the little airplane without difficulty.

Moments later McCafferty, who had seen a village which, from the air, looked to be not too far away, was strolling along the rudimentary path, looking like a purposeful tourist off the beaten track. He wore the backpack, his parka was slung over his shoulder, and he whistled, rather self-consciously, *The Happy Wanderer*.

He traded dollars for dinars from Mackie-Belton's pile at a huge loss, tossed back a couple of beers at a café, and bribed his way into the village post office which, as far as he could ascertain, housed the only telephone for miles around.

A fairly agonizing twenty minutes later, using the postman's sixteen-year-old daughter as an interpreter, Mac found himself magically connected with Philpott, cruising five miles overhead.

He gave the UNACO director the location of the castle—which he had learned from his new friends was called Castle Windischgraetz—and supplied directions to his village of Luka. Philpott set the time for their rendezvous in the early evening.

"I'll probably come alone," Philpott warned him. "I still have to case the scene in Yugoslavia. I've no idea what help or cooperation I'll get from the authorities, so I'd better not promise you an army of deliverance. The chances are it'll be just you and me, Joe."

"You'd better be in good form, then." Mac returned

142

cheerfully, though he felt far from confident at the prospect ahead of them.

Philpott signed off, and while McCafferty set out by donkey and on foot to reconnoitre the castle of Windischgraetz, the UNACO director's plane commenced its descent to Zagreb.

Feisal eased his slim body out of the hole and found himself looking down the sheer side of the mountain. He gulped and withdrew his head, then glanced up and to both sides. The fissure ran out in the mouth of the cave above the castle, and the boy scaled the remaining distance easily. He was now virtually on the castle roof, and he stepped gingerly onto one of the pyramid towers, from which he could see the cliff, the road, and the valley beyond, and just caught sight of the sloping eave in front of the sentry-slit in his own room.

He edged round the other face of the pyramid and descended to a flatter part of the roof. Looking up, he saw a flagpole projecting from the top of the tower, its fastening rope trailing from the bare stem.

The boy smiled, and was about to remount the tower when the sound of voices reached him from below. Feisal knelt and crept to the very rim of the castle. The voices came from a ventilation port set high into the wall of what he judged to be the trophy room, where the hostages were imprisoned. Mister Smith was speaking.

". . . so it would appear, gentlemen, that your respective governments care less for your lives than for the comparatively trifling sum it will cost to save them. At any rate, I can place no other construction on their request for a two-hour delay. I cannot believe they would be so foolish as to contemplate tracking us down at this place, since by so doing they will inevitably sacrifice all of you. Therefore, I repeat, I can only assume they are weighing your lives in the balance against a mere fifty million dollars in diamonds."

Smith had separated the ministers from the crew, who were valueless to him. He had Dunkels at one shoulder, Jagger at the other, both armed with Schmeisser machine pistols, and Fayeed leading a guerilla group which commanded the rest of the trophy room.

Hawley Hemmingsway, easily the tallest and strongest man in the room, folded his arms and said, with a disdainful sneer, "Maybe they just don't relish having to deal with scum like you, Smith. That would at least be understandable."

Smith regarded him with tolerant amusement, but the shaft had struck home. Smith never suffered criticism easily; it was part of the megalomaniac's armor that he must always be supremely right, above reproach, fêted, and admired for the aesthetic beauty of his crimes. Above all, though, he prided himself on his iron control, which rarely deserted him and which was needed now to suppress his rising anger. He was framing a suitably tart reply when Sheik Zeidan saved him the trouble.

The old Arab raised a cautionary hand and growled to Hemmingsway, "Easy, my friend, easy. Patience. You would not, would you, trade insults with a rabid dog? No, you keep your counsel and remove yourself from his solitary path."

Smith's teeth clenched and his eyes bored into Zeidan's, but he could not hold the cripple's burning, scornful gaze. But Hemmingsway, the Boston aristocrat with six centuries of traceable English and colonial blood in his veins, had never needed to curb his temper with such creatures as he saw before him.

He unfolded his arms and let them swing easily at his side, breathing noisily through parted lips, his eyes wild, the very marrow of his culture and civilization affronted. "I thank you for your advice, Your Excellency," he said, "but I have spent large portions of my life dealing with vermin such as these at various levels in war and politics. It is as well to make them completely aware that men such as you and I and your colleagues *cannot, will not,* be intimidated. We cannot and will not be used as pawns in the games of these sordid mercenaries, sold over their sleazy counter as merchandise to provide money for prolonging their disgusting lives, to give them—"

"Why don't you just button your lip, like the man says." The dry, softly spoken words from Cody Jagger cut through Hemmingsway's outburst and laid an aura of menace over the room which had not been there before. Dr. Hamady looked for the source of the sound and visibly

144

quailed when he met Jagger's cold stare. Dorani plucked nervously at Hemmingsway's sleeve, but the American shook him off. Sheik Arbeid tore his gaze away from Jagger's, then met other eyes everywhere he looked . . . dead eyes—of eagles, deer, boars, great fierce dogs—accusing and unforgiving eyes.

It was breaking point for Hemmingsway, though. Where Smith possessed at least the responsibility and lust of command, Jagger, the renegade American, the traitor for gain, was so far beneath Hemmingsway's contempt that what little control was left to him snapped.

"You, McCafferty," he breathed, *"you* . . . without *you* none of this would have been possible. *You* sold yourself and your country and your honor to this pack of lice to line your pockets and crawl away into whatever sewer will have you." Flecks of foam appeared at the corners of his mouth and he took one, two steps towards Jagger, until they were separated by no more than ten feet.

"Come back, Hemmingsway," Dr. Hamady pleaded.

"No nearer, pal," Jagger said. "I'm telling you." But Hemmingsway did not even hear them. He was shaking now with fury, and his eyes and senses could only encompass the man standing before him.

"That you should presume even to speak to me is so loathsome to me that I could vomit at the mere thought of you," he stormed. "Compared with you, Smith is a knight in shining armor. If it's the last thing I do, McCafferty, I will see that you suffer for your treachery. I will ensure that you pay for soiling the uniform you still wear. Because do you hear, you filth, you trash . . . do you? I'm going to tear your body apart with my own hands"— another step forward—"I'm going to rip—"

Without aiming, without even moving, Jagger tightened his finger on the trigger of the machine pistol and sent a stream of slugs into Hemmingsway, who was still coming at him, arms outstretched. One of the hands flew off, severed at the wrist; Hemmingsway's face disappeared, its contours and definition merging into a mash of blood and bone; his trunk was almost bisected as the bullets cut through him and the clamor and gunsmoke assaulted the senses of every man in the room.

Smith had made a feeble attempt to restrain his ringer,

but it would have been unavailing, for Cody Jagger was a man of the jungle; he had no conscience, no finesse, no scruples. And no control, since he had never needed to exercise any. Hemmingsway had genuinely believed he had dealt with the worst kinds of men, but he had never encountered Jagger's type, the totally amoral creature of the twilight underworld.

When it was over, Smith laid his hand on Jagger's arm and kept it there, looking into the ringer's face with a calm, level gaze until the killing light died in Cody's eyes.

"So, gentlemen," Smith said gravely, turning his false and handsome face back to the Arabs, "it has come to this. You have insulted my honor, and that of my men. I am, though you will not accept it, a man of honor. I did *not* plan this . . . you can have no conceivable doubt of that. Yet maybe it will serve as an indelible warning to you and to those governments who have so little regard for you that they have failed to take me seriously.

"As I have told you"—and his voice dropped so that they had to strain to hear him—"as I told you I am a man of honor. I keep my word. I gave my pledge to Malcolm Philpott of UNACO that if your nations did not find the ransom due to me immediately and inform me of it, I would execute one of you every three hours.

"I should, perhaps, tell you now that it had been my intention to dispose of Mr. Hawley Hemmingsway precisely at noon. By his own actions he has deprived himself of an hour of life. Such men are fools. You, I believe, are not."

Smith swung on his heel and walked out, leaving the hostages frozen in their horror like a ballet tableau trapped in ice.

Feisal clung to his tower and fought back the tears as the enormity of what was happening in the trophy room floated up to him on the light breeze. Then he completed his mission and used elbows, arms, and hands to ease himself back down the fissure.

His legs appeared through the gap in the ceiling, and Cooligan shouted, "Drop, sonny. I'll catch you." Feisal did as he was told. Bert carried him to the bed, and Sabrina bent over him anxiously. The boy's color was high, and sweat dewed his brow. Sabrina gave him a further injection and forced him to eat some gruel and black bread. Gradually, as before, the fever subsided.

Cooligan had been waiting patiently for the boy to recover, for both he and Sabrina had heard the shooting, and guessed that Feisal might be able to fill in the details. The Arab gasped as he choked on the food, and Sabrina patted his back and wiped his mouth. "Tell us, Feisal, if you can," she said gently.

He sat up, holding on to Sabrina's arm. "They killed him, Sabrina, they killed him," he sobbed.

"Who?" asked Cooligan.

"Mr. Hemmingsway, the American gentleman. There was a terrible quarrel between Mr. Hemmingsway and Mister Smith, and grandfather told Mr. Hemmingsway to be quiet, and then someone else spoke, and Mr. Hemmingsway t-turned on him, too, and called him things, and . . ." His voice trailed off.

"And what?" Sabrina pressed.

"And—and the other man shot him. He must be dead, I know. There were a lot of bullets. It went on for so long, and there was a time when nobody spoke, and then Mister Smith said he had been going to kill Mr. Hemmingsway anyway, but not y-yet."

Cooligan let the boy lapse into snuffles in Sabrina's arms. Feisal sniffed and blinked and said, "I know what you want me to tell you, Mr. Cooligan. And I will, as far as I can. The man who killed Mr. Hemmingsway was, I believe, Colonel McCafferty. I cannot be certain, but that's the way it came to me up there on t-top of the castle."

The agent straightened up. "It doesn't . . . it just doesn't . . . feel right. I know Mac's sold himself out, but God, he's no killer—not from anger or revenge. It . . . it doesn't gel. Could you have been mistaken, Feisal?" The Arab boy shook his head. "I don't think so."

Cooligan pursed his lips and stroked his chin. "That settles it then," he continued slowly, "when I get out of here, the first thing I'm going to do is put that hellhound where he belongs . . . six feet under with the man he murdered."

Only then did Sabrina, still cradling Feisal in her arms, feel the rope coiled tightly around his body. She fingered it wonderingly, and he allowed her to unloose it.

Cooligan dashed to the bed and grabbed the rope. "Where did you find it?"

Feisal explained that it had been attached to the flagpole He considered the rope would be long enough to permit Cooligan to drop to a lower level and make his escape. "You can get through the viewing slit"—he pointed at the external wall. "They have put no iron bars on the window here because they did not contemplate anyone being foolish enough to risk climbing out. But of course, if you have a rope?" Feisal had clearly recovered some of his aplomb, and was feeling in a didactic mood. Cooligan needed no second bidding.

He crossed to the wall-length window slit. "No time like the present," he muttered, casting around for something to use to break the glass.

At Zagreb Airport, Philpott was met by a càdre of anxious Yugoslav officials led by the deputy minister of the interior. "My government," the politician announced, "wishes to do everything in its power to bring this matter to a satisfactory conclusion. As a loyal member nation of UNACO, we are dedicated root-and-branch to the extermination of criminals such as this Smith, and the extinction of international terrorism."

"Very decent of you, minister," Philpott replied, guessing that Myshkin had already been busy. "I assume, then, that you will be prepared to offer me all the facilities I need to take Smith's stronghold by storm?"

"Eh—do you know where he is, Mr. Philpott?" Philpott confirmed that he did. The Minister queried whether a large assault force would be wise.

Philpott grinned, guessing that the deputy minister did not really wish to involve the Yugoslav armed forces in an action where they might possibly encounter Russians. He assured the politician that he, too, considered a small UNACO force would be able to penetrate Smith's lair while keeping a lower profile than a frontal attack group could. "May I have transportation, though?" he pressed.

"But assuredly," the deputy minister cried, "one of our most reliable helicopters is waiting for you at this very airport. It is yours to do with as you will."

He pointed to a far corner of the field, where a reliable

helicopter sat preening itself. Philpott learned that the pilot would have charts to cover the area of Smith's hideaway—wherever that might be—and any other location. Philpott expressed his thanks and began to make his way to the aircraft when he heard his name called. UNACO was on the telephone, the deputy minister said, with an urgent message.

As soon as Sonya came on the line, Philpott knew from the tone of her voice that she had unpleasant news. "Smith's issued his instructions for the ransom collection," she said when he had established his identify. "I'll give them to you now, shall I?"

"No," Philpott returned, "let's have the bad news first."

"Bad news?" she echoed. "Well, yes . . . there is some . . . Malcolm, he's killed Hawley Hemmingsway."

"Oh, my God," Philpott groaned, "I never thought he would actually do it. It's my fault, Sonya; I gambled with poor Hawley's life."

She reproached him for blaming himself, making it clear that Hemmingsway had not been executed according to Smith's announced plan. "He didn't do it personally. His radio message said Hemmingsway had been shot for being uncooperative and insulting Smith's integrity."

"Who did the shooting?"

"They didn't reveal that."

Philpott sighed grimly. "Then Smith let it happen," he pronounced, "because I'm still willing to bet it was part of his scheme. He may not have been able to prevent it, but I doubt if he tried very hard. It must have fallen very nicely for him that one of his men went ape."

Sonya let the comforting silence go on, then broke it to tell Philpott that Smith had now promised to kill all the hostages, Arabs and AF One crew members if any rescue attempt was launched.

"I think he means it, Malcolm," Sonya whispered. "I think he knows somehow that we may be closing in on him. He's been told of McCafferty's escape from Bahrain, and he must suspect the truth: that Mac followed the German—Dunkels, is it—to the castle. He knows you're in Zagreb—the Russians must have let on—and he probably imagines you're on your way to the castle with a large force. I believe he'd rather everyone died, himself included, before he'd consider surrender."

Philpott chuckled dryly, without a trace of humor. "Large force," he muttered. "A middle-aged has-been and a knocked-around flier. I ask you!"

Chapter Thirteen

Branches flailed at the head of Philpott's knocked-around flier as he cursed for the hundredth time after falling for what seemed to be the thousandth time. If McCafferty had not been too drastically knocked around before, he was now receiving more than his fair share.

His plan, which he still followed, had been to approach the castle not from below or from the level of the road, but from above. As Mac had ruefully admitted to himself, bidding farewell to his sad-eyed donkey, that meant climbing the mountain. He had taken the lugubrious animal up as far as he dared if he were to avoid either being spotted from the castle or thrown off the donkey's back, for by now they were struggling up near-vertical slopes.

Finally the donkey snorted and brayed his refusal to go any further, and McCafferty could not altogether blame him. He watched the donkey slide and plunge back down the mountainside and hoped the animal would still be around when he needed it later for his rendezvous with Philpott. He was not burdened with his backpack either, though he trusted that the now positively wealthy postman's daughter would not yield to temptation and search it.

So he had continued on foot, hanging for dear life on to the stunted shrubs, wiping dust motes from his streaming eyes, and being slowly flayed by the trees. He had brought a pair of two-way radios, and selected and assembled for arms, a sub-machine gun with a leather sling; as he climbed it began to weigh on his back like a Howitzer. At last he reached a ledge wide enough to allow him to lie at full length and get his breath back. He sat up, soothed his aching muscles, zipped his parka against the sharper chill of the air, and looked down upon Castle Windischgraetz.

The castle was even more spectacular from his lofty perch, which gave a true bird's eye view of it. He noted the twin courtyards and the chasm which the drawbridge would normally span, and the wooded country over to his left, the trees clustered thickly at the point where the hillside rose shallowly from the track, then thinning out a few hundred yards higher until, at his level, they were practically nonexistent.

Mac found that his ledge circumvented almost the entire mountain, and he decided to take the opportunity and oversee the castle and all its grounds. He followed the curve of the castle as it hugged the convex bulge of the mountain, and noted the Kamov still sitting on the jerry-built launchpad, its rotors spinning. To the left of the castle from the American's viewpoint lay a large parking area reaching back to the mountainside. It was tree-shaded, and the trees then wandered up the gentle slope. It was there that McCafferty first saw the running man.

He adjusted his field glasses and was so intent on focusing on the darting, crouching figure that the significance of the Kamov's whirling blades didn't strike him until the little helicopter had actually taken off and started to buzz the inclined woodland. At the same time, Mac became aware—and cursed himself fluently for not noticing before—that men were searching the lower slopes of the hill below the castle, with the helicopter snarling over them like an angry gnat.

But their quarry—and who could it be but the running man?— was above the castle. One up to the escapee, Mac thought, for the man must have gotten free from the castle . . . and now the hunt was on. McCafferty at last trained his binoculars on the fugitive, but even before identification became certain, he knew it was going to be Bert Cooligan. . . .

The agent had tied the rope securely to the king-post of the eave and lowered himself to the next level—a balcony outside an unoccupied room. He signalled to Sabrina and she unhooked the line and threw it down to him.

Cooligan smashed another window and repeated the trick until he dropped even lower, but still he was a full ten feet from the ground, and every second he remained visible on the castle wall he was in acute danger. He scanned the terrain beneath him, but could see nothing except, directly below, a tarpaulin shrouding a shape that seemed vaguely familiar.

Cooligan abandoned the rope and used footholds in the rock to make his final descent . . . and froze as an armed guard wandered out and dragged the covering from the courier's motorcycle. Had he raised his eyes by even six inches he must have seen the agent, clinging motionless over his head. Bert hardly dared to breathe; he couldn't believe his luck would hold, and no one else would come.

But the sentry remained a lone voyeur until, shaking his head—for he would never be able to afford such a bike—he wandered off and took up his post at the main gate.

Cooligan dropped the last couple of yards, landing almost on the motorcycle, and then he heard, coming from the eyrie above, the last sound he wanted to hear: a shout of warning.

He was protected to a degree by the natural bulge of the castle wall and the slight overhang at first floor level, which was why he hadn't spotted the bike at once. Bert got astride the machine, switched on the ignition and twisted the throttle until the engine roared its defiance at Achmed, who had discovered his absence from the attic room.

The Arab didn't have a clear sighting, only the noise of the motorcycle giving him a sense of direction, but he loosed off a volley of bullets from his machine pistol. They served to alert the guard at the entry arch, but by that time Bert had already passed through the inner court-yard, and was driving hell-bent for freedom.

The guard made the mistake of aiming his rifle at the swerving target and firing two single shots. He realized in time that he had no chance of hitting Cooligan, so he threw down the rifle and started to raise the drawbridge.

Bert could see the handle turning, and the thick slab of oak lurch off the ground on its rusty chains. He could hear, even above the engine noise, the aggrieved squeal of the mechanism, and when he passed the guard the drawbridge was already three feet up. But for Cooligan there could be no stopping.

As the Honda hit the drawbridge the guard let go of the wheel, and the bridge started an even more raucous and protesting descent. The motorcycle shot off the end and bounced perhaps a dozen feet clear at the other side. Bert yelled and gunned the motor as he sped away from the castle under a hail of bullets from Fayeed, still at the smashed slit window, and from two more guards at the bridge. Cooligan swerved and then caught sight of the guard up ahead at the closed steel road barrier.

At the moment he spotted the guard, Bert was swaying to the right, and that was the way he elected to go, taking the air once more as the bike left the road and crashed through a screen of trees and shrubs. The guard at the barrier was still two hundred yards short of him, the bridge sentries the same distance behind him—but everyone had seen the direction he had taken.

He fleetingly considered using the machine as a scramble bike and taking it to the floor of the valley, but twisting to avoid a pair of saplings, he crashed right into a rotting tree stump.

Bert was catapulted off into a bush, but clawed himself clear and began to run along the side of the hill. He figured that if he could get beyond the barrier he might stand a chance of crossing the road and taking to the higher ground, which could throw off his pursuers.

He made it undetected, and was still running for cover when McCafferty saw him. . . .

Sipping a long Scotch on the rocks, Philpott again scanned the notes he had taken at Sonya's dictation of Smith's plans to collect the ransom. He was waiting now for a picture to be wired from Rome to Zagreb, which the Yugoslav minister had promised would be brought right out to the airport by dispatch rider, but first there was another visitor. The man carried a bulky bag of soft chamois leather and juggled meaningfully with it.

"I have brought what you want, Mr. Philpott," said the diamond merchant. He handed the bag to Philpott, who didn't even check its contents. A member of the Amsterdam Diamond Exchange was entirely trustworthy.

The dispatch rider was admitted with the wire photo, and Philpott studied it with a magnifying glass. The picture showed a tiny island—Saucer Island, the caption said—accompanied by a map reference. The island appeared to jut no more than a few feet above sea level; the map reference identified it as lying off the Dalmatian coast. The rock could have been anything from fifty to five hundred meters wide and looked flat and bare, except for the pole and cross-bar like a hangman's gibbet someone had constructed at its very tip.

"Is that a gibbet?" Philpott asked doubtfully.

The deputy minister bent over the picture. "It looks like a gibbet, but logic dictates that it cannot possibly be that," he said. "Why bother to take someone all the way out there to hang him when you can shoot him comfortably in a prison yard?"

The vertical post with the supported arm protruding out over the water was fastened to the island by a guy rope attached to a bolt which had been driven firmly into the rock.

" 'Place the diamonds into a canvas sack secured at the top, and bearing at its fastening a steel ring precisely six inches in diameter,' " Philpott read out Smith's instructions disbelievingly. " 'Loop the ring over the projecting arm.' "

"Is that all?" the deputy minister asked.

"No," Philpott replied. "He goes on: 'Do not set foot on the island. The operation must be carried out from a boat. Be warned that the island is mined. The ransom must be in position by 2000 hours this evening, or another life will immediately be forfeit. And heed well this injunction: any rescue bid will be met with fire, and the deaths of *all*, repeat *all*, captives.' "

"Curious indeed," commented the politician, inquiring what Philpott wished them to do.

"Do precisely as Smith says," Philpott returned. "Take a boat to the island, don't land on it, merely place the diamonds on the projecting arm of the whatever it is, exactly as per instructions. No tricks; no substitute package. I want fifty million dollars' worth of cut stones in that bag, and I want it to be where Smith expects it to be at the time he cites. I'll be able to give you further directions later, I trust."

The Minister bowed, "You are, sir, as I believe I have pointed out, in full charge of the operation. So that, should it go wrong . . ." He let the possible consequences hang in the air.

"I take the point," Philpott said grimly.

"How do you think Smith is going to take possession of the diamonds?" the politician asked, halting Philpott's exit to the helicopter.

Philpott turned and said, "If I knew that I'd know how to stop him. But I don't." He stalked out to the airport's apron and made his way to the helicopter.

The sun cast a deep shadow on the mountainside, and McCafferty used the camouflage to sneak further along the ledge until he was above Cooligan. He risked a slow, careful descent, wishing neither to alarm Cooligan nor attract the attention of the helicopter pilot. When he was only a few yards short of the agent, he called out in an urgent voice, "Bert! It's me. Mac!"

Cooligan spun around, and did the last thing McCafferty expected: his face darkened with fury, and he launched himself at his would-be rescuer.

Mac could have used the machine gun to hold off the maddened agent, but he was so taken aback that he allowed Cooligan to close with him.

"*Now,* you filthy bastard, *now* here's where you get *yours* like you gave it to Hemmingsway!" Colligan gasped, as his hands reached out for McCafferty's throat. Mac staggered, still unwilling to use either force or his own weapon against his friend.

"For Christ's sake, Bert, what the hell are you saying?" he hissed. "And keep the noise down or we'll both be caught."

They grappled, and Cooligan fought like a berserk Viking, possessed with fury and hatred. He hit out blindly at Mac's face, and caught him a glancing blow on the cheekbone. Mac stumbled backwards, then his foot caught in a tree root and he toppled to the ground. Cooligan's eyes blazed as he leapt forward to dash his booted foot into Mc-

Cafferty's face. Mac rolled desperately to one side, babbling all the while that Cooligan was making a dreadful mistake, that he was his friend, the old Mac—that the other man was a ringer!

Cooligan missed him with the first onslaught, but spun on his heel and lashed out again with his other foot. Still refusing to unsling his gun, McCafferty caught the flying boot inches from his mouth, and twisted cruelly on it. With a cry of fear, Cooligan pivoted, trying to keep his balance with outflung arms, and failing. He fell awkwardly to land on his front, and the wind was driven from his lungs. It was the change Mac needed: he bunched his muscles and jumped from the ground to fall squarely on Cooligan's back. He twisted one of the agent's arms, and held it pressed between his shoulder blades.

"Now will you listen! Say *nothing—*just *listen!* There are *two* of us, dummy!. *Two* of us! *That's* how Smith managed to pull the trick on board AF One. They used a *ringer*—and he's out looking for you now! I got away from them in Bahrain and I'm here under Philpott's orders. I'm to meet him shortly down the valley! *Now* will you for Christ's sake stop fighting me and let me rescue you, asshole!"

All Cooligan's fury was spent in the struggle to get free. He lay on his face, exhausted, and for the first time heard what McCafferty was saying. *"Two* of you?" he panted. "Then you're—you're—"

"I'm Joe McCafferty, Bert. He's—I don't know, someone else. Someone Smith trumped up with plastic surgery to look like me, talk like me, act like me . . . well enough to fool everyone on board the plane and pull off this hijack. What we have to do now, Bert, is stop him. And I think I've an idea how we can make a start."

He rolled off Cooligan but, to be absolutely safe, held him at gunpoint. Cooligan sat up and eyed the weapon suspiciously. "I guess—I guess I have to believe you, Mac," he said slowly. "There seemed to be something not quite right about you—I mean *him*—at the hotel and on the aircraft, and I knew all along that, even if you'd sold out, you couldn't have done what they said you'd done back there."

He related the details of Hemmingsway's murder, and McCafferty shook his head in grief; he had known Hemmingsway, and like him for his unaffectedness and determination. Cooligan asked for the plan of action, and McCafferty inquired if the ringer was still wearing AF One uniform. Bert confirmed that he was.

"Then change clothes with me," Mac urged. "I'll go down the hill as the ringer, and tell them to call off the hunt. That'll take the heat away and give us time to think.

They swapped clothing swiftly, and McCafferty, keeping a wary eye open for his double in case the ringer had also joined the search, made contact with the guerillas and ordered them back to the castle. He separated from the task force on a hastily contrived pretext, and had just rejoined Cooligan when their attention was distracted by a loud thump from below.

"That's the drawbridge," Cooligan said, "something must be coming out."

As they watched, the minibus clattered across the wooden bridge and took off down the road, followed by a truckload of men and two jeeps. McCafferty clapped the field glasses to his eyes, and counted off the passengers in the bus.

He turned to Cooligan. "It's Smith and the hostages," he said, "I think they're all in the bus, except maybe one."

"Which one?" Bert demanded.

Mac hesitated. "I don't know if she was even among them, but she was supposed to join the flight."

"Do you mean Sabrina Carver?" Bert asked.

"Yes. They were all there but for her."

"Then she must still be back at the castle," Cooligan said, "and Mac—there's something you don't know. She's not just AF One crew: she's an agent of UNACO, your people. She'll be in deadly danger."

"I *do* know, Bert," McCafferty said, "and that's why I'm going to get her out."

McCafferty left one of the communicators with Cooligan and instructed him to stay under cover. "I've got a plan," he explained. "It's worked once already, and I don't see why it shouldn't work again. I'll keep your uniform on for the moment, if you don't mind."

He trotted back to the castle, the gun still slung over his shoulder, and was challenged by the guards. McCafferty, who was now in the curious position of playing himself in

157

the mad scenario mapped out by Smith, curtly told the sentries that one of the jeeps escorting the hostages' bus had broken down. Mac noted that many of the guerillas had already left the castle, and seized the opportunity to get rid of a few more to even up the odds. He ordered three sentries to help with the repairs to the jeep, or, if it couldn't be fixed, to get it off the road.

The remaining two guerillas guarded the main entrance, and Mac left them as he made his way to the attic room where Sabrina was being held, following directions supplied by Bert Cooligan. He mounted the narrow steps and rapped on the door, expecting Sabrina to reply, but it was a man's voice that he heard, raised in a hoarse and chilling shout of triumph. . . .

Sabrina had first of all feared that Cooligan would be captured or killed before he even reached the ground, so quickly was his escape discovered. It was sheer bad luck that Achmed Fayeed, inflamed by the brutal murder of Hemmingsway, had determined to follow Smith's suggestion that Sabrina Carver should be made to suffer for her deception aboard Air Force One. And suffer she would.

Achmed had brooded on the beautiful girl in the room at the top of the castle, and eventually reached a decision. He ran up the stairway, intending to isolate Sabrina and make her submit to him. He unlocked the door and threw it open; Sabrina and Feisal were still at the window monitoring Cooligan's progress. Achmed, who had himself imprisoned the Secret Service agent in the attic, realized immediately what had happened. He called for a guard to join him and ran to the window, smashing the glass with the butt of his machine pistol and loosing off a volley of shots at the hastily glimpsed target.

Fayeed cursed when he saw Cooligan shoot the drawbridge on the stolen Honda. He shouted at the guerilla who answered his summons to take Feisal to the trophy room and inform either Smith or Dunkels that the agent had escaped. Sabrina was about to follow Feisal, but Achmed caught her arm and pulled her roughly back into the room. He backhanded her and she fell to the bed, her head ringing from the force of the blow.

The Arab kept his gun on Sabrina as the door closed behind the guerilla and the terrified boy. Achmed said, "You have crossed us for the last time. I do not think Mister Smith will care too much what happens to you, and I know he shares my opinion that it would be a pity to waste your obvious talents by killing you too quickly.

"You owe me your body, you Yankee bitch, and you're going to pay up. If you haven't known an Arab before, I can assure you that we're experts in our treatment of women. You'll never have another experience like it." He laughed, but it was an ugly sound. "You won't, in any case, but your last lovemaking might just as well be your best."

Achmed cradled the machine pistol in the crook of his arm, leaving his other hand free to loosen the broad leather belt on his battledress trousers. "Get your clothes off, slut," he commanded, and when she stayed unmoving he drew from a sheath at his belt a long-bladed knife. "I said undress, or I'll cut you naked with this, and I don't care whether it's the clothes or your lovely fair skin that comes away."

Sabrina continued to look at him with utter contempt in her blue eyes. Achmed stole towards her, his belt half-undone, the gun in one hand, the knife in the other. "Which is it to be?" he whispered. "Easy—or hard? Pleasure—or pain? I'm going to have you whether you like it or not, whether you're willing or not, whether you fight me or not. I don't give a damn what state you're in when I finally get your legs open. I can use you just as well dead or alive."

Sabrina's flesh crawled with fear and disgust as she saw how unmistakably ready he was for her, even beneath the rough material of his uniform. She had hoped her refusal even to answer him might infuriate him, goad him into hasty action, but he held the knife like a trained fighter, and the pistol pointed unwaveringly at her face.

Still with her lips compressed and her eyes blazing with hatred, she knelt on the bed and shrugged off her AF One blazer. Her fingers flicked through the buttons on her blouse, and unhooked the fastener of her skirt. She rose from her knees to her feet without using her hands for support, and towered over him on the bed. The sounds of vehicles leaving the castle nagged at the edges of her mind, but she ignored them. She slipped out of the blouse and pulled down the zipper of the skirt. The garment fell to the counterpane, and she stepped away from it.

As a strip routine, it lacked even a scant suggestion of style or titillation. Hers were the actions of a woman who was about to be raped; her eyes never left his, and her teeth clenched in defiance. She would never, she swore to herself, go willingly to him, and Achmed would swiftly discover that Sabrina Carver had ways of defeating him even in the height of his lust.

Sabrina kicked the blouse and skirt off the bed, and stood looking down at him, her fingers laced before her, resting on her lightly tanned belly. "The rest," Achmed muttered hoarsely, "Take off the rest."

She made no move to obey. "Kneel!" he ordered, and she allowed her body to sag and fold until it slumped before him. "The rest," he said, gesturing again at her bra and panties with the point of the machine pistol.

More quickly than his eyes could follow, her hand came up and wrenched at the barrel of the gun, twisting his finger in the trigger-guard until he gave a howl of pain and yanked it out of her grasp. "You will pay for that," he panted, "by God you will pay for that."

Sabrina's eyes were on the snout of the gun, and she did not see the knife as its point came up to slit through the front of her bra and hook it off her body, leaving a faint line of blood welling on the creamy skin of her naked breasts. Her hands flew to cover them, and Fayeed hooked two fingers in her silken panties and ripped the wisp of cloth from her groin. She could not suppress the cry of pain and outrage—and now fear—that was the only sound so far to leave her lips.

Sabrina fell backwards and her legs parted. The Arab saw her open and unprotected, and tore off his belt to bare his own body. He spun the knife to lodge it quivering in a floorboard, and dropped the machine pistol to the ground. He bellowed in his native tongue a cry of victory compounded with lust, knelt on the bed in front of her, spread her legs wide . . . and slumped sideways over her as McCafferty crashed the butt of his sub-machine gun into the back of his head.

Mac dragged the Arab off the bed and threw him to the

160

floor, and Sabrina reached down for her clothing to hide her shame and humiliation, even greater revulsion flashing from her eyes.

"That's not a nice way to look at someone who's just saved you from a fate worse than death—and most probably death as well," McCafferty said. "You don't have to say 'Thank you,' but at least you needn't make me feel you'd rather I was down there on the floor and he was back on the bed having his evil way with you."

"In some ways," Sabrina spat at him, "I'd prefer Achmed to you, if it's got to happen. He may have been an animal, but it was honest lust from a straightforward lecher. You're so tricky, Mister, so—polluted, I think I'd rather die than know you've touched me."

Mac sighed. "Jesus, this guy really made a mess of my life without knowing the slightest damned thing about me."

Sabrina pulled the bedclothes up to cover herself, as much against the chill in the air as to cloak her nakedness. "What do you mean?" she asked. "Who are you talking about?"

McCafferty explained. Unsurprisingly, like Basil Swann and Bert Cooligan, she didn't believe him. But, again like her two colleagues, she came to be convinced, and was still avidly questioning him when Achmed seized the knife from the floor and struck at the American's stomach. Sabrina's warning half-scream alerted him, and he stepped back far enough to let the point of the blade pass through his shirt front and scrape the skin.

Mac swung the machine gun again, and Achmed, who had risen to his knees and was lunging forward once more with the knife, felt the gun barrel rake his face. He spat and sprang to his feet, blood leaking from his mouth. He sensed that Mac dared not fire the gun for fear of alerting a guard, and leapt at the American with the knife held high. Mac smashed the gun into the Arab's wrist and the blade flew across the room.

Mac's foot shot out and hooked around Achmed's bare leg. Fayeed swiveled and started to fall, and McCafferty, holding the sub-machine gun now in both hands, looped the sling around the Arab's neck, twisting the gun until the knot was tight. Using the weapon like a straight arm in a Chinese stranglehold, he imprisoned the Arab's head and rammed his knee into the small of Achmed's back, the rifle a rigid bar on the Arab's throat. No other noise came from Achmed Fayeed, pseudoprinceling of Bahrain, and he died in less than a minute, his face suffused, his sight masked by bursting blood vessels, his mouth engorged by the swollen tongue.

Chapter Fourteen

Slinging the sub-machinegun once more across his back, and partially concealing it with his parka in case anyone spotted it as American-made, McCafferty escorted Sabrina downstairs under cover of Fayeed's machine pistol. He had noticed another jeep in the interior courtyard, loaded with supplies, and three more in the parking area.

The castle seemed empty, but Mac was treading warily in the event that the ringer was still around, for he had not been among the passengers. Neither could he chance meeting a guard who might be on first-name terms with the ringer. When he reached the courtyard, an orderly was packing the last of the supplies on the jeep. He glanced curiously at McCafferty and the girl, but made no comment.

Sabrina whispered, "Where is everybody, for God's sake?"

"Gone," Mac replied tersely. "They left in a bus. Where to, I don't know. I only wish I did. What's more, I've no idea how we're going to find them."

"The boy, Feisal, too," Sabrina said, "was he with them? I've got to know, because he's ill, and I'm the only one who can treat him." Mac confirmed, low-voiced, that Feisal had been on the bus.

They made their way across the drawbridge, passing what seemed to be the only three remaining guards. One, who had been leaning against an entrance pillar, came upright and alert when he saw McCafferty. "Back so soon?" he inquired in thick, heavily accented English.

"Orders," Mac said. The guard's round, pockmarked face took on a puzzled expression, and he murmured something in Serbo-Croat to one of the others. Then he fixed his eyes on Mac again and said, carefully, "Orders from where? Mister Smith left long before you did."

McCafferty glanced at the parking area and saw only two jeeps: the ringer must have used one to join the main party at wherever it was the hostages had been taken. He plucked the communicator from his belt and sneered, "There are other ways of receiving orders than having somebody shout them at you, dummy. If you want to know, I was sent back to get *her*"—indicating Sabrina.

"Isn't the Arab looking after her?" the guerilla asked with a suggestive leer.

Mac grinned. "He was. Now he's recovering."

The guard laughed and translated for his friends. McCafferty said he had been told by Smith to bring Sabrina in immediately. Achmed and the other sentries were to wait a further half-hour, and follow in the last jeep.

"And the supply truck?" the guerilla inquired, waving his machine gun towards the internal yard.

"It's to go as soon as it's ready," Mac ordered.

"To the caves?"

"Where else?"

Mac prodded Sabrina towards the nearest jeep, and she drove it out of the parking lot on to the road. "Caves?" she mused.

"Seems like it. Anyway, it's the only clue we have. What we must do now is get behind the supply truck and follow it, and we've got only this one vehicle. As I need it myself, I don't quite see how we're going to manage."

They rounded a bend in the road and Mac could see in the distance the red and white crossbar of the road barrier. A guerilla lounged indolently beside the weighted end.

"Damn it," McCafferty cursed, "I was afraid of this. We have to pick up Bert Cooligan at some stage, and I wanted everyone from the castle to think we'd gone straight to the caves."

"What will you do?"

"What I have to."

He motioned to her to stop by the barrier, and got out of the jeep just as the sentry started to press down on the leaded fulcrum. "Speak English?" Mac asked the guerilla.

"A little," the man replied unsurely.

Mac pointed at the guard's chest, and then in the direction of the castle. "*You*—go back *there*," he instructed.

The Yugoslav nodded cheerfully, slung his rifle, and turned to leave. As he did so, McCafferty threw an arm around his throat and drove Achmed Fayeed's knife into his back. The sentry slumped to the ground without a cry, and Mac dragged him to the downward slope and rolled the body into a patch of undergrowth.

"Now what?" Sabrina asked. McCafferty ditched the knife and said, "I've just remembered that we do have more than one vehicle."

"That's right," Sabrina put in excitedly, "Bert got away on a motorcycle."

Mac nodded. "You take the jeep and follow the supply truck, and I'll recover the bike and use it to link up with Philpott."

"Why not the other way around?" she returned. "I'd be less noticeable on the bike, with a helmet, and Mr. Philpott would have a more comfortable ride in the jeep."

McCafferty shook his head wonderingly and replied, "I might have know it. I suppose you were the high school scramble champion?"

Sabrina winked at him. "Not quite, but I made him teach me how to ride."

They squared the ground where Mac thought the motorcycle might be, and Sabrina found it. "It's in one piece," she shouted triumphantly, hauling it upright and jumping on the starter. "And what's more, it works." They wheeled the Honda back up to the road, and concealed it and themselves behind a clump of trees. Presently the sound of an approaching vehicle caught their ears. Sabrina mounted the Honda, with Mac holding it upright, and started the engine.

The jeep, its swaying load tied down with ropes, passed them. Sabrina counted to ten, opened the throttle, and roared out onto the road. She had McCafferty's communicator in her belt, and banked on Bert Cooligan staying on high ground to receive her message when she had located

164

Smith's new hideout. She had not, though, been able to find a helmet.

McCafferty rejoined Cooligan up the mountain and gave him the details of the plan. They decided that when the coast was clear, Bert should return to the castle and await Sabrina's contact from there. He armed the agent with the dead sentry's rifle.

"Has Sabrina got a gun, too?" Cooligan asked, his voice worried.

Mac hesitated, then nodded. "The Arab, Achmed, tried to rape her. I managed to stop him, but I had to kill him. She's got his machine pistol. In any case, I've more guns back in the valley for when I pick up Philpott. We'll be a regular little army, huh?"

Cooligan grinned and wished McCafferty luck as he left to take the jeep down the hill into the village. The Secret Service agent squatted on his haunches, holding the rifle, butt first, on the ground before him, and saw the still-tenanted castle bathed in the amber glow of the late afternoon sun. He settled down to wait.

The track straggled off the mountain to the town of Knin, where four major roads converged. Sabrina kept the guards' jeep in clear sight until the terrain flattened out on the coastal plain of Hrvatska. She thought the jeep might be bound for the resort of Sibenik, but from Knin it diverted on to a minor road heading for Benkovac and the coast, and then threaded through a maze of tracks until it reached a spot which she judged must be twenty to twenty-five kilometers from the castle, and about ten inland. What was more, she was back in hill country again, though it was no match for the Dinaric Alps.

She had now to exercise greater care, for they had the road more or less to themselves. Luckily it was as winding as the castle track had been, so she was able to lurk out of sight around bends, and then sprint to catch up with the receding jeep. The sun was only a blazing segment to the west, and Sabrina mentally crossed her fingers that they would find the caves before the light failed.

The jeep started to slow down, so Sabrina eased the Honda off the track into the shelter of a scattering of boulders. The jeep swung right and began climbing the rock-strewn hillside. Sabrina switched her gaze to higher ground, and saw a barred gate fronting a vast concrete abutment set into the flank of the hill. The jeep stopped at the gate, and an armed guerilla materialized to check the visitor. Behind the concrete slab she could just pick out the dark mouth of a cave.

Sabrina propped the Honda against a rock and scaled the hill at an oblique angle to take her above the cave entrance. Leaning out perilously far, she saw that the concrete deck was wide and deep enough to take the minibus and several more vehicles, while still leaving a large unfilled space. She shifted her position, and craned her neck even further to look into the cave itself. A battered signpost, uprooted and reclining forlornly against the entrance wall, bore a skull and crossbones and the German warning, *"Achtung!"* alongside a device that suggested explosives. A wartime ammunition dump? she wondered. It would have made an ideal site. She spotted the points of stalacites hanging from the vaulted roof of the cavern, but could make out nothing beyond that, though the space was well lit by electricity supplied from a generator humming away in the background.

Sabrina grimaced, and pulled back. She needed to know more of the geography of the caves and, if possible, the exact location of the captives.

Carefully, for the sentry was still at his post, she climbed on up the hill until she reached the crest. She could see now that the caves must extend further than she had imagined—and that they were divided by a natural break.

The cavern which formed the entrance to the caves opened out on to a deep gorge over an unseen but audible river. A narrow bridge spanned the gorge, and the pathway at the other side disappeared into ᴜ‌ᴇ mouth of yet another cave. The suspension bridge was railed, but appeared none too safe. Sabrina grinned: she was sure she had located the hostages' hiding place, for Smith would not neglect such a spendid opportunity to make either escape or rescue as difficult as possible.

She activated her two-way communicator, and within a few seconds was talking earnestly to Bert Cooligan at Castle Windischgraetz.

When the minibus arrived at the caves, Smith himself had unlocked the gate. The hostages were shooed unceremoniously off the bus, Feisal holding tightly to Zeidan's hand as the crippled sheik was loaded into his wheelchair. A chatter of engine noise from above announced the arrival of Dunkels in the Kamov helicopter. One of Smith's guerillas activated the generator and pressed a switch to flood the gloomy cavern with light. The multihued limestone formations from ceiling and floor brought a gasp of admiration from Feisal.

Guards shepherded the captives through the cavern, and once more Sheik Zeidan was hauled from the wheelchair when they reached the flimsy bridge. Dr. Hamady took the first nervous step on to the bridge, clutching the rails and allowing himself to be led over with his eyes closed. Zeidan was next, chaired by two sentries and watched anxiously by Feisal in his wake. Dorani and Arbeid followed, with Fairman and Latimer heading the crocodile of Air Force One crew members.

Smith brought up the rear, but before commencing his crossing he ordered Dunkels to establish radio contact with the castle. "Check with Jagger whether they've caught Cooligan yet. If they haven't, get airborne again and give them a hand. At any event, I want the castle personnel here as soon as they've left everything safe. Tell Fayeed to get rid of the girl Carver—any way he pleases."

Dunkels hurried off, and Smith traversed the gorge to join the hostages, who were perched on an outcrop surrounded on three sides by a drop of a hundred feet, and under the watchful eyes of a pair of guards. Steps cut into the side of the cave descended to the ledge, and Smith negotiated them cautiously to stand before his captives. "Not quite the Ritz," he apologized, "but at least you're under cover."

Sheik Dorani regarded him under beetling brows. "When do you propose to release us?" he demanded.

"As soon as the ransom is in my possession," Smith returned affably.

"And when will that be?" Zeidan growled.

Smith consulted his watch. "By nightfall," he said reflectively. "Fifty million dollars in diamonds. The largest ransom in history, I believe."

"Kidnappers are notorious not for the size of their unlawful gains but the heinous nature of their crimes," Zeidan intoned. "If you are remembered at all, Smith, it will be as the common criminal you undoubtedly are."

Smith turned to face the old Arab, who leaned back in his wheelchair as if it were a golden throne and regarded his captor with abhorrence. Zeidan knew that of all the hostages, he alone possessed the ability to unsettle Smith's composure; it was a weapon he used sparingly, and always to great effect. Zeidan gambled that in these infrequent outbursts, when his dignity was affronted, Smith was inclined to tell the truth. That was what the sheik was seeking now to learn.

Smith's voice was a silky threat. "Would you rather I be remembered as a mass murderer, Your Excellency?"

"That is your prerogative," Zeidan grunted, "and could well be your epitaph."

"If it is *my* epitaph, Sheik Zeidan, I can promise you it will also be yours and that of your grandson."

Latimer snapped from the darkening lip of the ledge, "You must be certifiable, Smith, if you think you can get away with killing all of us, because that's what you'll have to do, and take the ransom as well."

Smith looked across at him, his good humor and confidence restored. "Fortunately for you, major, I am neither insane nor an instinctual killer. *But* . . . if you provoke me too much, any of you, or if you should attempt to escape, you have my promise that you will not leave this place alive." He turned and remounted the stone steps, and left silence, doubt, and terror behind him. . . .

McCafferty had just been able to make out Sabrina's Honda in the distance as he spun the wheel of the jeep to take the opposite direction for his appointment with Philpott. He reached the village without meeting another vehicle, recovered his pack from the postman's daughter, and fortified himself with a few beers to while away the time. He didn't have long to wait: he saw the helicopter before its engine noise reached him, and made a bet with himself, which he won, that the pilot would land in the same field where he himself had parked the UTVA. Mac saw Philpott stoop unnecessarily as he ran under the rotors, and appreciated how truly alone they were when the helicopter promptly took off again.

Philpott listened to McCafferty's account, and questioned him closely on key points. When Mac had finished, Philpott said grimly, "So we still don't know exactly where the hostages are, and we can't find out until we make contact with Cooligan."

"That's the size of it," Mac conceded.

"Or what Sabrina's doing, or whether she's in danger."

"That, I must admit, is the part that worries me most," McCafferty replied.

She was at that moment squirming back down the hillside, mostly on her bottom, to repossess the Honda. She got to it undetected, kicked the motor into life, and was wheeling the machine over to the track to take the same route back to the castle, when she looked up and saw the helicopter bearing down upon her.

Dunkels had been airborne before Sabrina arrived at the caves. His radio link with the castle had revealed not only that Cooligan had not been recaptured, but also that Fayeed had been strangled, and that Sabrina Carver was missing. The German had analyzed the confused message about the mysterious reappearance of Jagger at a time when the ringer ought to have been at the caves with Smith and the hostages.

He reported to Smith, who quickly grasped that the genuine McCafferty was back on the scene to ring the changes on his alter-ego by posing as himself.

"How can you be sure?" Dunkels asked.

Smith rounded on him, his control slipping, fury twisting his features. "Jagger was *here!*" he screamed, "so he couldn't have been up there, idiot. He's *still* here. Take the helicopter—now! Find Carver and bring her to me—alive. I must know Philpott's movements. Look for a motorcycle . . . they'll have abandoned the jeep.

"McCafferty will have gone by now to join Philpott's force, but Carver will be around here somewhere, on the motorcycle Cooligan used. *Get* her, Dunkels."

"How d'you know she'll be around here?" Dunkels asked unwisely as he turned to leave.

"Because she'll have followed the supply jeep here," Smith sneered, almost frantic with rage now. "The timing fits, you fool. Get out! Now! And do not return without her."

Sabrina ducked off the road and skidded to a halt under a stury beech tree. She could hear the Kamov circling overhead, and peered up into the branches. The sun was leaving the sky now, but the twilight air was crisp and clear, and she saw Dunkels at the controls ease the helicopter lower and lower until its blades threatened to decapitate her tree.

She unclipped the machine pistol, took careful aim, and fired a burst through the foliage at the grey, swooping shape. Dunkels jerked back on the stick as a stray bullet ricocheted off the fuselage of the Kamov. He rose above the little copse and flew out of range, then buzzed her hiding place like an angry wasp. He sighted a clear space to his left, and gained height again, banking sharply at the end of his spiral to signal his obvious intention of landing.

Sabrina took the bait. While the Kamov hovered a few feet from the ground she remounted the Honda, throttle up and roared away from the concealment of the trees. It was only when she heard the rising engine whine of the helicopter that she realized she had been tricked: Dunkels had merely made a landing feint to flush her out of cover.

She swore fluently and skirted a tufted hillock to crash through a hedge which she hoped might lead to another copse, only to find herself in an even bigger field. There was a wood at the other side, though, and she was streaking towards it when Dunkels caught up with her again. The first bullets from his own machine gun tore red divots out of the bumpy ground.

The German played cat-and-mouse with her, and she could see him through the perspex awning of the cockpit, laughing as he brought the helicopter down to block her path and force her to swerve dangerously away. Then he backed off and she resumed her course, but

170

wrenched at the handlebars again as the rushing blades of the Kamov fanned the air only a few yards from her face. Dunkels chased her this time, forcing her back the way she had come until she spun the Honda around and, ducking low in the saddle, drove it straight under his wheels.

But she had neither the speed nor the maneuverability to elude him, and the end was inevitable, for Dunkels had noticed something she could not have seen: between the field and the copse that was her target lay a small pond, sunk into a dip in the ground, and not visible from her vantage point.

As a sheepdog would, he herded her across the pasture, and like a rabbit fleeing the teeth of a snapping hound, Sabrina scuttled in the direction he wanted her to go, lurching and weaving to avoid the helicopter and the constant stream of bullets. She had hated being chased as a child, and when she was cornered, her resolve to fight always gave way to hysteria. She was sobbing now, and close to total panic when the Honda left the ground and backflipped her off to dump both of them in the middle of the pond.

Sabrina lay stunned and half-drowning in the murky water. She came to as Dunkels gripped her by the collar and hauled her to the muddy bank. He stood astride her, letting her lay there in her misery. Then he leaned down, grasped her hair, pulled up her head, and smashed his fist into her face.

For the second time she lost consciousness, and when her brain again struggled through the mists of returning awareness, the noise of the Kamov's engine completed her disorientation. She collected her thoughts and flexed her arms and legs. Dunkels had not even considered it necessary to tie her.

Above the roar of the helicopter, Bert Cooligan caught the few words she managed to get out before Dunkels shot Sabrina's communicator to pieces.

"Bert!" she screamed, "they've got me! They're taking me to the caves!"

Sonya Kolchinsky felt oddly comforted by the presence of Brigadier Tomlin standing beside her in the prow of the motorboat, cutting through the Adriatic off the coast of Dalmatia. Since Philpott had been told he was in complete charge of the operation, Sonya had used UNACO's authority to browbeat the Yugoslavians into yielding every ounce of assistance she could squeeze from them. With a fair-sized naval task force at her disposal, she had bludgeoned the deputy minister of the interior into conceding a NATO commanding officer. Tomlin had needed no second bidding, and jetted over from Naples almost before the words were out of the politician's mouth.

Now he looked gloomily over his shoulder at the waning light, and snapped on his torch to study a sea chart of the myriad of islands sprinkled around like seaweed between their embarkation port of Split and the Italian peninsula of Venezia Giulia.

Sonya sighed and looked for reassurance from the lights of Sibenik winking at them from the shoreline. The lights of the next coastal town of any size, Zadar, were more distant. She had been confident, based on the geographical relationship of the landing strip to the castle to the presumed location of the hostage caves, that Smith's ransom island would lie somewhere between Sibenik and Zadar, which tied in with his necessarily generalized map reference. But they had covered the territory once, and it was coming up to seven o'clock, only an hour away from Smith's deadline for placing the diamonds on the gibbet.

"We obviously missed it first time," Tomlin declared. "We'll have another look."

"But it's almost dark now," she protested.

"Nonetheless, we go on searching," Tomlin pronounced firmly. There were three other boats in his flotilla, and he was in touch with English speakers aboard each of them. "Quarter the area again," the brigadier ordered, "and bear in mind that the island could be a hell of a lot smaller than it looks in the photograph. What we're seeking may not be an island at all—just a rock."

Tomlin returned to his chart. They rounded the island of Kakan with Kaprije to starboard and the larger bulk of Kornati to port. Murter passed to starboard and Zut to port, and ahead of them, lying off the seaward coast of

172

Pasman Island, was another islet which Tomlin immediately identified. He stabbed his finger on the chart and said "Lighthouse," with immense satisfaction. Just then the beam of the light flashed on and swept the sea before them. Sonya stammered, "It's th-there! Over there!"

On its return trip the light confirmed the fleeting impression she had gained. It picked out the flat bulge of Saucer Island, lying like an upturned dinner plate in the sea and washed by breakers. On the starboard rim of the island stood the gibbet.

The helmsman of their launch followed her pointing finger and steered the vessel through the chunky waves towards the little island. Tomlin held up the photograph and glanced from the snapshot to the islet, now transfixed in their lights and those of two other vessels in their fleet. "Spot on," he said, "well done, Mrs. Kolchinsky. First-class piece of observation."

The boat made a complete circuit of the island before drawing up and backing in to take position next to the curious pole with the horizontal arm.

"Don't get too close," Tomlin warned the cutter's crew, "and no one, but no none, must make any attempt to land on the island. I don't want anybody slinging hooks near that pole or prodding it with guns or anything else. We don't want to berth there; we just want to get far enough in to let me drop this bag over that projecting arm, and we can do that while we're still on the move. If we miss, we'll try until we succeed."

As it turned out, they needed three passes before Tomlin found his range and encircled the arm with the metal ring. He rubbed his hands together briskly and his teeth gleamed under the pencil mustache as he favoured her with a glowing smile. "Excellent," he pronounced. "Now we lay off and take posts."

"Where do you suggest we go?" Sonya inquired, and Tomlin jerked his head at the neighboring island. "No sense in staying out here in the cold when we can be sitting down over a steaming mug of cocoa," he chortled.

"Cocoa?" she echoed blankly.

"Quite so," Tomlin replied. "Never knew a lighthouse-keeper yet who didn't make jolly good cocoa. That'll be our headquarters, ma'am, if you agree."

Sonya grinned at him appreciatively and said, "Spot on, brigadier. With you all the way. Cocoa it is."

Tomlin barked into his communicator, "All units. Calling all units. Proceed to designated stations forthwith. Flagship will moor at the island 30 degrees to starboard, and the command post, offering a full view of the rock at all times, will be the lighthouse. If you read me, please acknowledge."

Three Aldis lamps blinked in acquiescence, and Tomlin ordered his crew to proceed to the lighthouse while the flotilla, manned by armed marines, ringed Saucer Island and sat a quarter of a mile off like sharks waiting for dinner time.

Smith received Sabrina with icy politeness, trusting she was none the worse for her encounters with Achmed at the castle and Dunkels in the helicopter.

"Not at all," she said sweetly, "they behaved like the perfect gentlemen they obviously are."

"Or were, in Achmed's case," Smith pointed out. Sabrina tried to conceal her alarm at the news that he had learned of Fayeed's death.

Smith, however, forestalled any lies she might have invented. "Of course I know Achmed is dead," he said, "and what is more I am aware that he was killed by Colonel McCafferty—the real Colonel McCafferty, if you follow me, not our ersatz and somewhat shop-soiled model."

Again she wished she had a poker face, but what nature had not given her she found it impossible to assume. So she replied, evenly, "All of which indicates that you're on the point of losing, doesn't it, Mister Smith?"

"On the contrary," Smith beamed. "Philpott will be able to do nothing to prevent me from picking up the ransom, and I have prepared a little surprise to guard my back. I am beginning to find these Arabs decidedly tiresome. No, Sabrina, I have not lost; neither shall I. All Philpott is doing sitting off my island with a—"

"If you think *that*—" she began, and bit her lip in anger.

"I didn't really," Smith purred. "Indeed, I imagine him to be much closer to my castle than to the seashore,

174

since of course you were kind enough to supply him with the location of these caves through your communicator, and he would hardly have had time to get here yet, would he? No doubt he and Colonel McCafferty are at this very moment linking up with the agent Cooligan to plan how they can best launch their assault force on this stronghold."

Once more she tried to keep her expression neutral, and for the third time failed. Smith laughed in genuine amusement.

"My dear Sabrina." He chuckled. "There really is no point in submitting you to persuasion, when all one has to do is study your lovely face and get all the answers one needs. I have now learned that Philpott, possibly with McCafferty and Cooligan, are at or near my castle, and that far from possessing an army capable of defeating me, they may well be acting entirely alone. Probably they have some assistance at sea, where I would guess that the estimable Mrs. Kolchinsky is holding the fort—"

Sabrina flushed and her lower lip quivered. "Bull'seye again." Smith chuckled. "There we are, then, the complete picture." He beckoned to the grinning Dunkels. "Siegfried, give our beauteous 'Brünhilde' some hot food, then take her to join the others, that they may all meet their *Götterdämmerung* together."

He laughed, full-bellied, and strode into the main cavern.

Philpott groaned and swore when Cooligan brought him and McCafferty up to date with the news of Sabrina's capture.

"How long ago did you get her message?" he rapped.

"Not ten minutes," Cooligan replied.

"Damn, damn, damn," Philpott said, with feeling.

"Why so gloomy, chief?" McCafferty asked. "Sabrina's a tough cookie, isn't she? Surely she'll be able to take care of herself?"

Philpott's response was a resigned sigh. "It isn't that, Mac," he admitted, "it's just that we'll now have to assume that Smith knows everything, and act accordingly."

175

"How so?" Cooligan frowned as mystified as McCafferty.

Philpott grinned ruefully. "Sabrina never could lie with a straight face," he explained. "She's like an open book: plenty of guts, plenty of brains, but not a shred of guile.

"No—Smith will have found out as much as he needs by now. I was going to hold off trying for the caves until Smith had picked up the ransom, so as not to endanger the hostages unnecessarily, but all that's changed. We must strike at the caves first, and quickly. I have a suspicion that the hostages' lives may not be worth a row of beans after Smith's got his hands on the diamonds."

McCafferty objected, "But I thought you said he wasn't a murderer by design."

Philpott shook his head wearily. "I know, Mac," he replied, "but this operation seems to be different. He's already allowed Hawley Hemmingsway to die, and since he knows we're hot on his tail he may be starting to feel threatened. And we all know what rats do when they're cornered. I fancy I've always assumed that Mister Smith is some sort of gentleman bastard . . . but I've never seen his evil side, Mac. For everyone's sake, Sabrina's included, we must tread very prudently from now on."

As the "assault force" boarded the jeep to take them to the caves, Smith stood, arms folded, alongside Jagger at the side of the suspension bridge nearer to the captives on their cold, cramped ledge.

Smith looked approvingly, and Jagger grinned, the light from his torch picking out the guerilla who was placing a plastic explosives charge into a hole in the wall of the cave above the ledge.

Unseen by the hostages below, the man wired a detonator to the *plastique,* and rolled the coil of bright yellow cable across to Jagger. The ringer scooped it up and spliced the loose end into a reel. He backed across the bridge unwinding the cable, and Smith followed him, meticulously avoiding the wire snake.

Chapter Fifteen

Sabrina sat on a rock eating a peppery goulash and pondered the meaning of Smith's last remark. The connection she did make—the Wagnerian one between "Siegfried," "Brühilde," and *Götterdämmerung*—was not reassuring, since the "Twilight of the Gods" implied the destruction of practically everyone in sight.

At the end of Dunkels's gun she was conducted to the bridge over the river chasm, where they had to give way to Smith and Jagger returning from the hostage cave and sharing some secret diversion. Her eyes met the ringer's, and for an instant she knew the sensation of cold steel in her heart.

The fleeting insight of Jagger's gaze boring into her own made her now unswervingly sure of something she had merely suspected: that whatever fate Smith had planned for the captives, Jagger intended killing every last one of them.

She read the message unmistakably in the ringer's eyes as clearly as if he had spoken the words. And he did not hide the pitiless loathing he felt for her, for he knew that he would never see her again.

The realization brought her to a halt on the swaying bridge, and she felt the barrel of Dunkels's machine pistol drill into the small of her back. She looked wildly around at him, and down at the slatted wood under her feet, then back at the entrance cavern, and stumbled as she tried to move. Dunkels's arm shot out and supported her as she half fell—but before he pushed her roughly ahead she caught the barest glimpse (and again—and there, again!) of the yellow cable tacked to the side-runner of the bridge.

Anger swiftly replaced the fear in her, and she strode off the bridge barely acknowledging the bomb which she could see clearly in its nest of rock. Dunkels propelled her down the steps, where Feisal ran to her, and she caught the boy in her arms.

"Don't let her out of your sight," Dunkels said in Serbo-Croat to the single remaining guard, "and keep away from her yourself. She's dangerous. She may not look it, but she is." The guard nodded curtly, and Dunkels backed up the flight of steps and disappeared.

Sabrina eased the boy from her embrace, but allowed him to lead her to his grandfather. She guessed that neither Sheik Zeidan nor any of the other hostages knew that Smith had given Jagger the means to kill them all, and she preferred to tell Zeidan first and seek his counsel.

The old Arab heard her out in silence, and allowed his eyes to stray only once to the point high on the wall of the cave where Sabrina indicated the explosives were placed. Feisal followed his gaze, then turned his head back and looked steadily at Sabrina.

"If you recall," the boy said softly, "I am rather good at climbing. Should you or someone else be successful in persuading the guard not to look, I believe I could get up there and defuse that bomb."

Sabrina gasped and shook her head violently. "No!" she whispered. "Never! I couldn't forgive myself if anything happened to you."

Sheik Zeidan's hand fell on her wrist and he tugged it gently. "The decision would not be yours to make, Miss Carver," he said. "Nor indeed would it be mine. Feisal is of royal blood, my blood, going back untraceable numbers of centuries. He is brave like the desert lion and as fearless as a hunting falcon. If he wishes to do this thing, then he shall. Besides," Zeidan added with a twinkling smile, "he does know about chemistry."

"He does?"

"Oh, yes," said Feisal, "I have dealt with explosives before."

Philpott sniffed the air again. "Still smells like goulash to me," he said.

"Whatever it is," McCafferty replied, "we've found the place."

With Cooligan, they had driven to the approximate area

of the hostage caves indicated by Sabrina's directions, and spent a fruitless twenty minutes exploring the locale with shaded torches, until Philpott caught the odor of home-cooking.

"You stay here, chief," Mac directed. "Bert—over to the other side of that concrete outcrop there; it's obviously the front door. I'll get above them and flash you: once for all clear, twice for guards. Don't reply."

They were scarcely in position when all doubt was removed. The entrance cavern was flooded with light, the two sentries came to attention, and out walked Mister Smith into what McCafferty could now see was a parking area for the minibus, a collection of jeeps, and Dunkels's Kamov helicopter.

Smith halted before the bus, then turned and beckoned towards the mouth of the cave. Jagger came to join him.

From above and below, Joe McCafferty and Malcolm Philpott got their first in-the-flesh sighting of the ringer, and each man experienced a thrill of dread as they realized how appallingly difficult it would have been for AF One crew members—or anyone else who had known McCafferty—to tell the ringer from the real thing.

Smith's voice wafted down to Philpott. "As soon as the diamonds are in my hands," he told Jagger, "I'll signal you. Then you can clear out and leave the hostages. I'll make sure Philpott knows where they are."

"Do you have your insurance with you?" Jagger asked.

Smith held up his hand and revealed a small flat box fitted with a switch and an inset timing device. "I have it. Any trouble with the ransom and I'll use it. I'll warn you first, though, so that you get our people out of the way."

"Will the signal be strong enough to detonate the bomb from somewhere out at sea?" Jagger queried.

Smith grinned and replied, "Plenty strong enough. I made it myself."

While they were talking, Philpott had been inching through the rocks under the cave's mouth, and was now hauling himself up to the parking area. He crouched behind the minibus as Smith bade the ringer farewell and boarded the bus. Smith was talking earnestly to the driver and so missed seeing the next thing Jagger did. But Philpott saw it.

The ringer pulled from his pocket a small flat box identical to Smith's, glanced at it, and stowed it away again.

The engine of the minibus stuttered into life, and when the vehicle negotiated the steep incline to the road, Malcolm Philpott was clinging for dear life to the rear luggage rack. . . .

One of the guerillas commanding the entrance to the caves relieved himself noisily against the rock wall, called out something indistinguishable to his friend, and disappeared inside. The other guard pulled the gate shut after Smith's bus had left, and locked it. He was strolling back to his post when McCafferty dropped from an overhanging boulder and flattened him. The guerilla squealed as the breath left his body, and Mac chopped him crisply behind the right ear. The American whistled, and Cooligan ran to join him. Together they trussed and gagged the guard. Cooligan pulled the body into the parking area and lodged it under a truck.

"Now for Sabrina," Mac whispered, for the second time that night. Miss Carver, he thought, was getting to be a problem.

"Yeah, I wonder what she's up to?" Cooligan echoed.

Seduction, that was what she was up to. She sauntered over to the Yugoslav sentry who unslung the machine pistol from his arm and presented it to her barrel first so that she could see the rifling. His finger was on the trigger, and he said something to her in Serbo-Croat which, from the tone he used, Sabrina judged to be most unpleasant.

"That's not friendly," she murmured, "I was only trying to get acquainted. It's pretty boring here, you know."

His eyes showed he had not understood a word she was saying, so she continued in the same conversational tone, "Up you go then, Feisal. This guy's so intent on keeping me under close surveillance that I think we could smuggle in a troupe of performing elephants and he wouldn't notice."

Feisal slipped from behind his grandfather's wheelchair and used the other Arabs as a screen to get out of the sentry's line of vision. At the wall, Fairman hoisted the boy up the first few feet and enabled him to get a toe hold.

Sabrina moved closer to the guerilla until the gunpoint

180

lodged in the valley between her breasts. She licked her lips and purred, "Is that the best you can do?"

The guard flushed and backed away, but his eyes still held hers as, fleet and silent, Feisal gained height. The Yugoslav waved at her impatiently with the gun to keep her distance, and Sabrina made a face at him and wiggled over to the rim of the ledge. She stooped down—and the sentry's gun followed her. She looked back over her shoulder at him, grinned, and picked up a handful of pebbles.

She stood at the very edge of the rock face and peered down into the dark pit. Attractively oscillating her rear end, she tossed the stones, one at a time, into the void.

From his windy perch, Philpott saw the indicator light of the minibus wink left, and as the bus pulled off the road and slowed to a halt, he dropped off and rolled behind a handy bush. He peered into the darkness, heard the crash of waves, and smelt the sea. Smith instructed the driver to take the bus back to Castle Windischgraetz, and in a moment he was alone with the noises of the night and the waters and the sighing breeze . . . and Malcolm Philpott.

Philpott cautiously raised his head and saw a lone cyclist pass Smith, respond warmly to a greeting in the local dialect, and continue on his way. Smith crossed the road and stood for a moment framed against the skyline in the bright light of the moon. Then he disappeared from view. Philpott rose stiffly to his feet and gave chase. From the opposite side he heard the sound of Smith scrambling down an incline. Philpott waited until he reached the bottom, then followed him.

A standing lantern came on, and Philpott shrank into the shade of a stunted tree. He saw Smith haul from a hiding place under a rock an Avon dinghy with an outboard motor at its stern. Smith carefully emptied the boat of sand and fragments of brushwood, then unscrewed the lid of the gas tank and topped up the fuel supply from a small can of gasoline. He pushed back the sleeve of his brand new parka and glanced at the illuminated face of his watch. The deadline for the placing of the ransom had passed by a good half-hour, but Mister Smith was in no unseemly hurry. He smiled a satisfied smile, and looked calmly out to sea.

Ten minutes went by, and Philpott fidgeted uneasily, fighting the cramp that was stealing into his muscles. He held a gun in his left hand and clasped the tree with his right arm, but he was fast tiring of the crouching position he'd been forced to adopt.

Then Smith moved. He stooped and picked up from the sand a rope-line which Philpott hadn't spotted. He tugged on the line, and a row of bubbles erupted on the surface of the water and followed a straight course out from the shore.

Philpott half straightened and leaned forward to get a better view. The crumbling shale beneath his feet gave way, and with a manic shriek he pitched down the bank to fall practically at Smith's feet.

The gun flew from his grasp, and Philpott scuttled crabwise to retrieve it until Smith planted a boot firmly on his outstretched hand.

Sabrina dropped the last pebble into the abyss and turned her head to wink at the Yugoslav, who couldn't take his eyes off her. That was the moment of secondary sexual communication which Feisal chose to shatter by losing his hand grip on a sharp splinter of rock. He gave an involuntary cry and slithered down the rock face until he was suspended ten feet over the guard's head.

As the guard looked sharply up at the boy, Sabrina dived at the man's legs and tackled him. He lurched backwards and fell to the ground, but his finger still curled around the catch of the machine pistol, and when Sabrina dived after him and grabbed the barrel, the sentry pressed down on the trigger.

A spray of bullets spattered against the wall and bounced around the cave like demented fireflies. Sheik Dorani howled as a stray shot clipped his shoulder bone, and Sabrina strove mightily to bend the pistol back against the guard's hand.

With the fingers of her other hand she clawed at the man's face and drew blood, but he closed his eyes to avert the worst of the damage. He brought his knee up into her crotch, and she gasped and heaved. The Air Force One crewmen stood by helpless, not daring to intervene while the Yugoslav held on to the gun. Finally, with a massive effort, the guard drove his elbow into her face and pulled himself to his feet, with Sabrina still clinging to the pistol.

The guerilla punched her savagely again and tore the gun from her grasp, then bellowed in pain and surprise as Feisal landed heavily on his back.

The man and the boy crashed to the rock floor together, and once more the machine pistol stuttered and coughed. But it was Feisal who rose with his hands and shirt front drenched in blood. The Yugoslav lay on his back, his face, throat and chest shot away, one sightless eye staring at the crystal moldings on the roof of the cavern.

Sabrina threw her arms round the sobbing child and kissed his cheeks. Then she surrendered him to Dr. Hamady and ordered Fairman to get to his knees. She clambered on his back and gritted her teeth as she began to scale the rock face, for the bomb had still to be neutralized.

Jagger and Dunkels heard the burst of firing while they were supervising the clear-up operation in the main cavern. Most of the guerillas had already left, deployed to their secret mountain bases. Jagger swore and grabbed a sub-machine gun, ordered Dunkels to guard the approach to the bridge, and ran to investigate.

Cooligan and McCafferty were lying low in the entrance cave planning their next move when the sound of the shooting reached them. Cooligan immediately drew the wrong conclusion. "He's *done* it, the bastard," Bert choked, and started for the tunnel leading to the bridge. McCafferty grabbed his arm and pulled him back, explaining that the ringer was unlikely to launch a shooting massacre when all he had to do was explode the bomb.

The two agents used rock cover to get them to the tunnel, and it was sheer bad luck that Dunkels turned to look behind him just at the instant when a shaft of light glinted on the stock of McCafferty's gun.

Sabrina looked long and hard at the bomb. The detonator was wedged firmly into a crevice in the rock, and the wires, sunk into the viscous mass of pink *plastique,* might be delicately poised to resist dismantling. She dared not risk setting the explosives off accidentally, so she tried to

183

saw through the trailing yellow cable against a sharp edge of rock. Her head was bent to the task when Jagger's gun tickled the soft hairs behind her left ear and his voice said "Drop the wire."

She froze, and the cable slipped out of her hand. The ringer plucked the machine pistol from her belt and motioned her inside.

Then Jagger himself froze as another fusillade of bullets crashed into the wall at his side. He spun around to see Siegfried Dunkels stagger out of the tunnel on to the bridge, clutching his torn stomach. Slowly, almost balletically, Dunkels folded and draped across the suspension cable. He tried to right himself, but his head fell forward as he died, and his body toppled into the chasm.

McCafferty hurdled the corpse of the guard, brought down in the same burst as that which killed Dunkels, and at last came face to face with his other half—himself— across twenty feet of rickety bridge.

Mac raised his machine pistol and caught his trigger finger just in time when he saw, in the dim lighting of the second cave, that the ringer was using Sabrina Carver as a shield.

"Back, McCafferty," Jagger shouted, "or she gets it. You too, Cooligan."

Mac waved Bert away and retreated himself, still keeping the ringer in his line of vision. Somehow, Jagger knew that the odds were stacked against him, and played his last lunatic card. Fear of the Russians, of Karilian, of what they could do to him if he failed to carry out their orders, governed his life to the last. He groped in his pocket and brought out the detonator.

"Three minutes," he breathed, and pressed the time switch. "Three minutes and you're all dead."

He shoved Sabrina ahead of him to recross the bridge, and saw McCafferty and Cooligan withdraw further into the tunnel. When she and Jagger reached the other side, Sabrina rounded on Cody savagely and yelled, "You *can't*, you *mustn't*, kill those people. They've done nothing to harm you. What kind of animal are you, Mister No-Name?"

The ringer exploded and lashed at her face. She took the blow on the chin and crumpled to the ground, striking her head on a rock. "The name is Cody Jagger—do you *hear*?" he screamed at her senseless body. "Do *you* hear, McCafferty? I'm Cody Jagger, and I'm going to kill you and everyone else here!"

Mac's answer was a burst of pistol fire which sent Jagger reeling back unhurt into the darkness of the bridge. He snarled an obscenity when he saw that the detonator had fallen from his hand and was lying a yard from Sabrina's head. The timer showed two minutes before the bomb would explode.

Jagger began to crawl towards the detonator, but McCafferty had him in clear view now. "You're covered, Jagger," he shouted, "drop the gun."

Cody rose and loosed off another salvo until the firing mechanism jangled on the empty chamber.

The detonator's timing device clicked around to one minute.

Jagger threw the useless gun away and jerked out the machine pistol he had taken from Sabrina. He never got to press the trigger: McCafferty shot him twice through the hand, and the gun clattered onto the bridge.

Mac advanced, and his eyes flickered to the ticking remote-control box, then back to Jagger's face . . . his own face, warped with hatred, licking the blood from his hand.

"You son of a bitch, McCafferty, I should have killed you back in Bahrain, but the Russians wanted you alive."

"The Russians?" Mac cried. "You work for—"

Sabrina chose that second to moan and stir, and McCafferty's eyes left Jagger's long enough to search for her face. Cody heaved himself at the American and kicked out at his groin.

The electronic timer showed thirty-two, thirty-one, thirty seconds.

Mac took the kick on his thigh and rocked back as Jagger caught the gun in his wounded hand and crashed the other into Mac's face. But Jagger couldn't retain his hold on the pistol. Blood was pumping from his hand, and his fingers fell away. He tried to defend himself one-handed. Then McCafferty got a lock on him and splintered his cheekbone with the butt of the gun.

Cody's head came up, his lips slid away from his teeth, and his eyes glazed over. Mac used the gun butt on him again, and Jagger keeled over against the rail. It broke under his weight, and his dying shriek lasted until his body hit the pointed rocks of the riverbed.

Sabrina screamed when Mac turned to her. Her mind strove to cope with the man standing before her. Who was he? Who had won the fight? She clasped her hands to her pounding head, then reached for the machine pistol, and McCafferty cried, "It's me, you silly bitch."

She let the gun go, and in the hiatus that followed they heard the remorseless ticking of the timer. They both dived for it, and she was nearer.

When she switched off the detonator and disconnected the battery wires, the clock face showed two seconds to blastoff.

"You're not quite the last man in the world I expected to see, Philpott," Smith remarked urbanely, "but I honestly didn't imagine you'd suddenly drop in out of the blue in that vulgar manner."

Smith removed his boot from Philpott's hand, and kicked the gun into the sea. "Get up," he commanded. Philpott tried, but fell back grimacing with pain.

"I think I've hurt my foot," he apologized.

"Serves you right," said Smith. "You must have had a pretty rough journey, too. I suppose you rode on top of the bus."

"Something like that," Philpott admitted.

Smith's eyes gleamed and he smiled broadly. "Then you're alone. How convenient—for me. If you can make yourself comfortable on the sand, I would advise you to do so. You will not have long to wait, and I can promise you that what you see will be of consuming interest to you."

Philpott moaned and lay back, clasping his hands behind his head. "What were you doing," he asked, "when I inflicted myself upon you so rudely?"

Smith put a finger to his lips. "Patience," he said, "and all will be revealed." He took from his parka pocket a small flat metal box.

Philpott recoiled in horror. "Don't, Smith," he pleaded. "for God's sake don't do it. Those people are innocent. You'll get your ransom. They don't deserve to die."

Smith smiled and juggled dexterously with the little

box. "As I thought," he mused, "you know far more than is good for you. But on this occasion, Philpott, you're wrong. *This* box"—pointing to the one in his hand—"is *not* the detonator for the explosives at the cave."

He pulled another, seemingly identical, box from the same pocket. *"This* one is."

Philpott regarded him in amazement. "Two detonators for the same job? Or rather—three?"

"Three?" Smith repeated. "What are you talking about?"

It was Philpott's turn to smirk. "Now there's something *you* don't know about, Mister Smith. Your pet *doppelgänger* has one just like that," he said, indicating the bomb timer.

Smith looked apprehensive, and impressed. "How clever of you to find that out, Mr. Philpott," he murmured. "So our Colonel McCafferty—whose name, incidentally, used to be Cody Jagger—has designs on the hostages too, has he?" He remained in silent thought for perhaps a minute, then turned his blank grey eyes on the UNACO chief.

"I would only have considered killing the captives in the event of the direst emergency, Philpott. I think you believe that. Jagger, on the other hand . . . Jagger is all beast. Clearly I must waste no more time."

He dropped the detonator timer back into his pocket, and pressed a button on the second device. "Look!" he directed, pointing dramatically out to sea.

Philpott followed his arm, In a blaze of fiery sparks, a rocket scorched into the air from Saucer Island and drew a comet's tail track in the night sky.

Chapter Sixteen

Brigadier Tomlin stalked over to the tripod in the light room and jammed his eyes for the hundredth time into the socket of the telescope. "This is getting ridiculous," he barked, "nothing's happening at all."

"It's less than an hour since the deadline," Sonya Kolchinsky pointed out reasonably, "and Smith didn't guarantee to act immediately. Anyway, with all this hardware around, we may have succeeded merely in frightening him off. He's not to know, after all, that we're only here to have a look-see."

Tomlin straightened up and bristled at her. "It's not my job, ma'am," he said, "to make life easier for a bounder like Smith."

She was about to frame a suitably barbed reply when the lighthouse keeper drew their attention to the rocket, which neither of them had seen leave the island, being too occupied in glaring at each other.

"Damn and blast it!" Tomlin roared, "so *that's* how he's doing it."

He snatched a communicator from the table and snapped, "All units, repeat, all units. Track that rocket. Don't lose sight of it. Mark where it falls and recover it. Move!"

Smith watched the performance through powerful binoculars and chuckled as the watchdog ships peeled away. "So splendidly predictable, the military," he mused. "Do you not agree, Mr. Philpott?"

"I take it that the little fireworks display had nothing to do with the collection of the ransom," Philpott observed.

Smith wagged his head, and tut-tutted. "But there you would be wrong, my dear fellow. True, it served admirably as a *divertissement,* but its principal objective is important, indeed crucial, to my plan for picking up the diamonds."

Sonya Kolchinsky wasn't fooled, either. "We're going to the island, brigadier," she announced firmly.

"We are not, Mrs. Kolchinsky," Tomlin replied, equally firmly.

Sonya bridled. "You have more than sufficient units tracking that roman candle. We will take the command boat—the flagship, as I believe you call her—to the island."

188

"And why, pray?"

"Mainly because I say so. I shouldn't need to remind you, brigadier, that you are under UNACO command. I don't believe for a moment that the rocket has been magically oriented to pick up our bag of diamonds and take them to Smith's current lair. We will investigate."

Tomlin heaved a theatrical sigh and muttered, "As you wish, ma'am."

When the launch slowed to a halt at the gibbet end of the island, Tomlin pointed to where the pole had been and proclaimed, "There! I told you—it's gone!"

Sonya frowned, then peered into the water where the strong searchlights of the boat were playing. "It hasn't, brigadier," she cried, "it's still there."

Before Tomlin could prevent her, she stepped from the prow of the cutter and jumped on to the island. Tomlin shouted, "It's mined! For God's sake, be careful!"

Sonya turned to him and waved. "Don't be silly, of course it's not mined," she called out. She trotted over to the center of the rock slab and found the tube from which the rocket had been launched. A length of singed cord lay half out of the hole and she examined it curiously. Then she returned to the edge of the island and searched for the pole—which, as she had reported to Tomlin, was indeed still there, only now it was lying horizontally on the surface of the sea, with the crossbar projecting down into the water.

Tomlin followed her gaze. "By Jove," he mumbled incredulously, "the *bag* is still there, too. Shall I have it recovered, ma'am?"

"Please, brigadier," Sonya replied.

But as a crewman with a boathook leaned over to scoop up the leather bag, a dark, ghostly shape cleaved the water past the launch. Its nose speared the six-inch metal ring which Smith had insisted must be fastened to the end of the bag. The grey shadow swam away, and with it went fifty million dollars in cut diamonds.

Tomlin's eyes almost left his head. "What—what the blue b-bloody blazes was that?" he spluttered.

Almost in a dream, and half to herself, Sonya Kolchinsky murmured, "God Almighty, you've got to hand it to Smith, haven't you."

189

"What was it?" Tomlin demanded, his puce countenance turning purple in the garish light.

Sonya pulled herself together. "What was it, brigadier? A dolphin, of course. What on earth did you think it was—a submarine?"

McCafferty finished prodding the bruise on Sabrina's head and remarked, unfeelingly, "I think you'll live."

"Gee, thanks," she replied. "Are we ready, then?"

McCafferty bowed and conducted her into the cramped seat of the Kamov helicopter. "Your carriage awaits, m'lady," he joked.

They had collected the hostages and sent them back under Cooligan to the Kosgo airstrip, located for them by the Yugoslav Air Force. Mac suggested that the AF One crew should recover their aircraft and prepare it for takeoff. If all turned out well, and Smith was either captured or at least prevented from snatching the diamonds, Philpott's party would join them later for the trip to Geneva. "Anyway, Bert, I'll see you're kept informed," he promised, as the small convoy pulled out of the parking area and descended to the floor of the hostage-cave valley.

"Which way, skip?" Sabrina inquired as they took off.

"The coast," McCafferty answered matter-of-factly. "That's where the ransom drop is taking place." They zoomed up into the starlit sky and Mac banked the Kamov sharply to bring it around for a nose-down straight run to the Adriatic.

"A what?" Philpott echoed faintly.

"A dolphin," Smith said. "That's what I was doing when I pulled on the rope-line just now. It released the endwall of the dolphin's cage, and it was also the signal for her to start swimming.

"She needed to keep going for only three or four minutes, homing in on an ultrasonic direction beacon built into the pole of what you called the gibbet, which your considerable armada was frightened to examine in case the apparatus, or indeed the entire island, was mined."

"Which of course it wasn't," Philpott supplied dryly.

"Which of course it wasn't," Smith confirmed. He then explained at length how the dolphin had been purchased

190

and trained at an aquarium in America until she could have made the pick-up blindfolded. The rocket also operated a device linked to a cord which uprooted the guy rope supporting the pole, and tilted the gibbet down to sea level, Smith added.

Philpott listened in silence, then drew a deep breath and exhaled in a frustrated sigh. "I hate to admit it, Mister Smith," he said, "but it's impossible not to admire your style, if not your actual objectives or methods."

"Why thank you," Smith beamed, and gave the UNACO director a mocking bow. He looked out to sea again when Pilpott observed, "Your talented lady mammal has come back to daddy." The row of bubbles, effervescing more furiously than ever, had reappeared.

Smith picked up the rope again and waded into the water for perhaps ten yards. He hauled on the line, and the caged dolphin gradually emerged from the waves. "Well done, my angel," Smith boomed approvingly, patting the dolphin's snout and removing the ransom bag in one smooth gesture. "I may never see you again, but believe me, I am eternally grateful to you."

He turned and walked back, the chamois bag slung over his shoulder. "I'll leave you now, Philpott," he announced, "but let me add one cautionary word: should you feel that you can still prevent me from escaping, remember that I have another electronic device still in my possession. *This* one."

He pulled a metal box from his parka, and Philpott had no doubt whatsoever that it was the detonator for the bomb which could destroy the Arab and American captives—provided, that is, that Jagger had not already murdered them.

Glumly, Philpott watched in silence as the dinghy pulled away from the beach. He dug both hands into the sand beside him, picked up fistfuls of watery gravel, and threw them after Smith, as though he could stop him by a display of sheer bad temper.

The Kamov cleared the coastline and spanned the necklace of tiny islands, seeing the activity aboard the three naval cutters milling about looking for traces of a long-dead rocket, and spotting Sonya arguing with a tall, red-faced soldier—English, Sabrina thought—on another launch, moored next to an island which was hardly more than a rocky platform.

"Perhaps Smith's already gotten away," Sabrina shouted above the roar of the helicopter's engine.

McCafferty nodded, and jabbed his finger repeatedly at the little island. "Shall we land and try to find out what's going on?" he cried, miming the action in case she hadn't caught the words.

"What do you think?" Sabrina yelled above the helicopter noise. Mac thought for a moment, then shook his head. He indicated that they should return and search for Philpott. "He may actually be on to something."

They dropped until they were practically brushing the waves, and when they reached the shoreline, McCafferty guided the Kamov in a futile patrol of every promising cove, inlet and cliff. Each time they drew a blank—until Sabina spotted a signal fire.

Mac gave a jubilant whoop and spun into a tight turn. "It's him!" Sabrina yelled as they buzzed the beach. "He's still piling brushwood on the fire, and there's a gasoline can lying beside it. Smith must have left it behind."

McCafferty maneuvered the Kamov into the likeliest-looking stretch of firm sand on the small inlet, and set her down near Philpott's fire. He and Sabrina piled out, and quickly found that the UNACO chief was suffering from outraged dignity and a nasty ankle sprain. Sabrina soothed him with a résumé of the latest developments, and a cold compress.

Philpott had struggled to his feet, supported by McCafferty, when Sabrina reached the description of the killing of Jagger and the neutralizing of the bomb. He swore viciously and almost overbalanced. Sabrina rushed to help, but Mac was able to keep him upright.

"Well, what are you waiting around here for?" Philpott demanded excitedly. "Get after Smith! The only thing holding me back from having a go at him myself was that damned remote-control detonator, and this damned ankle. Naturally I couldn't afford to risk harming all of you, though I guessed when I saw you'd escaped that Mac had been able to pull something out of the hat.

"But now we can't afford to lose a second. He's out there,

in that blasted dinghy. Where he's heading, I don't know, but it's my opinion he's sailing off to join a larger boat, or taking his loot and landing it further up the coast. He'll have a vehicle stashed away somewhere. Anyway, that's the direction he took. After him, damn it! I can look after myself!"

They jumped back into the helicopter after promising to radio Sonya with Philpott's location. McCafferty spotted the Avon dinghy less than twenty miles away, weaving a path around the island of Pag to enter the Velibitski Kanal, a treacherous strip of coastal water strewn with half-submerged rocks and other traps for the unwary mariner.

Mac banked the helicopter again and motioned to Sabrina to take charge of both guns. "Shoot the bastard out of the sea," he yelled as hard as he could. "We'll worry about the ransom afterwards."

Smith was within five hundred yards of the shoreline, one hand gripping the wheel of the dinghy, the other resting lightly on the ransom sack. He wore a happy, even insane, smile, and the spray whiplashed his face and the wind tore at his hair, but Mister Smith was past caring. He had won, as he always knew he would! He was truly invincible, invulnerable. None could stand against him—not even the great Malcolm Philpott and all the resources of UNACO!

"I'm going to head him on to the beach, or crash him into the rocks," McCafferty shouted. "As soon as I get close enough, start shooting. Kill him if you can, but most of all I want him good and scared."

Sabrina shivered as she checked the guns. She was remembering another helicopter chase, when she had been the quarry. She did not believe she could ever expunge from her mind the horror and despair of being hunted by that huge fast bird, cleverer and more ruthless than any of nature's winged predators. She could almost feel sorry for Smith, but when she got him in her sights and emptied half a magazine of tracer rounds at the jinking boat, her hatred of him returned and she was a cold, calculating special agent again.

The idiot grin vanished from Smith's face as the bullets whipped the foam piling up on either side of the dinghy.

He looked back over his shoulder and saw the Kamov. At first he thought it must be Dunkels and that he had only imagined the shooting, but then Sabrina opened up again, and he spied her face in the helicopter searchlight, and the mane of brown hair streaming over her shoulders.

McCafferty dived as near to the dinghy as he dared and dropped speed, zipping over Smith's head and throwing Sabrina's aim. Smith opened the throttle and changed course. The helicopter banked and darted in for another searingly close pass. This time Smith was forced to wrench the wheel to starboard and turn the boat for the shore.

Mac bayed his triumph and settled on Smith's tail. "Take him while he's going straight," he shouted to Sabrina. She sighted on the hunched figure, but some instinct raised the short hairs on the back of Smith's neck, and as she pressed the the trigger he was already selling a dummy to port and bringing the craft into an agonizing right-hand bend.

The helicopter once more overshot its mark and Smith resumed his course parallel to the coast. For the third time Mac brought the Kamov in, then charged across Smith's bow, whipping up spouts of water and spray. Smith shut his eyes, hunched down even further, drew the sleeve of his parka across his face and doggedly held his line, dropping and increasing speed, twisting and tacking, handling the dinghy like a master to shake off the accursed helicopter—or to force McCafferty into a fatal error.

Sabrina pantomimed a lay-off position above the dinghy and matched Smith's speed, so that she could get a good, steady shot at him. Mac obediently held an escort station, and Sabrina riddled the side of the dinghy with bullets, but Smith, who had dived to the bottom of the boat, steering blind, rose unhurt.

Mac kept the position at Sabrina's insistence, and immediately regretted it, for Smith, holding the wheel with one hand and the leather bag between his knees, fired a machine gun from the hip. McCafferty throttled back and screamed away as the shots ricocheted off his undercarriage.

"You've annoyed him now, my pet," he said to Sabrina, who shouted back, "So what!"

"Leave it to me," McCafferty insisted at the top of his

voice, "I've got an idea that can't miss. Start shooting again when I tell you."

He brought the Kamov in carefully to starboard of the boat, then opened up and dipped to the seaward side, yelling "Now!" Sabrina pressed the trigger of the machine pistol and kept her finger down until the gun was belching nothing but hot air.

Distracted, Smith yanked the wheel over and plowed into a course for the shore. He fired back over his shoulder but his aim was erratic, and McCafferty, instead of beating a hasty retreat, managed to close until he was flying directly above the dinghy, knot for knot at Smith's speed.

Try as he might, Smith couldn't shake the Kamov loose, and Mac dropped the aircraft down until he was no more than a few feet over Smith's head. Lower and still lower he sank, while the down-draft from the helicopter's flailing rotors grew more violent.

Sheets of water strafed the boat, buffeting and blinding it driver. He could no longer use the gun, for he could not sight a target. He could no longer steer the dinghy, for he could not see where he was going.

He tugged and twisted the wheel this way and that, and each time he abadoned his course he somehow strayed back to it. He was an experienced sailor, but this was worse than the most awesome typhoon he had ever known. Smith shrieked his fury at the wind and the waves—and all the time, though he did not know it, he was sailing closer and closer to the rocky shore.

McCafferty looked ahead, peering through the spray, and saw the coastline looming up, now less than fifty yards away. Grimly he kept the Kamov at its post, tossed like a cork though it was in its own down-draft. At the last possible moment he pulled up and away and Smith could see—but it was too late. He spun the wheel frantically to avoid a rock, and instead struck a floating log a few feet offshore.

The sodden splintering wood acted as a launching ramp, and Smith's dinghy took to the air. It spun like a dart and thudded into the beach. Smith was catapulted through the windshield and flung to the wet sand like a rag doll. Fairy lights exploded before his eyes, and he was glad the torture was over. McCafferty spread the flats of both hands wide in a repeated sweeping gesture, and Sabrina got the message: there was no room to land the helicopter on Smith's beach. She jabbed her own finger towards his recumbent form on the sand, and Mac nodded vehemently. Sabrina checked that she had a full clip in the machine pistol, slung it over her shoulder, and heaved herself out of the Kamov. Her feet found the landing skids, and she vaulted lightly to earth, sending Mac off with a cheery wave to find another landing place.

She bent over Smith's body; he was starting to come around. Mischievously, Sabrina picked up the ransom sack and put it under his head as a pillow. Then she checked the shattered Avon dinghy, retrieved Smith's gun, unloaded it and threw the magazine away. The lantern he had brought with him still worked, so she propped it on a rock and switched it on.

Smith opened his eyes, and saw her pale face, framed by the now quiescent halo of hair, cast in the light of the full moon and the rays of the red metal lamp. His gaze fell to the gun she held trained on him. She was kneeling about four feet from him, and when he levered himself up to support his body on his elbows, she relaxed and sat back on her heels.

"Game's up, Mister Smith," Sabrina said laconically. "Too bad. You're quite a guy in your own weird, perverted way."

His head darted from side to side like a cobra's as he searched the beach for the bag of diamonds. Sabrina grinned and remarked, "Maybe you're not so smart, huh?"

"What have you done with them?" Smith asked. "Taken them back to Philpott? I can't believe you'd do that, Sabrina . . . you of all people. Your body would look so—exquisite—picked out in diamonds."

Sabrina gave an ironic chuckle. "Mister," she said. "I've stolen more diamonds than you've had lobster thermidors. What's so special about these?"

"They're *mine,*" Smith replied, "by right of conquest, planning, superb execution. They're *mine,* and I want them . . . but I will share them with you. Fifty-fifty?"

She shook her head. "It'd be no fun that way," she mused. "I get my kicks from stealing diamonds, not by being made a present of them. Besides, where would I spend them? I don't have your contacts, and Mr. Philpott would be very displeased."

Smith sat up, shaking off the last effects of his ordeal. "Then come with me," he urged. "I don't have to tell you we'd make a superb team. I'll share everything with you, Sabrina . . . and I have so much. Great houses, châteaux, a ranch, and an island in Micronesia—"

"Only one?"

Smith grinned. "I know you're mocking me now, but just use that agile brain of yours and *think*. You're still young and quite appallingly beautiful. So you want to waste your substance running from the police of a dozen countries, or risking your life for Malcolm Philpott's gratification?

"You're an odd girl, you know, very odd. You're quite splendidly amoral on one side of your existence, and I deeply admire you for your remarkable accomplishment as a jewel thief. And yet there's this grotesque puritanical streak in you that seemingly makes you want to deny to other people the pleasure you yourself derive from criminal activities. It's a disturbing mixture, and I am not sure I could easily accommodate to it."

"That's that then," Sabrina returned briskly. "I told you we'd never make it. Apart from anything else, what do I really know about you, Mister Smith? What does anyone know—you, even? Who are you, where are you from, what do you really look like? Oh, I know the face you've got now, but that's different from the one you wore when we last met. No—on reflection, I don't think *I* could ever accommodate, as you put it, someone so desperately anonymous as you, Mister Smith. Master criminal you may be, but you're not a person in the accepted sense. You're a kind of—kaleidoscope. And color patterns bore me, buddy. I like cool, glittering sparkles—lots of them."

Smith surveyed her with a sardonic grin. "Too bad. But at least tell me what you've done with the ransom sack."

She pointed behind him. "The metal ring which you were so insistent we fastened to it is at this moment about an inch and a half from the back of your right hand."

Smith jerked his eyes down and murmured, "Delightful, my pet. You are truly capricious. I like that."

197

She waved the gun at him. "That's as close as you're going to get to them, sweetheart. When McCafferty comes back, you return to the cooler and the rocks, unfortunately, to the Amsterdam Diamond Exchange. In fact, I think I hear Mac's engine now."

Smith cocked his ear and observed that she was probably right. Then he started a stream of aimless chatter, probing her about minor irrelevancies, praising her, praising Philpott, McCafferty, UNACO, the Savoy Hotel Grill Room . . . and by the time her suspicion that he was trying to distract her hardened into certainty, a boat had drawn up on the beach. A man clad in a black wet suit, holding a large torch in one hand and a gun in the other, stood behind her.

"You," the man said in guttural English, "the girl. You. Up." Sabrina straightened and swiveled on her knees to look into the barrel of his gun and seven others. A silent ring of men, wetsuited and anonymous, made it abundantly clear that if she fought them, she would die.

She climbed to her feet and tossed the machine pistol into a bush.

"Good," said the man, and turned to Smith. "You—into the boat."

"My friend," Smith cried. "I don't know who you are, but you've come at the right moment. I want to—"

He reeled back as the leader of the group cuffed him sharply on the mouth. Blood dribbled from his split lip, and Smith's eyes grew large and frightened.

"Into the boat. No time for talk."

Smith recovered some of his composure. "Of course, of course," he soothed. "I take your point utterly." He bent triumphantly to Sabrina. "Well, my sweet," he crowed, "it appears that, after all, you have lost and I have won. It's a great pity you did not accept my offer. It is, of course, unrepeatable."

"I'll live with the disappointment," Sabrina said dryly, although she was inwardly boiling with rage and frustration. How *could* she have been so dumb as to mistake the noise of the boat for McCafferty's helicopter? And where the hell *was* Mac, anyway?

Smith bowed—then his eyes flashed again as two men roughly seized his arms and propelled him towards the boat. He protested loudly, but they picked him up and dumped him over the side, still clutching the ransom bag.

The launch revved, the sea churned in its wake, and the wind rose, and above the noise Sabrina could hear Smith's voice, screaming, pleading, commanding.

As the boat pulled away from the shore with its passenger and wordless sentinels, a dark object flew through the air in a graceful arc and landed at her feet.

She picked it up by the metal ring and opened the chamois leather bag.

Fifty million dollars in cut diamonds glinted warmly in her eyes.

Philpott had fashioned himself a rude crutch and was now stoking his fire more for the comfort it provided against the chill night air than for its value as a beacon. He was engrossed in the task, but his keen ears caught the soft footfall behind him. His senses flared and he looked for the gun McCafferty had left him. It was lying by the fire, after he had used it as a poker.

"You won't need the weapon, Mr. Philpott," came Myshkin's soft, sinister voice. "I'm sorry to see that you are hurt. It is, I trust, nothing serious."

Philpott turned to greet his visitor, the flames dancing merrily behind his head. "Not too serious, general," he replied. "To what do I owe the pleasure of your company?"

Myshkin's lips tightened into a smile. "Merely that I wished to offer you my congratulations, Mr. Philpott. You have won at least half of your battle."

"Won? What are you talking about?" Philpott gabbled.

Myshkin's mouth actually relaxed. "You will soon learn everything, I am sure. Suffice it for the moment to say that your charming agent Miss Carver is in possession of the ransom money. Intact. No deductions for expenses."

Philpott gaped at him. "And Smith?"

Myshkin shrugged and spread his hands apologetically. "There, I'm afraid, is the half of the battle you lost. Mister Smith has been, shall we say, removed from the scene for a while. If he had been captured by your forces, you would have put him back into prison, and that, my dear Philpott would have been a criminal waste of an extraordinary criminal mind."

Philpott let out a cynical chuckle. "You mean you have him, general, and of course you want to make sure he keeps quiet about your own questionable role in this affair."

Myshkin shrugged again, and observed that Smith would probably keep a low profile for an acceptably long period of time. "Then—who knows?"

"Who indeed?" Philpott retorted. "And when, pray, did all these miracles happen, Myshkin?"

The KGB man studied his watch and said, "I think you will find my intelligence is accurate, Mr. Philpott."

Philpott inclined his head. "It's good to see you acting in the capacity of a loyal and upright UNACO member state, general."

Myshkin loosed an oily grin again. "I thought you'd take that view, Mr. Philpott. May I offer you a cigar?"

"You may."

Myshkin produced a handsome leather cigar case inscribed, in ornate gold letters: "With affection and respect, Warren G. Wheeler." Philpott accepted a Havana-Havana and a light, and drew the smoke gratefully into his lungs.

"Isn't that your transport?" Myshkin asked suddenly, pointing at the skyline. Philpott peered after his finger, and picked out the winking lights of a helicopter.

"It is," he confirmed, "and Mac's guiding one of our boats in so that I can get a more comfortable ride."

He turned back and began, "Well, I must say, general, I'm greatly impressed—"

But he stopped in mid-sentence, for Myshkin had melted away into the night. . . .

Philpott sat at a table in Air Force One, supporting his sprained ankle on a cushioned seat. He glowed expansively as Dr. Hamady said, "Naturally, I can only speak for the sovereign state of Saudi Arabia, but I think it likely, if only as a tribute to our departed and lamented colleague, Hawley Hemmingsway, that we shall consider the oil accord to bear every chance of success. What do you say, Your Excellency?" he asked of Sheik Arbeid.

The Iraqi grunted agreement. The Libyan, Sheik Dorani, followed suit. The Bahraini, Sheik Zeidan, smiled gravely, and Feisal nodded enthusiastically.

200

"I am sure the American government will be most grateful to you, gentlemen," Philpott beamed.

"They should be grateful to *you*, and of course to UNACO and its agents," Zeidan put in. "Without you we should not have been saved, and neither would the ransom, although that is of small conseuqence."

"Oh, quite," said Philpott.

Zeidan leaned forward and whispered into Philpott's ear, "Ought our gratitude not to be extended in perhaps another direction, too?"

"What do you mean?" Philpott whispered back.

Zeidan smiled knowingly. "Do not imagine for a moment," he continued, "that I, for one, believe Mister Smith could have mounted an operation on that scale without benevolent assistance, shall we say. His very presence in Yugoslavia, his access to men, arms, machines, would have been impossible unless . . ."

"Unless?"

"Unless he had the help of—a big brother? A big red brother? In any case, where is Smith? You don't have him? Shall we ever see him again, Mr. Philpott?"

"I suspect, Your Excellency," Philpott replied glumly, "that we shall." And he gave Sheik Zeidan a broad wink.

Sabrina Carver arrived at the table with a teapotful of Scotch and the promise of an interesting night ahead with Joe McCafferty in Geneva.

"Now then, Your Excellency," she said to Sheik Arbeid, "was that tea with milk and sugar, or coffee with cream and no sugar, or tea with cream and—"

Chief Steward Master Sergeant Pete Wynanski groaned on the sidelines. "That dame," he confided to McCafferty, "will never be anything but useless."